# Better Laugh
# Than Cry

# Better Laugh Than Cry

## Glenna Kauppila

**VANTAGE PRESS**
New York

Published by Vantage Press, Inc.
516 West 34th Street, New York, New York 10001

Manufactured in the United States of America
ISBN: 0-533-12826-9

Library of Congress Catalog Card No.: 98-90518

0 9 8 7 6 5 4 3 2 1

# BETTER LAUGH THAN CRY

by

Glenna Kauppila

| To my children: | Brian |
|---|---|
| | Erin |
| | Kylin |
| nieces: | Connie |
| | Charlene |
| | Patricia |
| | Torchie |
| | Tamara |
| nephew: | Wyman |
| and: | |

All future generations of the Belts/Wyman heritage.

Dear Family,

Realizing I was the only one of my generation left, I started writing down some of the facts, figures, and stories about the family, as some of you had asked me to do, but my notes seemed disconnected, uninteresting.

What I really wanted to do, I decided, was provide a record of what your ancestors were like, of what the times were like, and of how life was lived in those times—so I decided to try to make a story of it.

The material is drawn from my memories of the stories Mother used to tell about her early days on the farm in eastern Oregon and of our growing-up years in various places combined with my own personal memories. I have made no particular effort to verify these memories and am not at all sure that I could. If there are conflicts with stories you have heard from your parents, put it down to us all seeing life, or hearing about it, from a different perspective.

I hope you enjoy it.

With love to all of you,
Glenna Lou Belts Kauppila

# Better Laugh Than Cry

# 1

Now that I have given some thought to the matter, I find I know very little about my father's family background. I do not, for instance, know my Grandfather Belts's middle name, how many brothers and sisters he had, where the family lived before settling in the Pendleton, Oregon, area, or how he made his living. I would guess he might have had a cattle ranch, as all of his sons, my father and his brothers, were excellent horse- and cattlemen.

What I do know is that my Grandmother Belts's name before marriage was Helen Ogilvy. Her parents, my Great-grandfather and -grandmother Ogilvy, emigrated from Scotland, traveled west by wagon train, and settled on a sheep ranch in the Pilot Rock, near the Pendleton, Oregon, area. They had two children: a son, David Ogilvy, and a daughter, my grandmother, Helen.

My grandparents Thomas H. Belts and Helen Ogilvy Belts had five children: my father, Thomas Henry (called Tom) was the oldest, a sister, Florence, was next, then brothers, Douglas Clyde (called Clyde) and Charles L. (called Scotty). The baby of the family was a sister named Eva Belts.

In 1902, the first of the many tragedies to strike Grandmother Helen Belts occurred when her husband, my Grandfather Belts, was killed and she was left with her five children, my father and his four brothers and sisters, to raise by herself.

The second tragedy in Grandmother Belts's life

occurred around 1910 when her parents, my Great-grand-parents Ogilvy, were shot to death by a drunken sheep-herder they had fired the week before. The man was arrested for this double murder, tried, convicted, and sentenced to a long prison term. After serving only two years in prison, however, he was released on parole. My grandmother and her brother were convinced that the murderer of their parents had been hired by the cattle ranchers as part of the war to rid the range of sheep and that early parole was part of the bargain.

The oldest of Grandmother Belts's daughters, Florence, was the first of her five children to leave home when she married in 1912. Florence and her new husband, Charles Barlow, made their home in American Falls, Idaho. The Barlows had three sons, Charles Jr., Clyde (nicknamed Moony), and James (called Jim).

In 1913, shortly after Florence married, my father, Thomas Henry Belts, moved from Pendleton to work in the lumber industry near Oregon City, where he met and married my mother, Gladys Irene Wyman. With the inheritance received from the sale of his murdered grandparents' sheep ranch he bought a wheat farm on Butter Creek, near Pilot Rock, to support himself and his bride. Tom and Gladys Belts had four children: my sister, Catherine Maxine (called Maxine); my oldest brother, Thomas Henry Jr. (called Junior); my next older brother, Robert Eugene (called Gene); and me, Glenna Lou.

My father's brother Clyde went to work as a cowboy in the Pendleton area and made quite a name for himself in the rodeo circuit. I'm sure my mother once told me he won the silver saddle, first place in bronc riding at the Pendleton Roundup, but when I mentioned this to my sister she thought I must have misunderstood. Clyde never married. The youngest brother, Scotty Belts, worked with my father on the wheat farm and, like Clyde, never married. The youngest member of the family, Eva, married and moved to California but had no children.

Some years ago, when driving by myself from Seattle, Washington, to Sun Valley, Idaho, I took the time to explore the town of Pendleton, Oregon, then took a detour out of Pilot Rock and up a country road in search of Butter Creek. It was a summer day with the heat rising in waves above the dry, seemingly dead earth that stretched on and on until it finally disappeared in the purple haze-covered foothills of the Blue Mountains. The ground was a sort of whitish color from the grass that had grown a bit during the spring rain, then bleached in the scorching summer sun until there was no color left in it at all. There were rock formations everywhere, on top of the ground, in little gullies, and lying just below that dead, white grass.

I couldn't help wondering what my mother, born and raised in the cool greenness of western Oregon, might have been feeling on that first buggy ride with her bridegroom through that hot, dry, desolate country. Still, she was no shrinking violet but one of the four Wyman girls, who were all very attractive young ladies, strong-willed, determined, capable, with a keen sense of humor and a temper to match their various shades of red hair.

If the ride did not distress Gladys, she must at least have been dismayed when she arrived at the big, run-down, unpainted farmhouse set in a small grove of trees next to a huge, brand-new barn with its grand hayloft soaring high above the cow stanchions and horse stalls below. A run-down house for the bride and fine new barn for the animals were definitely in keeping with farm values of the day, but I doubt my high-spirited mother took it kindly or ever let my father forget it.

The newlyweds, my parents, Tom and Gladys Belts,

arrived at their farm on Butter Creek in the spring of 1914. Gladys, new to the area, quickly made friends with Tom's family and friends. She was warm, generous, and giving and had a winning way of laughing at herself and the many misadventures she had during those early days on the farm. A "runt of the litter" pig story she told many times over the years illustrates both her ability to laugh at herself and her strong will and determination.

Being raised on the outskirts of a small town where her parents raised a garden and kept a few chickens and a cow had not prepared Gladys for the more cruel aspects of nature she encountered on the farm. For instance, the day after the first litter of pigs was born she was shocked and saddened when one of the new babies died after the sow lay on it. That evening when Tom told her the runt of the litter would probably also die, of starvation, she was distressed and outraged that Tom could accept the survival of the fittest theory so casually.

The next morning, although she'd been told the sow could be dangerous, Gladys opened the gate, walked into the pigpen, and picked up the runty baby. The piglet squealed, so Gladys thought the sow was going to attack and ran screaming for the gate, which she barely managed to latch before the sow reached it. In the meantime, Tom and his brother Scotty heard the ruckus and came running out of the barn and started yelling at Gladys to put the piglet down, which, of course, she would not do. On reaching her, Scotty grabbed the piglet and ran one way while Tom picked her up and carried her kicking and screaming in the opposite direction. The old sow quieted down as soon as Scotty returned the piglet, but calming Gladys down was another matter.

Eventually, the men did go back to work, but Gladys was still determined to rescue that runty pig and she was not about to let that old sow buffalo her! Later in the day she got an idea and went to the storage shed, where she fashioned a net out of window screening and bailing wire, then attached it to a long pole. She waited until the sow's back was turned, then used the net to quickly scoop the piglet up and over the fence, where she clamped her fingers around its snout before it could squeal; then she ran for the house. Tom and Scotty returned that night to find the runty pig bedded down in a box by the stove, happily sucking on a makeshift bottle.

Six months later the runt pig was as big and strong as the piglets that had stayed with the sow. Gladys was delighted and had great fun teasing Tom by suggesting the money from the sale of that pig rightfully belonged to her.

Making a success of a winter wheat farm was not an undertaking for the lazy or fainthearted. From early spring until late fall the family was up at dawn with Gladys cooking breakfast while Tom and Scotty milked the cows and fed the mules that were used for the heavy farm work. After breakfast the men harnessed the mules and headed for the fields while Gladys took care of the milk, gathered the eggs, and fed the geese, ducks, and chickens. She slopped the pigs, then carried the water to heat it on the kitchen stove for doing the dishes and washing clothes. There was the house to clean, the bread/pastry to bake, and the noon and evening meals to prepare.

In addition to the daily chores, there were seasonal activities such as planting and cultivating the garden, then gathering the produce and preparing it for eating, canning, or storing for the winter. Some periodic requirements included harvest crews to feed, clothes to make, and animals to butcher when fresh meat ran low. But Tom and Gladys were young, strong, and hardworking and in spite of an occasional clash of tempers formed a satisfying, successful partnership.

The farm prospered during these first years, so there was money for periodic visits to Gladys's relatives in Oregon City and for entertaining friends and family who came east each year, especially at Pendleton Roundup time.

After the first baby, Maxine, was born in 1916, Tom's youngest sister, Eva, and Gladys's baby sister, Vera, now teenagers, spent their summers on the farm to help Gladys and for a change of scenery. The girls liked each other and enjoyed the social life, e.g., picnics, barbecues, barn dances, impromptu rodeos, and mule team pulling contests. Tom was known as a good man to work for and Gladys set one of the best tables in the territory, so there was no lack of young farm hands around for the girls to flirt with.

Tom, with his special love of animals, used the first of the farm profits to buy the finest mules he could find. He was soon winning most of the mule team pulling contests and gained a reputation as one of the best mule skinners in the state. A more frivolous but important acquisition was a beautiful five-gaited bay thoroughbred saddle horse named Fritz.

Tom was a slender six-footer with a generous amount of dark, wavy hair and a handsomeness marred only by a nose that had been somewhat flattened by a kicking horse when he was a toddler. How proud and a little vain he looked sitting tall in his ornate saddle as he put Fritz through his paces during the opening day ceremonies at the Pendleton Roundup.

In the spring of 1918, two weeks before their second child, Thomas Henry Jr., was born, Tom's brother Cylde was killed in an accident that involved horses, possibly at a rodeo. A letter Gladys's mother, Lucinda Simmons Wyman, wrote to Tom regarding the birth and death follows:

6

Oregon City
May 10, 1918

Dear Tom,

We received your wire and your letter and were very glad indeed to get both.

We send heartiest congratulations. Am so glad you got a boy as you wanted one so bad. They are all nice.

We were very sorry to hear of Clyde's death. It certainly must have been a shock to you, such a sudden death. I assure you, you have our sympathy.

We are in need of rain here. We did have some but not enough.

I have written Gladys twice, just a short letter. I certainly am glad she is getting along so nicely. No doubt you will be very glad when she can come home.

Dad is home tonight so it is not quite so lonesome. We join in wishing you success. We hope you have a splendid crop and the best of luck in everything.

Respt,
Mother and Dad*

During the great flu epidemic of 1918, that same fall, word came that Gladys's mother, Lucinda, had the flu and was getting so weak they were afraid she might not live. Gladys, with Maxine and Junior, hurried to make the trip to Oregon City, but by the time they arrived her mother was gone. One of the letters with news of Gladys's brothers and

* Letters in this book by Lucinda Wyman are used by permission of Lois M. Koerrelman, Dorothy Henry, Lauri Greimes, Torchie Corey, Connie Mayes, Alan Green, Gail Bonniksen, Patricia Beltz-Moore, Charlene Whidbee, Tamara Belts, Wyman Belts, Suanne Jasso, Charles Andrus, and Henry Wyman.

sisters (Bertha, Paul, Hazel, Henry, and Vera) that Gladys saved from a few months earlier follows:

Oregon City
August 1, 1918

Dear Gladys,

Your letter came a few hours before Henry left. I know you and Vera were disappointed and I was myself. I did so wish you could have come here or he could have gone over there. He tried for an extension on his furlough but could not get it.

Henry is looking fine. Is awfully tan and is husky I tell you. Is a little taller than he was and more manly. Seems so much older, all his kiddish ways are gone but is just as spirited as ever. He likes to tease just like all of the Wymans.

He never talks about the war and never reads the newspapers very much.

It is so dry here nothing grows unless you water it. Bertha was in and stayed a week so she could visit with Henry. I hope Vera comes home pretty soon, it is lonesome here. It has been all summer but worse now.

Paul and Bernice are planning to marry soon but can't decide on a date.

Well, I want to answer little Maxine's letter she sent me a few weeks ago. She is so cute and sweet. I sure envy Vera. She has such a good time with Maxine and Junior.

Hazel wishes you would hurry and come here too.

Lovingly, Mama

In spite of each losing a loved one, these years from 1914 through 1920 were happy ones for my parents, Tom and Gladys, but then the tide began to turn. In January 1921, Gladys realized she was pregnant again though nei-

8

ther she nor Tom wanted any more children. We were loved when we did arrive, but we were not included in their original plan.

In August word came from American Falls that Tom's sister Florence had committed suicide. The eldest of her three boys was only eight years old. It was decided that Tom would take Grandma Belts and his sister, Eva, to American Falls, Scotty would stay to run the farm, and Gladys, beginning her ninth month of pregnancy, would take Maxine and Junior on the train to Oregon City to stay with her family until the baby, my brother Gene, was born. In the end, they brought Florence's body back to Pendleton to be buried in the family plot, but Gladys stayed on in Oregon City until Gene was born in September 1921.

The death of a son or daughter, especially by his or her own hand, is a tragedy from which some mothers may not recover, but Grandma Belts had already survived the death of a husband that left her with five children to raise by herself, the murder of her parents, my great-grandparents, and the death of her second oldest son. At fifty-seven she was still strong, with a down-to-earth attitude and a will of iron. Her way of coping with her grief was to return to Pendleton to pack her belongings, sell her home, and move to American Falls to keep house for Mr. Barlow and raise her three motherless grandsons. Her explanation was direct and to the point: "It needs doing and I am the best one to do it."

If Grandma Belts felt any guilt or remorse about her relationship with her daughter, she never talked about it. Her only comment was to repeat one of her favorite sayings: "No point in crying over spilt milk." It's not that she was uncaring, merely practical.

Two years later a second accidental pregnancy baby arrived when I, Glenna Lou, was born in October of 1923.

These were sadder, more stressful times for Tom and Gladys. They had new babies to care for, Grandma Belts no longer lived close enough to provide strength and comfort, and their younger sisters, Vera and Eva, were now married, so they no longer spent their summers on the farm.

My father, Tom, by nature a restless, quicksilver sort of man, often charming but also capable of considerable temper when crossed, and my mother, Gladys, strong-willed and with a bit of temper of her own, found themselves at odds with each other more and more frequently. My uncle, Scotty Belts, a sweet, mild-tempered young man who moved in with them full-time when Grandma Belts left, was often pressed into service as umpire of the increasing number of bouts between the two.

Gradually Tom withdrew from interaction with the family and began investing his time and money into breeding a new type of horse, the palomino. Gladys responded by concentrating on her children and spending more time at the Indian village where the only neighbors within a reasonable riding distance lived.

My grandmother Lucinda Wyman was a true Christian lady without bigotry or racial prejudice, and she had passed these values on to her children, at least to Gladys. So, in her early days on the farm, Gladys had responded to the Indians' request for help with a sick child as she would to any neighbor. The child recovered, and some time later, on hearing a banging on fence posts and voices calling, Gladys went outside and saw a band of Indians waiting outside the gate at the end of the lane about a quarter of a mile away. With good grace and some feeling of amusement, she walked down the lane and opened the gate so they wouldn't have to dismount from their ponies until they reached the main house. They had come to thank her.

Many of the farmers in the area attributed the Indians' behavior regarding gates to what they thought was natural laziness. Mother, however, insisted it was a stubborn refusal on their part to deal with the white man's fence, which had destroyed the landscape and their own traditional way of life. They came many times over the years, but if for any reason someone did not come down to open the gate for them, they assumed it wasn't a good time to visit and turned their ponies around and headed home— seemingly without hurt feelings or resentment. They never once, however, got down off their ponies and opened the gate for themselves.

When Gladys first visited the Indian village, she was appalled by the deplorable living conditions. Not as a do-gooder but as a neighbor, she visited as often as she could and over time was able to teach them some badly needed principles of sanitation and nutrition. Whenever she had more cows' milk than she could use, Gladys would saddle up a horse and ride over to deliver the excess to the village until Maxine was old enough to send by herself. It was an errand Maxine (and Junior later) was delighted to do because she was allowed to spend at least part of the day playing with the Indian children.

Now, feeling a need for an independent interest of her own to keep her mind off her troubled marriage, Gladys visited the Indian village several times a week. She had learned a few Indian words of greeting, etc., but had never been able to pursue her desire to learn the language well enough to talk with the older family members who knew more about the beliefs and customs of the ancient tribes.

One of the old customs still being practiced illegally by some elderly Indians was that of choosing for themselves a time to die. One special friend to Gladys, an older lady in poor health, announced one day that she had set the date for her death ritual and wanted Gladys to attend the ceremony preceding that event. Gladys was shocked by what she saw as a cruel custom actually being carried out and saddened by the prospect of losing her dear friend, but it was a great honor to be invited and she could not refuse.

The death ceremony was held in the communal area of the village. As I visualize it, food was laid out on a table, there was a dance area, and on the front porch steps of her shack sat the death ritual lady dressed in her ceremonial gown with all of her possessions arranged in a semicircle around her.

After the eating and ceremonial dances were over, the guests gathered around the front porch to receive the farewell comments and gifts that had been carefully prepared for each. My mother, Gladys, was presented with a wool Indian blanket, her friend's favorite woolen shawl, and two beaded carryall bags. When all of her possessions were given away, the lady, escorted by her guests, walked to the wickiup that had been built for her and entered to await her passage to the happy hunting ground. Three days later Gladys received word that her friend's passage was complete.

The wheat crop had not done well in 1925 and Tom's palomino venture was not yet paying off, so money was scarce and tempers were getting shorter each day. Grandma Belts came that year to spend Christmas with her boys and Gladys and, seeing what bad shape the family was in, arranged to stay on for a while. It was a welcome change for everyone. Finally, seeing that the chain of dissension had been broken, Grandma Belts was able to return to the Barlow household in American Falls feeling confident that Tom and Gladys would make it through.

A short time later the final straw to break the backs of the farmers on Butter Creek was dropped when my mischievous brother Gene stole some matches and headed for the barn with me in tow. Once inside, we climbed the ladder to the hayloft and settled down to watch the matches burn. Finally, my brother burned his fingers and dropped the lighted match in the hay, then piled more hay on top to put the fire out. As the flames grew higher, he climbed back down the ladder and headed for the house while I came toddling after.

By the time Tom and Gladys saw the fire it was too late to save the barn or my father's beloved saddle horse, Fritz. Tom's palominos, also kept in the barn during the winter months, were so crazed by the smoke and flames, as horses are, that they would not leave the building though the stalls and doors had been opened for them. They were all destroyed.

Mother used to laugh about how funny she must have looked as she ran from the house toward the barn with a bucket of water in each hand to fight that massive blaze, but it wasn't funny then. Apparently, I made it out of the barn only seconds before the roof caved in, and, at two and a half, my making it down the ladder, through the fire, and out the door at all was a miracle. Though Gladys and Tom were thankful Gene and I were safe, the fire was one disaster too many.

As soon as the roads opened up that spring, Tom put the farm up for sale and left to visit some of his relatives in Eugene, Oregon. It was his intention to look for a situation there that would provide a new beginning for himself and his family. He wanted no more of farming or raising livestock for a living, and eventually he bought a small mountain of tall virgin timber with a lumber mill at its base. He felt that the experience he'd had in the lumber industry all those years ago at Oregon City was enough for a start. Then, too, he was an adventurer.

In early summer of 1926, the farm on Butter Creek sold quickly for enough money to complete the purchase of the mill near Eugene, Oregon. So, no more setting a dish of whole milk on the back porch for the cream to be skimmed off by the blacksnake encouraged to live there to keep the rattlesnakes away. And no more geese, kept for the same reason, to attack us children if we moved in beyond their hissing range—no more bitter cold winters and no more scorching hot summers. There would be other problems, of course, but at least they would be different.

# 2

When we left eastern Oregon in the summer of 1926, my father, Tom Belts, was about thirty-four years old and my mother, Gladys, was thirty. Oldest to youngest, our ages were: Maxine, ten; Junior, eight; Gene, five; and I, Glenna Lou, three. Mother took the four of us to visit her family in Oregon City while my father went to Eugene, Oregon, to find us a place to live, as his lumber/logging acquisition did not include housing.

It was a proud, happy Tom Belts who met us that August at the train depot in Eugene and loaded us into the brand-new two-seater automobile he had just purchased. We were beside ourselves with excitement, wanting to know everything at once, but all he would say in his teasing way was, "Wait and see."

Tom drove out from Eugene through Cottage Grove, up a gravel road for miles and miles past the farmland area, over a wooded hill, and down into a clearing where a store and the Lynx Hollow School sat at a crossroads. Here he turned up a rather narrow dirt road and, after a mile or so, pulled into the yard of a large, square, shiny white two-story house. It looked like a mansion to us, so we thought he had just stopped to visit someone. When we asked, "Who lives here?" Tom responded, "We do." We were off exploring in an instant.

It was not in my father's nature to say he was sorry, but this fine five-bedroom house, freshly painted inside and out, with a small unpainted barn situated across the creek, was enough of an apology for Mother. It was the exact opposite of the old, run-down house with a big, new barn that had been such a great disappointment to her in eastern Oregon.

During their first twelve years of marriage, my father, Tom, drank very little, although there was plenty of opportunity, even during prohibition years. Now, in a business venture with loggers, who were often hard-drinking, hard-living types, he got into the habit of having a few drinks of bootleg whiskey with the boys after work, and it brought out the darker side of his personality. It was as if there were two Belts families. My older sister and brother, Maxine and Junior, could remember their early childhood with a father who was a cheerful, teasing, loving man, while Gene and I thought we had a somewhat cross, impatient, demanding father given to sudden bursts of violent temper. Years later, Mother said it was as if he had a chemical imbalance that turned him into an alcoholic the moment he took that first drink with the loggers. In addition, sometime during that first year in Lynx Hollow Tom set up a still somewhere on his mountain, and eventually he had a bootlegging operation, but that is getting ahead of my story.

Our arrival at the Whites' Place, named, I assume, after owners named White, in keeping with the custom of the day, rather than because it was painted white, was the beginning of a different kind of life for us. I have only two memories of the year that I, then three years old, lived on the Whites' Place, and both of them involved my father's quick temper. The first incident happened shortly after we arrived. It was a warm fall afternoon when I was happily using a tobacco can to scoop up dirt for mud pies and was suddenly picked up by my father and held in midair while he spanked me with his leather glove. Later I learned the can contained the only tobacco he had left instead of being empty, as I had assumed. The second incident happened in the spring when the stream between the house and the barn was flooding over the plank used as a bridge. I had been warned not to try to follow my brothers to the barn as I usually did because it was dangerous, but I did try to cross and I did slip and fall into the water. My brothers yelled for my father, who ran on the bank alongside me as I was swept downstream until I reached a point where he could grab me. Finally, he pulled me coughing and sputtering out of the water, then spanked me all the way to the house for disobeying him.

Since the spankings were both justified and not really that hard, I assume it was my sensing the violence of the anger in Tom that frightened me enough to make me remember those events. My feelings were hurt rather easily, so it didn't take much to persuade me to behave, but my brother Gene was a much tougher, more independent type, even then at age five. Mother, realizing spankings weren't improving his behavior, told that she knew making him sit on a chair for a half hour as punishment was the best approach when he begged her to "just give me a spanking and let me go!" That story always brought a laugh, probably because it described Gene so well.

The Whites' Place had been rented until our own home could be built on a piece of property about a mile farther up the road toward the logging camp and sawmill. The site chosen for the house was about a quarter of a mile off the mill road at the edge of the woods above the inside point of an L-shaped meadow with a year-round stream flowing through it. The long side of the L was pasture for horses, with the shorter base used for cows. There was a small barn situated to serve both animals, plus a chicken house and a lambing/storage shed.

In the year before we moved to what was now the Belts

Place, Mother had occasionally filled in for the cook at Tom's logging camp and the men had really enjoyed the meals she prepared. Now that she was within walking distance of the camp, the six to eight loggers who stayed in camp during the week asked if she would consider cooking for them on a five-day-a-week basis. Partly because she enjoyed having her cooking appreciated but mostly because she liked the prospect of earning money of her own, she accepted. The arrangement she made allowed her to prepare most of the food at home and carry it to the camp, where she would serve breakfast and deliver packed lunches; then she would go home for the day and return to serve dinner in the evening.

Now that Mother was working, Maxine, almost twelve, in addition to her regular milking duties, was put in charge of the house when Mother was gone. Junior, nearly ten, handled the rest of the outdoor chores while Gene and I tagged along. My father was already gone when we got up in the morning and rarely home at night before we were in bed. And with his bootlegging operation keeping him busy on weekends, we rarely saw him, which was a relief to me.

Such a life today might be seen as neglect, but from my point of view it was a wild, free, happy life. I had an older sister who was already a good little cook and housekeeper, an older brother who looked after me in a rather patient, teasing though kindly manner, and a next older brother who could always think up some exciting devilment to get into if we ran out of interesting things to do between morning and evening chores.

One springtime chore was caring for the runt pigs Mother still insisted on saving and any orphaned lambs or calves. Mother's "runt of the litter" pig story being retold each spring finally prompted Junior to decide, since I was the smallest in our brood, to nickname me Runt. My dislike of that name made it so much fun for the others, it stuck.

My father, Tom, believed a saddle horse was essential to the proper development of a child and had a spirited, though manageable, big bay riding horse waiting for Maxine and Junior when we arrived at the Whites' Place. Late the following summer, at our new Belts Place, he had a white pony delivered to Gene for his sixth birthday.

Gene's new pony had been used as a packhorse and did not take kindly to being ridden, but every time it threw Gene off he got up and remounted. Finally, after throwing him at least twenty times that first day, the pony suddenly decided to accept this feisty, stubborn little redhead as his new burden to carry. From then on, however, if Gene got too careless or too rough, the pony would throw him again as if to remind him of who was really the boss.

I was as thrilled as Gene was with his birthday present because that freed up the space behind the saddle on the big bay horse for me. All I had to do to win that spot was learn to ride far back on the horse's rump and hang onto the saddle strings, show no fear, never cry, and never, never tattle on the boys. It was a small price to pay for escaping having to wait for the boys by the barn or hang around the house with my sister, who was busy with twelve-year-old-girl activities that were of no interest to me.

That fall, 1927, Gene started first grade and I, though I don't really remember this, was determined not to be left at home alone another year, so I spent the winter pestering everyone to help me learn to read and write. There is one happening, however, from the following spring, 1928, that I do remember in great detail.

It was a hot afternoon in late May when some fairly new neighbors, Mrs. Smith and her four-year-old son, Basil, came to our house and Basil and I were sent outside to play while our mothers visited. We didn't know each other very well, so we just stood around for a while shuffling our bare feet on the hot, hard-packed dirt by the back porch wondering what to do next.

Basil finally said something about his feet being hot, and I told him we could cool them off in the creek down in the pasture. He said, "OK," so we climbed over the fence and picked our way through the cow pies and molehills that spotted the pasture until we finally walked into the marshy area at the edge of the creek. At first we just stood there enjoying the feel of the cool, wet mud oozing up between our toes, and then, as friends will, we joined hands and began jumping up and down, laughing to see the fountains of water and mud splashing high into the air.

Suddenly a frog jumped. Basil leaped to catch it but missed and it jumped again, so I joined in the chase. Up the creek, under the fence at the high end of the pasture, and into the woods beyond we went in our quest to catch that frog. After we left the pasture, the marsh at the edge of the creek gradually dwindled away into a definite edge next to shallow, clear water over a gravely, rocky creek bed. When we finally stopped to rest, we were deep in the woods, out of sight of the house and even the pasture fence.

I was startled to see that Basil was covered with mud from head to toe, and then, looking down at my own muddy dress, I thought about how angry our mothers would be. I ran into the stream and started splashing the water onto my dress in an effort to get it clean, but that wasn't working, so I just took it off and, seeing that my bloomers were muddy, removed those also. I washed the dress and bloomers in the stream, rubbing the worst spots and wringing them out like I'd seen Mother do, then hung them over a branch in the sun to dry.

Poor Basil throughout this performance was sitting on a rock crying helplessly in anticipation of his mother's fury.

I finally talked him into taking off his pants and shirt, but he would not relinquish his underwear, so I washed just the pants and shirt and hung them on the branch beside my own. After that we splashed in the creek, played tag among the trees, and finally put on our almost-dry clothes and headed for home.

Shortly after Basil and his mother drove off in their Model-A Ford, my brothers and sister came home from school. We had all gone in to change our clothes and back out into the yard to play when Mother suddenly came charging out of the house with a threatening, "jig-is-up" look on her face.

Now, one of the important things I had learned in my four and a half years was not to try to lie my way out of trouble when Mother had that "jig-is-up" look, as she meant business. So, when Mother, being fair, asked me to explain my side of the swimming-naked story Mrs. Smith had just called her about, I told it the way I saw it. Seeing I was making good progress, I finally pushed my luck too far by saying, "I don't see why you're so mad, 'cause Basil didn't care!"

With that my brothers and sister doubled over with laughter. "Ha, ha, Basil didn't care! Ha, ha." That did it. Mother headed for the nearest willow to cut a switch while I fell to my knees crying at the top of my lungs—I had already learned that louder crying resulted in lighter punishment. Needless to say, that "Basil didn't care" phrase became a standard saying in our household for years to come.

Later, as I lay on the grass at the side of the house with my arm around our old dog, Sport, I cried at the injustice of it all. Finally, having cried myself out, I rolled over on my back and watched the approaching sunset as I reviewed the happenings of this day. I had made an independent decision to brave the creek in spite of having nearly drowned the year before. True, I was punished, but that eradicated guilt. I had handled the muddy clothing problem with appropriate, positive action, though not being able to convince Basil to let me wash his muddy underwear had resulted in discovery and did detract a bit from complete success. I had made a friend without help from my family, although, in the end, his betrayal (modesty) probably made him unworthy of my friendship.

All in all, I decided I felt good about myself and if Basil's mother thought I was a bad girl—that was her problem. And if my brothers and sister thought the "Basil didn't care" comment was hilarious—so let them. This was the beginning of a confidence in my ability to manage some things on my own, and life was never quite the same again.

That summer was a glorious time. My father was often gone for a week or two at a time, and Mother was busy with her cook shack duties, expanded garden projects, new social activities, etc. To my brothers, Tom's being "out of sight" meant his rules were "out of mind," so the day after school was out they headed for the millpond, which was strictly off-limits, to try out their log-rolling skills while I stood guard with the horses.

Having been warned about how dangerous walking on the floating logs could be, the boys were fairly cautious for the first few days, but as their confidence grew they became more careless and, finally, Junior slipped and fell into the water. The force of his fall started the logs bobbing in such a way as to keep pushing his head underwater. If this had happened on a weekend he would have been a goner, but this was on a weekday so the mill hands heard our shouts for help and fished him out, barely breathing and deeply shaken. In spite of the boys' protests, one of the mill workers called Mother.

When Mother came to pick us up, she could see the boys had learned their lesson and said only, "Why do you always have to learn these things the hard way?" Now I could truthfully answer, "It runs in the family." Even if I had thought of it then, I would never have dared to say it.

Late that July, in 1928, shortly after Tom left on what he expected to be a lengthy absence, we found ourselves in a quite unusual and, in a way, ridiculous predicament when one of the workhorses died. It was a very hot July, and the carcass in the pasture by the barn started to decompose rather quickly to become an unsightly, unsanitary mess that stunk to high heaven in a very short time. It doesn't sound like such a big deal now, as I write this, but imagine how a woman and four children could move and dispose of a rotting carcass of this size. The situation was serious.

After numerous family conferences on the matter, it was decided to harness up the remaining workhorse and try to drag the carcass to a hole at the lower end of the pasture where the last of the roots from a burned-out stump were still smoldering. Junior got the harness on the horse while Mother and Maxine tried to get ropes around the carcass. After several tries, they did finally manage to rig up a network of ropes that appeared to be holding, but they couldn't be sure because the single horse could not get the carcass moving. One of my mother's favorite sayings was, "It's better to laugh than cry," and we laughed a lot that afternoon—but we did not get that carcass moved.

The next day Mother drove the car into the pasture to help break the body loose, but she wasn't much of a driver and finally Junior had to take over to get the car positioned. Then the car scared the horse and only Junior, who had Tom's touch with animals, could handle him. So Maxine steered the car while Gene operated the pedals—it was a wild day, but by sundown that dead horse was in the stump hole.

It was Mother's idea that we could burn the horse's body down to a much smaller size, then cover it with dirt for a proper burial. Maxine tended the fire while we carried dead branches from the woods to keep it burning. Once the fire got going, however, we discovered the only thing that smells worse than a rotting carcass is a burning rotting carcass, and the prevailing wind blew the smoke straight at the house for the whole two days we persisted in this hopeless task.

Although my mother did drive the car back and forth to cook at the logging camp sometimes, she had never driven to Cottage Grove. However, she knew of a chemical, probably lime, she could buy there that would speed the decomposition of the body and kill the smell and she was desperate, so off we went. When Tom finally got home and we were telling him this long story, the biggest laugh came when Gene, who admired Tom's speedy driving style, told about Mother driving to town and ended by saying in disgust, "And the only thing she passed the whole way was the fence posts!"

Since there were fewer than three dozen children in Lynx Hollow, the school consisted of only two rooms, with each teacher handling four grades. When the first-to-fourth-grade teacher came to visit us before school started in the fall of 1928, I told her I could already read and write and would be attending her first-grade class that fall.

The teacher and Mother both tried to explain to me that at four I was too young to go to school, but I begged and pleaded and eventually they gave in. They thought because I was on the go and talked a lot I would not last where I had to sit still and be quiet. If that didn't discourage me, they were sure the two-mile walk to and from school would. But I did sit fairly still and keep reasonably quiet, and for that whole first year my eleven-year-old brother, Junior, carried me on his back when I got too tired to walk.

The road we walked to school on was bounded by woods, with a private lane leading off to a house here and there, so this was the perfect place for some of the boys to harass the little girls. One of their favorite tricks to play on the first-graders was to run up behind a girl, pull up her dress, pull down her bloomers, then run laughing and hooting as she cried from embarrassment or anger as she struggled to hang onto her books and pull up her bloomers at the same time.

No one dared to bother me when my brothers were with me, but one day when they both had to stay after school some boys decided to pull the bloomer trick on me. Since my brothers had trained me not to cry or show fear, these boys didn't get much satisfaction out of my response. I just set my books down on the road, pulled up my bloomers, picked up my books, told the boys they had better watch out 'cause I was going to tell my brothers on them, and marched for home.

By the summer of 1929, Junior and Gene had heard of our father's still and bootlegging activities and couldn't stand the thought that there had been something going on all this time without their knowing about it. The day after school was out we set about correcting that situation by spending all of our spare time riding up every steep ravine and down every gully on the mountain searching for the still—but we never did find it.

What we did get out of our mountain search was the idea that we were great horsemen and that led Gene to suggest we develop our skills so we could join the circus. We spent hours riding bareback practicing a variety of tricks— sitting sideways and backward, on our knees, and standing up. Finally, the trick that made Mother put a stop to our ambitions was riding at a full gallop across the pasture with one foot on each horse with me in front, Gene in the middle, and Junior in the back. It really was a trick that belonged in the circus, as the big bay was at least six inches taller than Gene's pony. Mother did laugh about it later and suggested maybe we could have been billed as "The Lopsided Belts Family."

Later that same summer an airplane, the first we'd ever seen out our way, flew over our place and we watched, entranced, as it disappeared into the trees, and then we heard an explosion and saw flames and smoke in the distance. By the time we got to the house, Mother had already called the sheriff and talked to a man at the mill who said a rescue party was on the way to the crash.

It was dark when the call came that the rescue party was returning and Mother, after refusing to let us come with her, left to see if she could be of help to survivors, if there were any. The front door had barely closed behind her before we were out the back door, through the woods, and hiding in the bushes near where the rescue party was gathered. It turned out that none of the occupants of the plane had survived, and we watched with wondering eyes as the men lifted the three bodies off the packhorses and put them into the back of the sheriff's paddy wagon. We couldn't actually see much, as the bodies were wrapped in blankets except for one with two blackened feet sticking out. My brothers said they'd been burned black, but the only burns I'd ever seen made red welts or white blisters. I couldn't ask anyone else about it, of course, because we weren't supposed to be there, but I wondered about those feet for a long time.

Life in Lynx Hollow was not all close calls and exciting events, nor was it as isolated as it may sound. There were special events like baseball games, the circus in Cottage Grove, and visits back and forth with neighbors and relatives. There were individual events also, like when Maxine dressed up like a hobo, played the mandolin, and sang "Hallelujah, I'm a Bum" at a school function. Another time, Junior, at twelve, became a local celebrity when he substituted on the men's baseball team and hit the winning run.

Maxine was an almost straight-A student, bright, witty, capable, and as strong willed and determined as Mother. Before I was born, Maxine had hoped for a baby sister, but when they brought me home, she took one look at me and expressed her disappointment with, "She's too little to do me any good." With eight years' difference in our ages she was right, of course, and here on the Belts Place she rebelled against caring for me anymore, so Mother sent me outside into Junior's realm of responsibility.

Junior did not like school too well and, though he was probably the smartest of the four of us, often got poor grades. He was quiet, capable, and practical. So, when he saw he could not escape looking after me, he set about training me to give him the least amount of trouble possible with the no being scared, no crying, no tattling, I mentioned before.

Gene, surprisingly, did reasonably well in his studies but was often in trouble for fighting, which he did with regularity and ferocity. By the time he was eight years old, though small for his age, he'd whipped almost every boy in school, including Junior. Gene had a great gift of gab, a clever wit, and great determination and was a bit of a prankster—which sometimes got the rest of us in trouble.

Shortly after I entered the second grade, I learned one of life's great lessons when I was taken in by Gene's prankster instincts. One day when Junior was not walking home from school with us, I let Gene and some other boys talk me into pulling the bloomer trick on a first-grade girl who had just moved from town to Lynx Hollow—not a tough country kid like us. We expected tears, yelling, or threats, but this girl just stood stock-still, frozen, in the middle of the road, her bloomers around her knees, sobbing as if her heart would break.

The boys were so shocked they ran for home, but I was so ashamed of having hurt her feelings like that I stayed there with her. I tried everything I could think of to make her stop sobbing, including pulling up her bloomers for her. She finally did stop and we walked on together and became friends, but I knew I never wanted to do anything so mean again—pranks like that were sure not fun for me.

I don't know if it was because of the Great Depression or for some other reason, but that winter, 1929–30, Tom shut down his mill and logging operation. In the spring he and the neighbors cleaned out one end of the millpond so it could be used for swimming. Maxine, Junior, and Gene built a raft and had a grand time on the pond that summer while I stayed near the shore teaching myself to swim. The first day I swam all the way out to the raft they cheered me on and bragged about me to Mother when we got home. She made a party of supper that night with chocolate pudding, my favorite, for dessert—what a celebration.

During that same summer, 1930, there was a violent windstorm and some of the sparks from the still-burning sawdust pile at the mill blew into the woods and started a forest fire. Many neighbors and firefighters from the state came to help. The next day my father, Tom, sent word for Mother to send Junior to the upper camp with extra food for the firefighters. Junior was to ride the horse to the mill, then go the rest of the way on foot.

When Tom came home that evening to get a few hours' sleep, he told Mother that the wind had changed the direction of the fire so they had to move the camp and he wondered why Junior's horse was still at the mill. Mother said she thought Junior was with him, Tom, and suddenly they both realized that meant Junior was either lost in the woods or overcome by the fire. Looking for him at night, in the dark, with the roar of the fire shutting out any sound of voices calling, was hopeless, so Tom tried to get some sleep before starting a search at first light in the morning.

My mother, Gladys, maintained a confident, optimistic outlook for all our sakes, but I thought a lot about the blackened feet of that corpse from the airplane crash the year before. Mother found keeping busy the best way to get through a crisis and created chores to distract us—but we were scared.

The next day, miraculously, a telephone call came from some people who lived on the other side of the mountain saying Junior had just knocked at their door asking to use the phone. We all joined hands and began dancing around singing, "Good old Junior," over and over. We could hardly wait for the time it took to send word to Tom, on the mountain searching, and then for him to drive over and bring Junior home.

It was a glorious reunion. Junior was so proud when Tom bragged about how well he had handled himself in such a crisis. Actually, he had worried that he would be in trouble for getting lost. Later Junior told Gene and me that he never would have made it but for the knowledge of the mountain he'd gained in our search for Tom's still the summer before.

Living in Lynx Hollow was very different from living on Butter Creek for all of us but especially for my mother, Gladys. Tom's drinking had come as a most unpleasant surprise but for a while she had gone along with his new partying style of life in the hope he would soon return to what she considered normal. When it became obvious that wasn't likely to happen anytime soon, she concentrated on encouraging him to do his drinking away from home in order to minimize contact with us children. Now, looking back, I better appreciate the effort she made to protect us from the knowledge of, and exposure to, their gradually worsening marital problems.

It was on Gene's birthday, September 7, 1930, that for the first time, so far as I know, my father hit my mother. Why I happened to be in the house at the time or what they argued about I don't remember. I do remember seeing Mother lying on the floor with her bruised face, her hair askew, and her glasses knocked off onto the floor beside her. I ran for the barn as fast as I could go to get my brothers and my sister to come and help her. Gene, typically, was all for us ganging up on Tom and beating him up, but then we heard the car roar down the lane and we knew that he was gone.

By the time Maxine and Henry finished the milking and we went into the house, Mother had changed her dress and combed her hair and, except for the bruise on her cheek, looked as though nothing had happened. When Maxine asked what had happened, Mother said, "Just an argument between your father and me. Why don't you all go in and change your clothes and we'll go visit Joe and Lila. Then we'll sing Happy Birthday to Gene and cut his cake when we get home."

We were delighted at the prospect of playing with the kids at our neighbors', Joe and Lila's, so we hurried to get ready while Mother used the meatloaf she'd made for dinner to make sandwiches to eat along the way. She made the two-and-a-half-mile walk into a moving picnic, eating sandwiches, playing games, and singing. By the time we arrived at our destination we children had forgotten all about the violence from earlier. After we'd played for a while, Mother came out of the house and told us that Joe was going to drive us to Eugene to stay with relatives for a few days.

Once we arrived at our relatives' house, there were innumerable conferences among the adults, phone calls back and forth, etc. After a few days, Mother told us she had decided it would be best, because of the drinking, the boot-legging, and the physical abuse, for us to pull together to start a new life away from Lynx Hollow. Pulling together, however, at least for a while, meant being separated. She said arrangements had been made for Gene and me to live with Aunt Bertha (Bert) and Uncle Joe McComb, who lived in Viola, Oregon. Junior would stay with Aunt Hazel and Uncle Ralph Green in Oregon City, and Maxine would be with Mother in Eugene, Oregon, where she could work for her room and board helping Mother with the house-keeper/practical nursing job she'd gotten.

I can still see Gene's uncut birthday cake, chocolate with pink frosting, sitting on the dining room table when we arrived back in Lynx Hollow to pack our belongings for the move. I also remember being terrified the whole time we were there. I was afraid my father would come back and catch us before we could get away, but it didn't happen. I never saw my father, Tom Belts, again.

# 3

I have no recollection of the trip from Eugene, Oregon, to Aunt Bert and Uncle Joe McComb's place at Viola, near Estacada, Oregon. I do, however, remember some of my impressions from our arrival in September 1930 at this little farm that was to be home to Gene and me for the next year.

Being used to a more casual country style, I was, first of all, impressed by the large size and the orderliness of the front yard. The path from the front gate to the house seemed very long indeed. It was bordered on the right by a solid bed of iris cut off to a six-inch-high stubble with a row of flowers, probably dahlias, in bloom along the wood-rail-and-chicken-wire fence that bordered the far right side of the yard. To the left of the front path was what seemed to me a huge expanse of quite level, neatly mowed lawn extending across the front and around the side of the house. The house itself seemed small and oddly put together because of the strange chicken coop slant to the roof and the various bleached brown shades of wood siding that looked as though it had never, ever been painted.

As we walked up the path toward the house, Aunt Bert came out onto the front porch to welcome us. She was taller, heavier, older, and not as pretty as my mother, I thought, but I liked the pleasant, matter-of-fact way she greeted us and told us to go on in and look around while she and Mother visited for a bit.

Gene and I were glad to escape and moved quickly to

do as we were told. Just inside the front door, I stopped dead in my tracks at the sight of the most awesome, most wondrous piece of furniture I'd ever seen. It was an old pump organ of golden oak, ornately carved with little shelves on either side of the slanted sheet music holder in the center. There was a row of knobs (music stops) above the ivory keys, and down below the wide, slanted foot pedals for pumping still had some of the original red felt covering around the edges.

I would have stood and stared all day, but Gene urged me on and we quickly crossed the living room, peeked in at the bedroom across the end of the house, then moved into the big kitchen at the back. Here we took in the massive wood stove against the back wall, the cupboards across the end, and the big, old dining table with its high-back chairs at the other end before we ran out through a sort of tacked-on porch to the backyard.

To the right of the back steps was a long, low building, somewhat newer than the house but also unpainted. The far end of the building was used for a chicken house, the middle section for storage, and the end nearest the house as a bunkhouse for the McCombs' two sons: Albert, in his early twenties, who helped Uncle Joe run the farm, and Lester (Buddy), a teenager, who worked in the woods with the loggers and came home on weekends.

Almost straight out from the back steps was a well with a big iron pump. Beyond the well and slightly off to the left, on the downhill side for drainage safety, was the outhouse (a one-holer as I remember it).

After exploring the points of interest near the house, Gene and I started down the path that sloped off to the left behind the house and through a garden area to the barn. Approaching us on the path was a man of slight build with a brown, weather-beaten face beneath a shock of grayish white hair. As he got closer we thought he looked stern, but there was a playful twinkle in his eyes as he said, "Well now, who have we here: Mike and Mildred?"

We fell for the joke, of course, and in all seriousness identified ourselves as Gene and Glenna Lou, whereupon he said, "In that case, I'm your Uncle Joe and we better hie ourselves on up to the house so I can say hello to Gladys. I'll have Albert take you out to look over the barn and the rest of the place later."

After lunch Albert did take us on a tour of the barn, the pasture with its grass and stumps, the uncleared, wooded area behind the barn, and the rows and rows of loganberries that were the family's cash crop. That evening Albert played the organ and a few tunes on his steel guitar for us. I was thrilled.

The next morning, Sunday, Albert drove us all down the hill to the little church at Viola Crossroads for services. After dinner we again piled into the car and he drove a couple of miles up the highway toward Estacada to visit Mother's father, our Granddad Arthur Wyman, and our Grandma Jennie—the lady Granddad had married after Mother's mother, Lucinda Simmons Wyman, died in 1918. After we left Granddad's, we stopped to visit another relative, our Great-aunt Ellen Simmons Lankins, who lived in a tiny cottage next to her son and daughter-in-law's home.

The next morning Mother enrolled us in the little one-room schoolhouse located near the church we had gone to at Viola. I was six, almost seven years old, and in the third grade. Gene was barely nine years old and in the fourth grade. When we got home from school that night, Mother was gone, as she had said she would be.

Aunt Bert and Uncle Joe were warm, hospitable people and from the very beginning made Gene and me feel welcome and loved. Not loved in a huggy, kissy way, as Mother's family was somewhat reserved about displaying affection, but in a cared-about and well-taken-care-of way. Life with the McCombs was orderly, like the front yard, and lived in a straight line, like the loganberry patch.

Every Sunday night Aunt Bert wrote to Mother with a report on our behavior and well-being. At least once a month our aunt insisted that Gene and I also write to Mother and occasionally to Maxine, who had stayed with Mother in Eugene, letters to be included with Aunt Bert's. We, of course, liked receiving letters much better than writing them.

I'm not sure exactly when or how Junior (Henry), then thirteen years old, arrived at Aunt Hazel and Uncle Ralph Green's in Oregon City, but there were letters from him as well as from Gene and me in Mother's things. Using those letters to tell the story of this year of separation seems a good way to share them. (All have been slightly edited for spelling and readability.)*

Oregon City, Ore.

Dear Mother, XXOO

How are you and everybody up there?

I like school better down here that I did up there. Please send my grades down fast but for gosh sake don't send the bad ones because they make me feel so ashamed.

I left my toothbrush up there too. Will you get that and send it down please and anything that I didn't have that night we left?

*Letters in this book by Henry Belts are used by permission of Patricia Belts-Moore. Letters by Gene Belts are used by permission of Wyman Belts, Tamara Belts, and Torchie Corey.

Well, breakfast is just about ready and I have to eat and go to school now.

Your son, Junior Belts X X O O

Estacada, Ore.
October 1, 1930

Dear Maxine,

I like school just fine and I can skate and I can box. I learned a new game and it is lots of fun.

A man stopped and talked to us on the way home from school and Aunt Bert didn't like that.

Send me Junior's address and tell him I can lick him boxing. I box almost every Sunday.

I may get to go in to Alan Green's Friday night and Alan is a couple of inches higher than I am.

Your brother, Gene Belts

Estacada, Ore.
October 1, 1930

Dear Maxine,

I like school fine. Gene had a scrap the first day of school. I go to Sunday school every Sunday and like it fine. Gene got his fern patch done in one night. I help Aunt Bert set the table.

Love, Glenna Lou

Estacada, Ore.
October 18, 1930

Dear Mama,

I have just got through with my homework. I haven't got my report card yet and I like school just fine.

Has Junior got his paper route yet?

I had a chance to get a bicycle for two dollars and I got it Tuesday.

Love, Gene Belts

Oregon City

Dear Mother X X O O,

I received your letter last Saturday. I am just fine now. How are you? I hope you can come down Christmas don't you? How is Maxine and have you heard from Aunt Eva?

Gene and Glenna Lou are just fine. There is not much doing down here now. Have you heard from the ranch lately?

Yours truly, Junior Belts X X O O

Estacada, Ore.
November 4, 1930

Dear Mama,

We got your letter yesterday just in time before Aunt Bert was just driving off to town. Bud got home from hunting but did not get any deer. I like school just fine. I have a little curl and I have been a good girl.

Goodby now, Glenna Lou

Estacada, Ore.
November 11, 1930

Dear Mother,

I am sorry I never wrote you last Sunday but I will

write you an extra long one this time.

Teacher said I was improving in my studies. I only missed one word in spelling yesterday.

Junior was out last Sunday and we had fun wrestling and boxing and he licked me once. And another boy and Buddy and Albert wrestled too.

Aunt Bert is sick and Glenna Lou and I washed the dishes this morning and Uncle Joe has a sick turkey. Buddy is plowing up at Grandpa's today. Uncle Joe and I clean out the chicken house every other Saturday.

Love, Gene Belts

Estacada, Ore.
November 24, 1930

Dear Mother,

Can you remember when Grampa's birthday was? Aunt Bert and Aunt Hazel and Aunt Bernice and all the rest were there last night for a party.

I tried to get up the hill from school in 10 minutes tonight but it took me 25 minutes so I got home 5 minutes before time. I got 100 in spelling today and here they are: 1-date 2-kept 3-roll 4-use 5-please 6-faint 7-hunt 8-paint 9-tease 10-easy. I am going to sign off now. Lots of love to Mother.

Yours truly, Glenna Lou

Estacada, Ore.
November 28, 1930

Dear Mother,

I was in to Aunt Hazel's for Thanksgiving and Buddy and Albert too. I went with Junior on his paper route and he sure has a long paper route. It covers about 5 miles. And he hasn't got any good news either. He sure must be tired when he gets home from that work.

Aunt Bert took me to town today and got me a pair of shoes and a pair of gloves to haul wood and go to school in.

Yours truly, Gene Belts

Oregon City, Ore.
December 5, 1930

Dear Mother X X O O,

I am sorry that I haven't written sooner but I have been pretty busy. I haven't written to anybody yet that you told me to.

I will get paid Friday $2.00 and after that $8.00 or $9.00 a month. I think there will be no more time for you to come down if you don't come down for Christmas so come down, be sure.

How's Mrs. Morton feeling now? Is there any news from the ranch about the blackberries?

Gene and Glenna Lou was here Thanksgiving. We saw Oregon City vs. McMinnville in football Thanksgiving Day. Hank was here and Paul and Bud. Somebody broke into the high school Thanksgiving night and stole $300.00 cash and valuable papers.

How is Lila and Joe and kids now? I will write to them some day. I just hate to write letters to everybody else but you.

Your son, Junior Belts  X X O O

Estacada, Ore
January 5, 1931

Dear Maxine,

I sure do wish that you could have come up for Christmas this year. Old Santa Claus sure was good to me. He gave me a bunch of clothes for my doll and a doll bed too. I think I am getting too big to play with dolls. Oh well, that is all right.

I guess next Sunday I have to say a poem at church. Oh well, they are going to have a business meeting after anyhow. I sure don't like it when the preacher comes 'cause he talks too loud. I have to go every Sunday. I don't have time to write any more.

Yours truly, Glenna Lou

Estacada, Ore.<br>January 5, 1930

Dear Maxine,

I am sorry that I didn't write before but I thought we were out of paper but Aunt Bert said that it was all right to use this kind.

I sure was glad to see Mother when she came out of Aunt Bert's bedroom Christmas morning and said Merry Christmas. I just stared at her and when I went out to wash up, Buddy and Junior grabbed me. I sure wished you were there.

Did you have a program Sunday night? We did. We sang and said pieces just like you used to do. At the last, Santa Claus came along so he gave us candy and nuts and then Wednesday we broke the nut press.

There is a lot of misspelled words in this letter but I am getting the hang of spelling now.

I must close now with love from Gene

Oregon City, Ore.

Dear Mother X X O O,

I received your letter with pleasure. I didn't know what happened to you. How was Maxine's report card this month? Mine was not so hot. I am going to write to Pete soon. How is he?

There was a wreck out in front the other night and a boy got his face caved in. Uncle Ralph took him down to the doctor and brought him home. It sure seems nice to have a payday once in a while now. I like my paper job pretty well. How is Mrs. Morton? Has Joe and Lila gone now or is Joe still working?

I hope to see you soon.

Yours truly, Junior Belts

Estacada, Ore.
April 30, 1931

Dear Mother,

Grampa and Grandma are here tonight. I just got the dishes dried. Every morning I wash and dry the dishes before I go to school and I haven't been late yet. Tomorrow I do not have to work as hard as the other days of the week.

I am sorry I did not write last week. I did not know that Aunt Bert wrote. Are you close enough to Maxine to tell her to write and send her address to us and ask if her address is the same as it was?

Gene learned the states and capitals and how to spell them. It is growing near the end of school. I haven't seen Junior for about 4 or 5 weeks. Bud has sent only 1 letter.

Lots and lots and tons of love, Glenna Lou

Estacada, Ore.
April 30, 1931

Dear Mother,

Will you send Maxine's address so I can write? I will

put the letter to you so that you can read it. I wrote Junior a couple of weeks or more ago, but he has not wrote back. Gramma and Grampa came down tonight.

I know all the states and their capitals. I had to learn them before I could come to the next P.T.A. Us kids down at the school is going to put on the best play.

I counted up the days till school will be out, 17 more days without counting Saturdays and Sundays. Well, must close, but I must not forget to ask how you like my deportment.

Love, Gene Belts

Oregon City, Ore.
April 3, 1931

My Dearest Mother,

How are you? I am not so good as I have the measles and won't go back to school until the 13th of this month. I will write to Dad as he sent me an Easter card today. What was that about the prune yard? I sure hope that I can come out to Pete's this summer. I collected from Miss Hadly and some other people but some people just don't want to pay their money.

Lots of Love, Junior

Estacada, Ore.
May 29, 1931

Dear Mother,

I have just been to the barn and seen our baby kitties. They sure are cute and we have been thinking of names for them. They are about 9 or 10 days old, but this is the first time that I've seen them. I think that I will call one of them

Flaky and another Whity, but we might not have them for long.

I received a letter from Daddy Thursday and he wants us to come and visit him. He said the houses were all full and about 10 kids or more are there, 6 are started to school. School was out Friday up there and it was out here on Tuesday.

Well, I can't think of much more, but I know that I do help Aunt Bert quite a lot. I think I will close, but there is more, I am in the fourth grade next year.

Lots of love to you and Maxine.

Good-bye, Glenna Lou

Estacada, Ore.
May 29, 1931

Dear Mother,

Our school was out the 26th of May and we had a picnic.

We got a letter from Daddy and he said he gave you $15.00 to get our Easter things with and he read the letter that you got from us.

When are you coming down?

Is Maxine still playing the mandolin? Can she play "Old Black Joe" yet?

Well, I must close. Love, Gene

Oregon City, Ore.
June 5, 1931

Dearest Mother,

How are you and Maxine? We got our report cards today and I failed in two subjects darn it all anyway.

I am going out to Grandfather's today. I did not see Billy but the kids there knew her. You know that guy that stole my cap was there.

Are you coming to Eugene many times now? There is plenty of hot weather here. I went swimming at the park yesterday and had a good time.

We went to the ocean last Friday night and stayed until Sunday night. Well, goodbye.

With loads of love, Junior

As the contents of these letters illustrate, the Wymans were a close family who visited back and forth a lot. This was the first time Gene and I had this kind of extended family experience, and we really enjoyed it—especially cousins to play with.

In addition to celebrating all the standard holidays, birthdays, etc., the Wymans also got together on Memorial Day to decorate the family graves located in the Oregon City cemetery. Afterward, they gathered in the local park for a big family picnic. In the old, pioneer section of the cemetery were the graves of our Great-grandparents Wyman and our Great-grandparents Simmons plus a great-aunt and -uncle or two. In the newer section were the graves of our grandmother Lucinda Simmons Wyman as well as many other of our family members and those of the in-laws: the McCombs, the Greens, and the Andruses (Aunt Vera's in-laws).

When Gene and I and our cousin Alan Green got tired of helping distribute the flowers, we walked around—no running was allowed—looking at gravestones, some dating back to the early 1800s.

My aunts and uncles had performed this ritual for so many years, they had it down pat. At 10:00 A.M. they met at their mother Lucinda Wyman's graveside to decide who would decorate which graves; then they set off with good cheer to get the job done. By dividing the graves among them they managed to get done by noon; then it was off to the park for the picnic that was planned. The afternoon was spent remembering little things about this one or that one with fondness and much laughter. Gene and I were amazed to see death, which we thought of as a pretty scary thing, treated in such a comfortable, almost jovial manner.

Early in June 1931, a car we had not seen before pulled up in front of Aunt Bert's house. We were surprised and tickled when Junior, Maxine, Mother, and a man we'd never seen before got out. The man, it turned out, was our new stepfather, John Kinnick, and they were on their way to Montana, where John owned forty acres of irrigated farmland with no buildings on it.

"The place to be in a depression," said John, "is on a farm where you can grow your own food—at least you can always eat. And this depression looks like it is going to last awhile."

John Kinnick was at least twenty years older than my mother, a rather short man with a pleasant face, and he wore a suit and tie every day—not work clothes like the other men. I liked him right away.

The plan was for the four of them to drive on to Seattle, Washington, to visit my Uncle Henry Wyman, then go to Port Angeles to see Aunt Vera Andrus. Maxine was going to stay with Aunt Vera while John, Gladys, and Junior drove on to Montana, where they would camp out on John's land until they could get a house built. Gene and I were to take the train from Portland to Montana later, in time to be there for school in the fall.

During that summer at Aunt Bert's, Gene and I picked loganberries for money—I earned about two dollars and Gene earned three or four dollars. We had additional chores to do, church functions to attend, family picnics, etc., to enjoy. Suddenly it was August and time to go to Portland and board the train for Montana.

When we got to the train depot, Albert went to check our luggage (paper boxes) while Aunt Bert and Uncle Joe took us out to the boarding platform. They explained our situation to the conductor, gave Gene the tickets to carry, and boarded the train with us to get us settled. We had with us a rather large suitcase, and a big bag full of sandwiches, fruit, cookies, and two jars of loganberry juice. And we had our suspicions!

One day soon after we'd entered school at Viola, a man had stopped his car to talk to us as we walked up the hill toward home; then he asked if we'd like to go for a ride with him. We were under strict orders to be home a half hour after school let out and he was headed in the opposite direction, so we declined and ran on up the road, as we were late. Before he could turn around and come back, which he did, we were cutting across the pasture to the house. When we told Aunt Bert about this encounter, she was very upset, and her warnings regarding strangers were so frightening that, from then on, we hid in the woods whenever we heard a car coming up or down the road.

Looking back, I can imagine how amused the other train passengers must have been by this seven- and nine-year-old pair who kept strictly to themselves, who stood guard over their suitcase and lunch as though their lives depended on it, and who rejected every kindly offer of help or attempt at friendly conversation. We never left our seats except to go to the rest room, taking turns so our belongings would not be left unguarded, until we had to change trains that evening.

In Seattle, where the train for Montana left from a different depot, the conductor introduced us to a nice couple who offered to help us make the transfer. Gene, who was in charge, stubbornly refused to go with them, so the conductor finally gave up in disgust and loaded us into a cab, which Gene had money to pay for, and had the cabbie deliver us to the conductor of the train we were to take. The new conductor then helped us board the train and get settled into facing double seats that we had all to ourselves— we were pleased with that.

On this train was a concerned, kindly porter who was also the first black man we'd ever seen up close, let alone talked to, and we were very worried about his intentions. When he brought us two bananas, which we loved, we reluctantly refused them because we thought they might be poisoned. Later, when he offered to show us to the dining car, we wouldn't go for fear he was trying to get us out of the way so he could steal our things.

Between the black porter and other passengers who, in trying to be friendly, commented on how good our sandwiches and jars of loganberry juice looked, we decided we had better stay awake and guard our food and suitcase— after all, we had lots of good eats and other stuff that many people might like to have. I finally fell asleep, but my brother Gene, who took his new responsibility seriously, stayed awake all night to protect me and our belongings. The next morning, after I awoke, he did nap off and on until the conductor came by to tell us we were pulling into the whistle-stop station at Dixon, Montana.

There are no words to express our delight at seeing Mother and John Kinnick waiting for us by the steps the conductor set down for us. He need not have bothered for my sake because I took one look and leaped straight from the train into my new stepfather's arms. Finally, at long last, Gene, Mother, and I were together again.

# 4

From the moment I leaped off the train at Dixon I loved Montana. I could see! It wasn't just a matter of looking out across the pasture to the stand of trees beyond but of seeing for miles and miles and miles across the broad expanse of the Flathead Valley all the way to the Rocky Mountains, which to me, at age seven, looked rather small and insignificant in the distance. The air was hot and dry, with a little swirl of dust dancing here and there above the ground as a small gust of wind picked it up from between the patches of stiff brown grass and clusters of dried-out tumbleweed. How different from the green of grass and trees we'd left in Oregon. But to me, holding tight to my mother's hand as we stood beside the car waiting for Gene and John Kinnick to bring our boxes from where they had been set down from the baggage car, it was the most beautiful, most wonderful place on earth.

As the train started moving slowly down the track and we were waving and calling, "Good-bye! Good-bye!" to the conductor and black porter, John and Gene arrived with our boxes and loaded up the trunk; then we all climbed in the car and breathed a sigh of relief as the engine started with a roar. As we moved off down the road, I climbed up on the seat to look out the back window and was startled to see nothing back there but an empty dirt road next to some railroad tracks with a big DIXON sign standing high between them—it was as if we had never been there.

Gene immediately started asking questions, beginning

with a casual, "What's Junior up to these days?" We were surprised when John, rather than Mother, answered.

"By now, I'd say, he should be about half-done cleaning the barn. That boy's a good worker, all right, but a bit too know-it-all and lippy for my taste." John said with a quick sidelong glance at Mother. Then he gave a little laugh and leaned over and patted her on the knee. "Let me tell you, this woman's been driving me near crazy over meeting you kids. She was up before dawn and wanting to leave by five. I managed to hold her back till six-thirty but even then we got there an hour early." It was sort of a complaint, but you could tell he was happy all the same. And Mother's comment: "Now, John, they aren't interested in hearing about all that," sounded more pleased than scolding.

Gene's next question was about Maxine, and this time it was Mother who explained that Maxine was working for a neighbor to earn money for her school clothes, but she would be home to see us at suppertime. There were more questions about the farm, the animals, and the neighbors and some talk about our trip; then Mother turned to me.

"Glenna Lou, we haven't heard a word out of you. Cat got your tongue?" she teased.

"I'm listening." I said, but the truth is I was pondering a very serious problem. When I'd turned from looking out the back window and settled myself on the seat behind the driver, I was looking at the back of John Kinnick's head and suddenly realized I didn't know what to call him. It made me feel shy. It seemed to me the only way to avoid saying the wrong thing was to say nothing at all, so I remained sitting quietly looking out the window. Not that there was much to see. The countryside was much like Dixon, flat and parched, with the only signs of life the prairie dogs sitting upright by the little mounds of dirt they'd scooped out of the earth to make their underground homes.

John Kinnick's driving style was slow, steady, middle-of-the-road, without accommodation for road surface variations, though on the long straight road across flatland there had been only a minor bump or two. When we moved into the hilly terrain we'd been viewing in the distance, however, there were ruts and potholes the first of which we hit so hard I was thrown clear off the seat onto the floor. All conversation stopped as Mother took up the role of spotter. "Slow down, John," she'd say. "There's one ahead." And while he might swerve to miss it there was no change in speed. "John, why can't you slow down? There is just no need for this," she'd add in an exasperated tone as we hit bottom again, but he'd just laugh and make some cheery remark like "Keeps us awake," or, "Good exercise," and keep right on going at that same steady pace.

Once Gene and I got the hang of how to brace ourselves, the bouncy ride was rather fun, especially after Gene made a game out of counting the number of times the underside of the car scraped on the ground. We were a little disappointed that it was over so soon as we drove down from the hills onto a smoother, well-kept gravel road. A mile or two farther on we found ourselves riding beside lush green fields bordered by ditches filled with water.

"Now this is God's country," said John proudly. "It's irrigated land like ours. Best soil in the world when you get water to it. Handled right, it'll keep you eating and a little money in your pocket, but some of these folks just don't know how to work it or are just plain too lazy to do it right. But you kids don't have to worry none about that. I worked a farm here during the last depression and we made it through just fine and that was with a woman who wanted to sit around all day, not like your mother here, who does her share and more. Now there," he said, pointing to a run-down house and barn in the midst of some scraggly fields.

"There's the farm of a man too lazy to work and make a decent living for his family—being foreclosed on, I hear." Then, ignoring Mother's protest that the man was sick, John changed the subject as he pointed up ahead, "Now look up there. I bet you kids never saw a round barn before."

John's earlier comments had left us a little stunned, for we were not used to being talked to about such grown-up matters but the barn was something we understood, so we looked quickly in the direction he was pointing. Sure enough, it was a round barn, a huge two-story building painted dark red with crisp white trim. It looked so neat with the green fields around it and in the front a big white house in a grove of trees with a bright green lawn stretching all the way to the road. I felt a twinge of envy as I wondered about what kind of family might live there.

"That's Old Man Bates's Place," John said. "It's one of the best in the county, and he's known as the hardest-working man around."

"Too hardworking," Mother commented in a tight-lipped way that told us there was more to say, but it wasn't fit for the ears of children.

The time passed quickly now, as John filled us in on who lived on each farm we passed and gave us his opinion of their farming skills while Mother supplied statistics on the number of children they had and what their ages were. Finally, with a note of excitement in her voice, Mother said, "That hill you see straight ahead up there is Round Butte, and that big white building in front of it is the school you'll be going to next month. It has four teachers, so you'll be in different rooms—Glenna Lou in the third- and fourth-grade room, and you'll be in with the fifth- and sixth-graders, Gene."

Gene poked me and I poked him back as we fidgeted and giggled at the prospect of being in different schoolrooms and because, as Mother had written that our house was only a mile from the school, we knew we were almost home. That was the longest mile in history. When John finally turned into a driveway and stopped the car with a hearty, "Well, here we are," we froze in place like statues, too thrilled to move or speak—it was so fine, so beautiful, so all brand-new, such a contrast to the old, unpainted buildings on the farm we'd left in Oregon the day before. The long, low house and small one-story barn were freshly painted a clean, light gray with sparkling white trim. There was a big green lawn, sunflowers and hollyhocks in bloom beside the pasture fence, and in the pasture a pond of water for the cows and horses. Seeing Junior come sauntering around the corner of the barn just then brought us back to life, and we leaped to open the car door, then paused to look at Mother, as we were still uncertain how to act in this new situation, what with John and all. But Mother just laughed, happy with our amazed reaction to the place, and said, "Go on and say hello. I'll go on in and get dinner on the table and call you when it's ready."

Gene, being bigger and faster, got to Junior first, and while they pounded each other on the arm I grabbed Junior around the waist and hugged him as hard as I could. The boys adopted a sparring stance and threw a few fake punches at each other though Junior was at a disadvantage with me hanging onto him. Then, with my face pressed tight against Junior's chest, I asked the question that had been burning on my tongue all morning: "Do we call him Daddy?"

"*No!!*" It was more an explosion than a word. "Tom Belts is our daddy, and don't you ever forget it. When we asked him, he said to call him John or Kinnick, and we chose Kinnick, and that's what we'll all call him. You hear?" Without even being able to see the tears welling up in my eyes, Junior added in a calmer, more teasing tone as he loosened my arms from around his waist, "Now, Runt, don't you cloud up and rain all over me. He said to call him Kinnick, and that's what we'll do, that's all."

Suddenly the fog I'd been in all morning lifted and I felt good. Junior was in charge again. Life was back to normal. When Mother called us to come and eat I skipped all the way to the house singing, "Cat gave me back my tongue; now, cat gave me back my tongue."

"I'm so glad," Mother laughed as I skipped into the kitchen. "I thought sure I was going to have to put you to bed for the rest of the day. If Glenna Lou isn't talking she must be sick, I said."

The boys went on in to eat, but I stayed behind and whispered to Mother, "Are we really s'pose' to call him Kinnick?"

"Supposed to," Mother whispered back, for proper speech was a big thing with her. "Yes, that's what he said to call him. Why?"

"Because I wanted to call him Daddy."

"I'm sure he'd be pleased by that—whatever you decide." Then in her regular voice as she handed me a dish of pickles she added, "Here, carry this for me and let's go eat."

That first meal in our new house was a memorable one. I sat down on the empty chair beside Gene and started chattering up a storm until Kinnick, for deep down I already knew I'd not be able to defy my brothers and call him Daddy, not out loud anyhow, broke in with an announcement: "We won't have no unnecessary talking at the table in this house. We're here to eat. Now your mother will say the grace."

I saw my brothers exchange looks and duck their heads to keep from laughing as Mother murmured, "Won't have any," before she said the blessing and started passing the dishes of food around for us to help ourselves. There may have been no sound of talking as we ate, but it was not a silent meal. I had never realized, because there had always been conversation and laughter at the tables I had eaten at before, how noisy eating really was. Utensils scraped on dishes as food was scooped up or meat was cut. The sound of chewing came through loud and clear even when we kept our mouths shut as we chewed. And there were smacking sounds and little snorts and grunts. I felt a giggle coming on when I thought how much we sounded like pigs at the feeding trough, but a frown from Mother helped me choke it back.

The three of us raced through dinner quickly, excused ourselves, ran for the back door, and barely made it out of earshot before breaking into howls of laughter. Finally Junior, still laughing some, said, "That's nothin'. If you think that's funny, wait'll you see him try to milk the cows or put the harness on the team. He ain't no farmer—I can tell you that—nor carpenter either. He claims he built a lot of houses but he sure didn't do the work himself from what I saw. Why, within three days after we started on the house I was doin' two to his one on studs and rafters."

"Sounds like I don't have to worry none about conceit," Gene teased, " 'cause you already got it all." A friendly scuffle followed; then Gene, picking up on Junior's negative tone, said, "Well, he's sure no driver either. You shoulda heard him start up the car down at the train. He revved the motor up so high it hurt my ears and smoked so bad I thought it was on fire. And I swear he don't know how to use the brake. He hit every rut and hole full blast. If we hadn't hung on we'd of bounced clear through the roof. I counted fifteen times we bottomed out, and there was at least a couple times before I started counting."

Junior, not yet ready to let it go, went on about what a sissy Kinnick was, what with wearing a tie every day even when he was working in the fields and never swearing, not even when he hit his thumb with the hammer or when the horse stepped on his foot, and how he wouldn't ever take a drink when the whiskey bottle was passed around and all the other men would take a swig. Then Junior talked about how smart Kinnick thought he was just 'cause he'd made a little money here and there, but what really made him mad, Junior said, was how Kinnick bad-mouthed the other farmers and even our own mother, when she'd worked so hard cooking and canning and trying to get everything fixed up nice before we came. Eventually Junior did quiet down, but there was still a touch of sarcasm in his voice as he gave my shoulder a little squeeze and said, "Hey there, Daddy's girl. Now whadaya think?"

"I think you're mean!" I yelled as I twisted out from under Junior's grasp and ran for the barn before he could use his knuckles to Dutch-rub me on the head to clear my brain, a favorite trick of his when I dared to disagree with him.

When the boys came into the barn where I was lying on a bale of straw, they switched from talk of Kinnick to happier boy talk as they set about finishing up the cleaning job Junior had started earlier in the day. The next thing I knew, Gene was shaking me and saying, "Glenna Lou, wake up! Maxine's riding up the lane, and we're goin' out to meet her."

Sure enough, there was Maxine, hair flying in the breeze as the neighbor's horse she was riding came trotting up the drive. "Hey, Runt and Red!" she called as she pulled the reins, then threw her far leg over the horse's mane and slid off its bare back to the ground in one graceful swoop. "You've grown," she said as she looked us over, then laughed. "So now you're even bigger brats than ever." Maxine and Junior thought her joke hilarious, and Gene and I laughed, too, not at the joke exactly but because this was the kind of greeting we felt comfortable and happy with—it was when they were sweet and kind to us that we were wary, because we knew that somewhere down the line there was sure to be a price to pay.

Mother came out of the house just then with a pitcher of lemonade in one hand and a plate of cookies in the other and suggested we do our visiting in the shade beside the house. It seemed like no time at all before John came in from his fence mending and he and the boys went out to do the evening chores while Mother, Maxine, and I went into the house to finish getting supper ready. Gene fell asleep on the floor right after supper—he hadn't gotten a nap as I had, so we let him sleep while we went out and said good-bye to Maxine and waved as she started down the road back to her job. Mother put Gene to bed, then decided she had better do the same with me, as it had been a long and exciting two days and I was probably tired.

When I came out of my bedroom the next morning, I was surprised to see Kinnick all dressed up in a neat brown double-breasted suit with a starched white shirt and tie, standing with one foot on a chair as he shined his shoe. "Where you going?" I asked. It was obvious he would not be doing farmwork dressed like that.

"I'm going to Ronan to cut some hair like I do every Saturday," he answered.

"How come? I thought people went to a barber in a barbershop for that," I said skeptically, because I had been to a barbershop in Oregon with Albert once and knew about such things.

"Well, by trade, I am a barber," he said as he switched feet on the chair and started buffing his other shoe. "You know, when I was young there wasn't much a fellow with a fifth-grade education could do to earn a living but barbering or farming. I didn't want to be a farmer, so my daddy got me into barbering. It's a trade that's served me pretty well, something I can always go back to, like now, to earn a little cash till the crops come in." Looking over his shoe and finding the shine satisfactory, he put his foot back on the floor as he added, "Time to go." He picked up the little black bag that was sitting on the table, kissed Mother goodbye, went out to the car, started it with a roar, and drove off toward town.

I followed him out the door, and after watching the car move down the road with a big dust cloud billowing up behind it I saw my brothers come out of the barn carrying pails of milk. I joined them in their walk to the house, where they set the pails down beside the separator on the back porch and we trooped on in to breakfast—we were pleased to find that talking at the table was allowed when Kinnick wasn't there. After breakfast, Gene went out with Junior to work on the fences while I stayed in, sticking so close to Mother as she ran the milk through the separator, slopped the pigs, and fed the chickens that she started reciting from a poem:

" 'I have a little shadow that goes in and out with me,
And what can be the use of her is more than I can see.' "

She laughed and gave me a little hug to let me know it was all in fun. Then we went into the house and she stayed in the kitchen to do her chores while I went on to explore the other rooms.

Our house was the simplest, most economical shape

there is—a perfectly plain rectangle with no extra little corners or windows that might add interest but also add to the building cost. The end of the house next to the driveway was divided lengthwise down the middle, with the living room across the front facing the road and the back porch, kitchen, and dining alcove in a row across the back. There were three small bedrooms across the far end of the house opening directly off the living room and dining space. Mother and Kinnick had the front bedroom facing the road, Maxine and I were in the middle room, and Gene and Junior were in the back. The bathroom was an outhouse quite far out across the driveway toward the barn.

As one walked into the back porch, there was a washtub on a stand, a sink with a pump for drawing water and washing up, and a big icebox along the wall next to the living room. On the other side was a long screened window above a counter where the small cream separator sat with room underneath for the milking pails and a bucket to hold vegetable cuttings and plate scrapings for the pigs. Inside the kitchen next to the living room wall was a worktable beside a big iron cookstove with cupboards and a window on the outside wall. It was simple and utilitarian, as was the rest of the house and furniture, though everything was clean and polished.

When the boys came in to eat, Mother decided that Gene looked tired and we should both stay in for the afternoon, so we could visit or maybe get out a deck of cards and play some rummy. We voted for the card game, and as soon as the dishes were cleared away Gene dealt a hand that we played by ourselves until Mother finished the dishes and joined us. It wasn't long before my natural inclination to tell everything I knew, and some I didn't, led me into saying, "Junior says Kinnick isn't much of a farmer."

"Well, you better learn to take what Junior says with a

grain of salt," said Mother. "He's had a chip on his shoulder ever since we got here. John's been patient with him, but every man has his breaking point and I'm afraid Junior will push him too far one of these days. I don't know what I am going to do with that boy. But what you should do is not let him tell you what to think, but wait awhile and make up your own minds for yourselves. Now, let's play cards."

Since I had already let the cat out of the bag, Gene apparently decided to bring up the rest of it. "He says Kinnick is a sissy and that he brags and bad-mouths people, even you."

Mother's face turned red as she laid down her cards, got up from her chair, ran into the kitchen, and shut the door. We were astounded. She had been angry, so angry her hand was shaking as she laid down her cards. We heard noises from the kitchen, but it didn't even occur to us that she was crying until she came back to the table with glasses of lemonade for us and we could see that her eyes were red and puffy. But she was calm now, steely calm, as she set a lemonade in front of each of us and, sitting down, said, "Just this once, I'm going to talk about this so as to get it settled now, right off the bat.

"John Kinnick is a good man," she began after taking a long, deep breath. "Let me tell you, there aren't many men who would take a wife with four children to raise in good times, let alone hard times like these. He had the money to buy this farm and build this house, and we should be grateful to him for sharing what he has with us and help him any way we can. As for being a sissy, well, that's the silliest thing I ever heard." She gave a little laugh to emphasize the point, then continued, "John worked as a barber where he had to wear a tie for years and years, and if that's what makes him feel comfortable, then what's the harm? I think it's kind of nice. Oh, I know what Junior says about him not swearing or drinking, but believe me, that makes him twice the man in my eyes as those who do."

Mother paused a minute like she was trying to make up her mind about something, then went on, speaking slowly and careful. "It's true farming doesn't come as naturally to John as it does to some, but that just makes me admire him more, for he has to work even harder to get the job done—but he does know what needs doing and he does get it done, and that's what counts. Sometimes, when a person feels himself at a disadvantage due to lack of education or ability to do something as well as others can, he may talk in a way that isn't considered proper in order to remind himself and others that everyone else isn't perfect either."

Then, with a straight, hard look at each of us, she said sternly, "As to talking about me, well, that's my business and you just let me worry about it. There are things between a man and wife you're way too young to understand. What you can understand is that John's earned the right to brag a little whether we think it's the thing to do or not. When Junior's grown up and done as well for himself, then he'll have earned the right to criticize and not before, and that goes for the two of you as well. Now, that's the end of it. There will be no more talk. You hear?"

We nodded solemnly, a little overwhelmed by her response and more than a little relieved when she smiled and stood up, saying, "Well, nature calls," then hurried out the back toward the outhouse, calling playfully, "When you gotta go, you gotta go!" I felt happy and satisfied with what Mother had said, though I didn't really understand it all, but Gene still looked serious and worried.

"I think Junior plans to run away," he said.

"Did he say so?" I asked.

"Not exactly," Gene replied.

"But what did he say, exactly?" I persisted.

"He said," Gene answered in an exasperated tone, "that he was just waitin' till we got here before he made his move."

Before Mother came back in the house, we speculated on what Junior meant by "made his move". We thought maybe he meant to pick a fight with Kinnick or pull some kind of trick on him, but even at our ages we knew it would still end up the same. One way or another, Junior was going to leave. But then, in the spirit of accepting what we could not change, we brightened up and went outside to play.

After supper we were allowed to pick one each of the white and pink peppermints Kinnick had brought for us from town, but Junior angrily refused the candy and took off walking down the road to visit a friend. Though I didn't realize it at the time, of course Junior would have resented any head of the house right then, for he already considered himself a man and, having gotten his growth early, did actually look much older than his fourteen years. Junior was quite tall and lean and muscular from the farmwork he'd been doing, for he was a hard worker, so fast and efficient that the neighbors had already taken to hiring him over others to help with the haying and the harvest. Then, too, there was considerable attention from the girls, even some much older than himself, for he was a handsome fellow with his dark, curly hair, slim face, slightly crooked nose, and deep-set hazel eyes.

The following morning, Sunday, when Junior was called to get up and do his chores he came out of the bedroom looking as if he hadn't even been to bed. Later we heard Mother getting after him for coming home late and accusing him of drinking and carousing around like a no-good hoodlum. Afterward, he told us he'd gone to a dance in town with some older boys and they'd had a few beers and a fight or two, for as Junior put it, "When a man works hard all week, I think he's earned the right to go out with the fellows on a Saturday night and have some fun."

# 5

Many of the farmers at Round Butte worked straight through, seven days a week, but Sunday at our house was not a regular workday. Soon after arriving in Montana, Mother joined the little church located a half-mile up the hill from Round Butte School, but though he would drive her there and pick her up afterward, Kinnick steadfastly refused to attend the services, as did Junior, though Maxine would sometimes go. Mother had been looking forward to having Gene and me go to church with her and wanted to get us started in Sunday school right away while we were still in the habit of going, as we had in Oregon. On this, our first Sunday here, however, she decided it might be better to wait a week to give us time to settle down and give her time to take care of the string beans she'd neglected due to our arrival. Junior went in to take a nap while Gene and I helped Mother pick the beans, then pulled the strings and snapped them while she packed the jars for canning. "Now that I've had all this good help with the beans," Mother said as we finished up, "I'll have time to make some ice cream. Run out and ask John if he will please get a block of ice from the dugout for me."

At last, the mystery of the dugout was about to be revealed. When we had asked Junior about the big mound of earth behind the house, he had told us it was the "dugout," but children were not allowed inside by themselves for fear they might leave the door ajar, which would let the warm air in to melt the ice. Junior went on to explain how he and Kinnick had dug a big pit in the ground, eight feet wide by twenty feet long by six feet deep, then built a roof of heavy timbers to support the two feet of dirt it was covered with—it was that roof that supported the mound of earth we saw. The word had apparently gotten out when it was finished, because some neighbors came over the following Sunday to visit and to donate a few blocks of ice and some produce from their own dugouts to see us through the summer.

Now, knowing we must play it right to get ourselves invited inside the dugout, we walked quietly up to Kinnick and very politely delivered Mother's message. Sure enough, he told us to come along and take a look. Standing on the steps as Kinnick unlocked the door, I felt a shiver of excitement, for I had never been in an underground room before. It looked dark and eerie as the heavy door swung open until Kinnick reached up and turned on a light so we could see it was just a little storage room with dirt walls, sawdust-covered floor, shelves of potatoes, carrots, and turnips near the door, and blocks of ice intermixed with sawdust at the other end. The real mystery of the dugout was why the ice, stored in such a simple manner, had not melted away completely during the long, hot summer. It seemed a wondrous thing to me then and it does still, though I've heard the logical explanation for it many times, i.e., how the temperature underground does not change as fast as the air above it, so it stays cooler in summer and warmer in winter.

Gene and I knew the pampering was over when Mother started right off Monday morning assigning regular chores for us to do. I was to set the table, dry the dishes, make the beds, and feed the chickens. Gene's chores included getting the cows into the barn for milking, catching the horses and feeding them their morning oats, slopping the pigs, and washing the supper dishes. It was that last assignment Kinnick begged to differ with, for he had very rigid, old-fashioned ideas about what kind of work was appropriate for males versus females. Men built the fires and did the barnyard chores and heavy farm work. Women did the cooking, cleaning, washing, and canning. The light outdoor chores like tending the chickens, pigs, and vegetable garden could be shared. But Mother was determined that all her children learn to cook and clean so we would at least be able to take care of ourselves in a decent manner when we were grown. She prevailed.

The following Friday evening, exactly a week after we arrived, as Gene and I were doing the supper dishes, we heard a commotion and ran outside to see what was going on. What we saw was too ridiculous to be real. It was a slapstick comedy in our own backyard, a hilarious clown act from the circus. There was Junior, young, tall, fast on his feet, running around the dugout with his shirttail billowing in the breeze, being chased by Kinnick, short, middle-aged, flat-footed as a duck, with his full-cut work pants flapping about his legs as he paddled along balancing a shovel up high ready to lower on Junior's head, providing he got close enough—though it seemed to us there was little chance of that. Junior, far out in front, stopped, turned, and adopted a boxing stance as he called out, "Put the shovel down and fight me like a man. I dare you!" But Kinnick just kept on coming until, thinking he was close enough, he brought down the shovel, which Junior deftly sidestepped, and it landed on a rock with a loud, metallic ring.

What could we do but laugh? Unable to get Kinnick to fight on his terms, Junior, seeing he now had an audience to play to, took to jumping and cavorting about as Kinnick picked up the shovel and started after him again. Suddenly Junior ran to the top of the dugout and put his thumbs to his ears and waved his fingers. We laughed so hard we had to hold our sides, until Mother, who had been shouting, "John, get hold of yourself. Put the shovel down!" and, "Junior, go in the house. Right now I say!," grabbed us roughly by the scruff of the neck and pointed us toward the house, saying, "You're just making matters worse! Get out of here! Go!"

We ran around the driveway end of the house toward the front as Junior ran down from the dugout around the other end. He leaped another time or two with hands to ears as he crossed the lawn, then took off running down the road toward his friend's house. We ran down the road after him calling for him to stop and wait for us, but Junior just kept on going as though he couldn't hear us. Finally out of breath, I stopped; then Gene stopped, too, and turned around and came back to where I was sitting in the middle of the road. "Well, that's it," Gene said. "He won't be back."

I got up and Gene and I trudged back toward home shaking our heads about how unpredictable life was. In this past week we'd talked of various scenarios for Junior leaving like Mother might be crying, begging him to stay, or Kinnick might apologize and say they really needed him, then Junior would look noble as he said he was sorry, but he thought it best he go—we had heard such dramas on the radio by then. But never, in our wildest flights of fantasy, had we imagined he'd be chased off by a shovel. "Wow, that was some noise when the shovel hit the rock, wasn't it?" Gene asked, then grinned. "Well, anyway, Junior did go off with a bang."

When we opened the back door to go into the house, Mother, looking grim, came out from the living room and told us to go on and play and not come near the house again until she called. We never did know exactly what she and Kinnick talked about, but there must have been an understanding reached, for when Mother finally called us to come in and get ready for bed she sounded pretty much as usual, except for that certain tone to her voice that told us we had best just do as we were told and do it quietly.

Saturday morning, after Kinnick left for town, we tried to get Mother into a conversation about Junior leaving the night before in hopes of finding out how the chase got started, but all she would say was, "What's done is done. Junior's capable. He'll be all right."

Saturday evening, Kinnick came home from town with three surprises. The first, for Mother, was news that Junior had gone to work at the Bates Place for room and board and a dollar a week. "You kids remember that place." Kinnick said, "The one with the round barn. It's a dairy farm and they have to hire men for milking 'cause they only got one boy of their own. About Junior's age, I think he is—maybe a little older. They have those big black-and-white Holstein cows that give a lot of milk, but so thin you'd take it for water if you couldn't see the color in it. It takes a Guernsey like old Bess out there to give milk rich enough to drink. Now that little Jersey heifer we got, the one that's hard to milk, gives milk that tastes like pure cream, though there isn't as much of it. Well, anyhow, that boy'll learn a thing or two with Old Man Bates all right."

Mother looked serious as she shook her head. "He's picked a hard row to hoe," she declared.

Their comments sounded ominous and we would have liked to ask some questions, but Kinnick handed me his second surprise right then, a big bag of candy with chunks of milk chocolate in addition to the pink and white peppermints he liked. The third surprise was for Gene, but it was Mother who was the most surprised when Kinnick went out to the car and came back carrying a .22-gauge rifle.

Mother, shaking her head unhappily from side to side, said, "John, what on earth were you thinking to buy such a thing? Gene is way too young to have a gun. Besides, there's nothing here to shoot except the birds, and I'll not have that."

"Same age I was when my daddy brought my first rifle home," Kinnick countered. "I thought the boy might do us some good shooting those gophers that are digging up that back field so bad. I figure it's worth a nickel a gopher to be rid of them. That'll give him money to buy his ammunition with and a little left for spending. Now don't you worry none; I'll make sure he learns all the safety rules before he goes off on his own. We'll start right after supper." Seeing Mother was not convinced, Kinnick tried a softer tone. "Why, my daddy took me coon hunting —raccoons, they're called out here—just three weeks after I got my gun, and I shot a coon all on my own. Biggest thrill of my whole life. I got to thinking about that today when that fellow came in the shop with this rifle for sale."

"Hmmph!" Mother snorted. "More likely guilty conscience than nostalgia, I suspect." But she could see Gene standing there looking anxious, barely breathing, as he awaited her decision, so she clamped her jaws together in that way she had of showing her displeasure and gave a little shrug of resignation. She was not pleased, but Gene could keep the rifle.

"Well, I best change my clothes and get to the milking," said Kinnick, knowing when to accept his winnings and move on before Mother had a chance to change her mind.

"I'll help," Gene offered quickly as he ducked his head to hide the smile that had spread across his face. "I've already been milking Ole Bess all week, anyhow."

*What a faker.* I thought resentfully as I watched Gene trying to match Kinnick's stride as they walked to the barn together later. *He's taking over Junior's place already. I bet Gene's glad he's gone.*

After supper, Mother offered to wash the dishes for Gene so the shooting lessons could begin. "If you're bound to do it, you might just as well get at it," she said.

A couple of days later, Kinnick declared Gene ready to start shooting gophers. "The boy's a quick learner," he said. "Gene, get the gun and show your mother the proper way to handle it."

Gene, pleased, moved quickly to do as he was told, for once, and proudly demonstrated how to load and unload the rifle, how to put the safety on, and how to carry the gun with barrel pointed to the ground away from his feet. We even went out back to the target range Kinnick had set up so Gene could demonstrate his shooting skill. Mother agreed he seemed to be doing well, so far as she could see, and gave permission for the gopher hunt to begin the following afternoon.

I don't know exactly what I expected gopher hunting to be like, but I was not prepared when the first gopher Gene shot sat there upright for a moment then fell to the ground and flopped around and twitched awhile before it finally lay still. I was shocked and saddened, but I must also have been fascinated, for I did continue going on the hunt with Gene, though I would turn my back each time he aimed the gun and wait for his triumphant, "I got him!" or disappointed, "Darn it all!" before I turned to look.

One especially hot afternoon, we came back to the house earlier than usual because there were so many gophers to shoot at that Gene ran out of bullets. Mother was in favor of our staying in but Gene, foreseeing her objections, had left the gunnysack of gopher bodies in the field. As long as he had to go back for the sack anyhow, he argued, he might as well take a few more shots—that nickel per dead gopher Kinnick had offered was a powerful incentive. Mother grudgingly gave in and I watched as Gene carefully loaded the rifle and put the safety on; then, as he turned to go out through the back, I heard a shot. I don't remember feeling anything, but I did look down and saw a stream of blood spurting far out from my leg. "I've been shot!" I cried with all the drama I could muster.

Mother was not the kind of lady who went to pieces in a crisis, and this was no exception. She did gasp when she saw the spurting blood but quickly recovered and helped me to the couch, where she proceeded to elevate my leg with pillows to help stop the bleeding. As she turned to go for cloths and her first-aid kit, she said, "Gene, get John! Quickly now! He'll have to drive us into town to see the doctor."

I was amazed to see Gene standing there with tears streaming down his cheeks, looking so white his freckles stood out like bits of paper pasted on his face. When he turned and ran out the back door without a single word, no laugh, no cute remark, I knew he was scared, really scared, but thought he was afraid of being punished. It didn't even occur to me he might be afraid for me, as being shot seemed no more serious than other cuts and scrapes. In fact, this wound hurt less than many a skinned knee I'd had. "It's not Gene's fault," I said to Mother as she returned. "I saw him put the safety on, and his hand was off the trigger."

"I know," she said, "but let's not worry about that now. Ah, good; I see the bleeding's slowing down. We'll just clean this up a bit so I can see—does that hurt?" she asked as she uncovered the wound and used a wet cloth to clean off my leg around the hole. Now, squatting down to take a closer look she saw blood dripping from the couch into a pool on the floor. "Uh-oh, I'm going to have turn you on your side to see in back. Now, just relax." she said as she gently lifted me from the side and rolled me partway over. "Good Heavens, child, that bullet went clear through. There's another hole in back. I'll have to make a tourniquet. Can you balance there on your side a minute?"

I nodded and concentrated on lying still while she ran to the kitchen and came back with a dish towel and a table knife. She put the towel around my leg above the hole and made a knot with the knife run through it, then turned the knife until the cloth tightened up to where it hurt my leg— but it seemed to slow the bleeding. I whimpered at the hurting and Mother talked to me soothingly as she alternately turned the knife backward to loosen the cloth and check the clotting, then forward again to tighten it. Finally, she pronounced the blood flow nearly stopped and bandaged my leg with the gauze and tape from her first-aid kit, then wrapped it with a strip of cloth torn from an old sheet she'd saved for rags. "Can you lie still there by yourself a few minutes while I get some things to the car?" she asked. "I want to be all ready to go the minute John gets here to drive us."

I remember very little about the trip to town except that I kept drifting off and Mother kept waking me up and urging me to take another sip from the jar of water she had brought. "You need the liquid to replace the blood you've lost," she'd say, and when I resisted, "You do as I say," she threatened, "or I'll climb back there and pour it down your throat." I whimpered, but I drank the water.

The doctor we went to was an older, white-haired gentleman who had treated a great many bullet wounds as an army doctor during World War I. "You are a very lucky young lady," he said cheerfully to me as he examined the hole in my leg, though he was really directing his remarks to Mother, who was holding me still on the table. "That bullet just grazed the main artery, so you got a good blood flow to cleanse the wound but not so much that you couldn't get it stopped—which would have been the case if it had pierced the artery. Your brother is a good shot. You tell him that for me, will you?"

I nodded and smiled along with Mother and the doctor, although I wasn't exactly sure what I was smiling about. Mostly, I guess, I was relieved that the doctor wasn't angry at me for causing him so much trouble.

When Kinnick came in to carry me to the car, the doctor told him what great nursing skill Mother had shown in taking care of me and what a brave patient I had been while he cleaned and bandaged the wound. Mother, never able to accept a compliment graciously, blushed and protested that it was nothing as she quickly picked up our things and hurried to the car. I, on the other hand, felt pleased and happy with the compliment and began to think, right then, that this getting-shot business might not be so bad after all.

The next few days floated by in a haze, as I was weak from the loss of blood and mostly slept on the little cot Mother had set up for me in the dining area so she could keep a close eye on me as she went about her household chores. The doctor had told her that the main dangers from a gunshot wound were dehydration, excessive bleeding, and infection. She was to give me liquids every two hours, day and night, keep me quiet to avoid further bleeding, and cleanse the wound and change the dressing often to avoid infection. In addition there was the medicine to give me, meals to prepare, bathroom chores to handle, and entertainment to keep me quiet. It was a tall order, but she managed and by the end of the first week, when we were due to go back to the doctor, I was wide awake and feeling fine, except that my leg still hurt too much to stand or walk on.

Ah, how sweet it was! I had my mother all to myself,

really paying attention to me, really concerned for me, really talking and listening to me. It was a whole new experience to have her undivided attention, for up to that time I had pretty much viewed her from a distance filled with two brothers and a sister. Then, too, Gene was being unusually kind and considerate, like bringing me crayons and paper when I asked or deferring to my choice of radio programs. And Maxine, full of laughter and stories about the children she looked after on her job, had been to visit me twice during the week. It was truly grand.

The first Wednesday after the accident, we were all anxious to see if there would be an article about the shooting in the weekly newspaper. Gene and Kinnick were in for lunch when the mailman arrived, and Gene ran to the mailbox and came back waving the paper to show that it was here, then handed it to Kinnick, who was always the first to read it. It seemed like it took him forever to look through the paper, but finally, near the back, he found a small notice to the effect that Glenna Lou Belts had suffered a gunshot wound in the leg as a result of her having stepped into the line of fire as her brother, Gene Belts, shot at a gopher out in a field near their home.

"But it isn't true!" I shouted. "We were in the house. How could they write something like that that isn't true?"

"A good lesson on life," responded Kinnick, showing none of the resentment the rest of us were feeling. "Those fellas that write for the paper think they have a license to make minor changes here and there to spark up a story. It's a good thing to remember when you're tempted to believe all you read about other folks. Nothing to do but learn the lesson and move on."

Shortly before we left for town to see the doctor for my first follow-up visit, Mother called Gene into the kitchen and whispered something to him; then he went to his bedroom and came back carrying the little tobacco pouch he kept his gopher money in. "Here, buy yourself something to play with while you're laid up," he said, as he handed me the bag of nickels and made a shooting-marbles motion with his other hand off to the side so Mother couldn't see. I felt bad, for I knew the money meant a lot to him, but before I could think of something to say Kinnick arrived to carry me to the car for the trip to town.

Our visit to the doctor was a great success. He was pleased with my progress, and while he had complimented Mother on her handling of the accident when we first saw him, on this, our second visit, he was positively effusive in his praise of her nursing skills. To Kinnick, whom he knew from the barbershop, he said, "You'd better watch out, John. If my nurse ever decides to leave me, I'll be trying to steal this wife of yours away from you to come to work for me."

Kinnick puffed up with pride as he responded, "Well, I stole her away from a family in Eugene, Oregon, where she was doing practical nursing, but I warn you, I won't give up easy on that one. She's a worker all right, but she's got all she can do right where she is, and I intend to keep her there."

Mother, embarrassed but pleased, said, "Now that is enough nonsense out of you two. John, you just get Glenna Lou to the car so we can get on with the rest of our shopping. This day is going to be gone before you know it. Then, too," she added, smiling at me as Kinnick picked me up and started for the car, "somebody I know has some deciding to do about what to buy with all that spending money she got this morning."

"I already know what I want!" I called excitedly to Mother, who had stayed behind to talk to the doctor. "I want a book of real paper dolls and a bag of marbles."

Kinnick sat in the car with me while Mother did the

grocery shopping, then he went in to carry the groceries to the car for her while she talked to me about the purchases she was to make for me at the dime store. "Are you sure Gene didn't ask you to get him some marbles?" she asked, knowing full well they were probably not for me. I shook my head to indicate he hadn't, which was, strictly speaking, true. She stood there a minute, then, apparently deciding it was better to encourage my generosity than to pursue punishing Gene, gave me a skeptical look to let me know she knew what was going on here and headed for the dime store. She soon returned and handed me a big paper sack to explore on the trip home.

A perfect moment is when you experience the joy of receiving something you have longed for suddenly, unexpectedly, toward the end of summer with your birthday and Christmas still months away. In the book of paper dolls were drawings of two little girls painted with perky faces, luxuriant long, curly hair, one brunette, one blond, each wearing bloomers and an undershirt. There were pretty dresses, coats, capes, hats, shoes, even a pair of gloves, all designed to fit both dolls. And the marbles, so smooth, so round, so colorful, viewed with the anticipation of pleasing Gene, were perfect. Then at the bottom of the sack to find, surprise, a box of crayons—and to realize as Kinnick frowned and shook his head at Mother's extravagance that she had wanted to please me more than she wanted to please him.

On the drive back from Ronan to Round Butte, Kinnick broached the subject of Maxine coming home to help Mother through the next two weeks of my convalescence: "Gladys, since Doc says Glenna Lou won't be able to walk for two more weeks, I wonder if you should maybe bring Maxine home to help you out. You're getting so worn out trying to do it all you're liable to make yourself sick—then where'd we be?" he said.

"You mean have her quit her job?" Mother asked. "Oh my, I would really hate to do that. She's counting on every penny of her wages for school clothes, and it is so important to her. She had a really rough year in Eugene, with old clothes, no spending money. You just can't imagine what it means to her, what with starting a new school and all." After a short pause she added tentatively, "Well, perhaps, if we could make up the difference. It wouldn't really be that much."

Kinnick humphed and hahed and somehow managed, without ever actually committing to a financial arrangement, to talk Mother into bringing Maxine home. Maxine, as Mother predicted, did not take kindly to the idea and for the first few days was a whirlwind of resentful action. Instead of telling me funny stories as she had on her earlier visits, she hissed at me each time she walked by me on the cot in the dining room.

"Mother, Maxine hissed at me again!" I'd call, and the first time or two Mother clucked and scolded at Maxine. Finally, tired of this repetitive battle, Mother tried a different approach.

"Glenna Lou, do you remember what you used to say when the kids teased you?" she asked as she sat down beside me on the cot. " 'Sticks and stones can break my bones, but hisses can never hurt me.' Just think of that and ignore her and tend to your own business. She'll soon quit hissing if you don't respond."

I giggled at Mother's substitution of *hisses* for *words* in our old saying, but I determined to try it. How satisfying it was to see that sudden flash of disappointment on Maxine's face the first time I applied this new approach. It worked!

On my third weekly visit to the doctor, Maxine went to

town with us to do her shopping for materials and patterns so Mother, an expert seamstress, could begin making her school clothes. The house became a flurry of cutting, stitching, fitting, and arguing, crying, screaming. Maxine was a pretty girl but slightly pudgy—not fat, but pudgy. She believed that tighter-fitting clothes made for a slimmer look. Mother disagreed. With both of them equally strong-willed and determined to prevail, the house became a battleground, and I, now able to get around on the crutches the doctor had loaned me, spent most of my time outdoors feeling sorry for myself about having my moment in the sun so suddenly eclipsed.

There was one lovely happening that week, however, when Junior, having heard of the shooting accident, came to visit me. It was Saturday afternoon, while Kinnick was gone to do his weekly barbering, that I heard a noise and looked up to see a horse bearing down on me at a full gallop. He came to a halt so suddenly, so close to me, I thought for sure he was going to run me over; then there was Junior, happy, laughing, as he slid off the horse's back and came over to me. "Hey there, Runt, how's that gunshot leg by now?" he asked as he reached over to Dutch-rub my head in a playful manner.

"Quit that!" I shrieked as I knew he expected me to, then yelled to anyone within hearing range, "Junior's here! Come quick! Junior's here!" In just three weeks' time Junior seemed to have grown taller, older, as though he'd been gone at least a year. I was so tickled to see him. "Where'd you get the horse?" I asked, for I knew better than to say anything mushy about how glad I was he'd come. But before Junior could answer, Mother, Maxine, and Gene came running up to extend their greetings.

There were hugs, smart remarks, and arm pounding as each of them welcomed Junior in his or her own particular style. I was grateful, actually, to have his attention diverted just then for I was feeling shy, overcome with the knowledge that he cared enough to come and see me. It wasn't long before Mother took Junior by the arm and said, "You come with me while I make some Kool-Aid. I want to talk to you." It was clear from her tone and the look she gave the rest of us that this was to be a private talk—we were not invited.

The afternoon flew by quickly. Junior's first big announcement was that we were to call him Henry or Hank, as the fellows called him—no more Junior. He didn't have too much to say about his job except that it was "all right," but he glowed with pride when he talked about the beautiful little sorrel horse he had ridden up on. He had been a wild pony, Junior said, that Old Man Bates bought and could never get broke for riding until he, Junior, took over. He talked about how fast it was, how quick, how strong. Junior hoped to talk Old Man Bates into letting him ride the pony in races and split the winnings with him. I talked a little about getting shot. Maxine told Junior about having to come home from her job early to help with the housework so Mother could spend more time with me—hmmph! Gene bragged about how well he was doing on Junior's chores. But the highlight of the afternoon was when Junior told us about how the incident leading up to his leaving home got started.

"Well, I went out after supper that night to work on the chicken fence Mom had been after me to build. I had the postholes all laid out nice and even and was using the posthole digger on about the fourth hole when I hit a rock I couldn't budge with the digger, so I went and got the shovel and started digging it out. Now, here comes Kinnick, poking his nose in as usual, saying to fill the hole I'd started and dig a new one a foot or two farther over. I said I'd rather keep the holes spaced even for a decent-looking fence, but Kinnick said that was silly and kept insisting on doing it his way till I finally got mad and handed him the shovel, saying, 'Here, old man, you're so darn smart—you do it!' and I walked away. Well, then I heard this kind of grunting noise and looked around, and there he was coming at me with the shovel, looking for all the world like a little ole banty rooster with his feathers all ruffled up." Junior laughed and shook his head. "I couldn't believe he'd get so mad over just one little thing like that, but I wasn't in the mood to stand there and get my brains bashed in either."

We all laughed then, including Mother, for she couldn't keep herself from seeing the humorous side of things, but she soon stopped laughing and addressed the more serious aspect of the conflict. "Now, that is enough!" she said sternly. "One day you'll understand what 'the straw that broke the camel's back' really means and then you'll have more sympathy for John. He had been putting up with your defiant, disrespectful attitude ever since we got here, Junior—Henry, that is—and it was all of those incidents lumped together that caused him to lose control, not just that 'one little thing,' as you put it. Now, you've told your story and you've made your move, though I expect you'll live to regret your choices as I told you earlier, but it's best for now to put the matter behind us and move on. Maxine, why don't you show Junior your new school clothes while Gene and Glenna Lou help me get these glasses and things picked up?"

Maxine shrugged and headed for the house knowing full well that last question was not a question but Mother's way of putting an end to the discussion. Junior made a face, but he did get up and follow Maxine toward the house.

"Are you getting any new school clothes?" Gene asked Junior as he walked away.

"Naw, I'm not going back to school," Junior answered. "Who needs book learnin' when they can get an education out of livin'?"

Junior not going on to high school—that was a shocker! Knowing how much our education meant to Mother, I glanced over to see how she was taking it and was just in time to see the tears begin to flow before she turned her back to us and pulled up the bottom of her apron to wipe her eyes. Gene and I stood there for a minute or two while she sobbed quietly. Then she gave her shoulders a little shake to help regain control and said, with her voice still slightly shaky, "Come on, you two; let's get these dishes into the house before the afternoon's clear gone."

# 6

The month of August 1931, our first month as a family in Montana, was finally over. It had been a "test by fire" for Kinnick, and while he occasionally looked baffled by or sometimes disapproving of our behavior, he still seemed comfortable and happy with the family situation so far as I could tell. The state of the economy in this year of deepening depression was, however, quite a different matter. On Saturday nights, when he returned from his day in town, and sometimes into Sunday there was bound to be one or two loud, angry discussions about farms being foreclosed on and the steadily dropping price for wheat and oats, two of the big cash crops in the Round Butte farming area.

Kinnick was an ultraconservative Republican with a very simple "work or starve," black-and-white philosophy of life, but the worsening economy was creating an environment that fell into a gray area between these two extremes, and his thinking pattern was having trouble coping. Many of our neighbors were in deep financial trouble, and while he could dismiss a few as being lazy or inept, he knew that most were decent, hardworking folks caught up in a situation beyond their control. Furthermore, he could see his own plan for surviving the depression might not work out, and it made him furious. He would lash out at President Hoover as a "disgrace to the Republican Party," but it was the Democrats with their talk of a moratorium on farm foreclosures, make-work programs, and personal income taxes, whom he most despised. He saw them as the "ruination of the country."

Gene and I were a little frightened—at least I was—of Kinnick's political discussions what with his stomping, shouting, and fist banging on the table to emphasize a point. After the first time or two, I tried to tune out his angry tirades, but Gene, always open for a new adventure, began to listen attentively. Gradually Gene picked up on those points that made Kinnick the angriest and started introducing them into the discussion from time to time in his own special innocent-sounding way; then he would sit back and watch the fireworks. At first Mother was pleased to see Gene taking an interest in national affairs, but she soon caught on to what he was doing and put a stop to it.

Provided the fields were planted early and the weather cooperated, the grains were ready for harvest in late August, sometime before Labor Day. In response to this big influx of cash in the area each fall, the businessmen in Ronan organized a three-day Labor Day Weekend Festival. They brought a carnival to town, sponsored a rodeo and horse races, and provided games for children, competitions for men, and entertainment for the ladies. It was the one big celebration of the year, and almost every family attended for at least one day. With a single trip to town the farmers could purchase their children's school clothes and supplies and have plenty of time left over to enjoy the festivities. Although our grain fields had been planted late, so they wouldn't be ready to harvest until the middle of September, Kinnick agreed to let us all ride into town with him on the Saturday before Labor Day, his regular barbering day, to attend the opening day celebration and buy the shoes and other things we needed for school. Mother knew that money was tight and assured Kinnick she would keep the purchases to a minimum.

The night before we were to go on our trip to town,

Mother fixed Kinnick's favorite dinner: a pork roast with lots of mashed potatoes and gravy and apple pie for dessert. She also fixed green beans and a salad, but Kinnick, being strictly a meat and potatoes man, would rarely eat cooked vegetables and called green salad "cattle food— unfit for human consumption."

After supper, as we were sitting in the living room, Mother brought up the reason behind the special dinner: "John, Maxine still has shoes and underthings to buy for school, so she needs the wages we owe her for the work she did here these past two weeks."

"We owe her! We owe her!" Kinnick exploded. "We owe her nothing! It was her mother and her sister she came to help, and she should have been happy to do it for free." Then he looked at me. "You were there when we talked about this, Glenna Lou. Did I ever once say I'd pay her?"

Before I could jump in and say he actually hadn't said he'd pay, Mother leaped to her feet and faced Kinnick belligerently with hands on hips. "Don't you dare try to bring Glenna Lou in on this," she hissed. "It's not her business, nor Maxine's either for that matter; it's between you and me. You made a commitment to me and I mean to see that you keep it!" Then turning to Gene and me, she said, "You kids go on outside and play. We don't need any extra sets of ears in here right now."

When I stood up to follow Gene my legs were so shaky I had trouble making it to the outside, where I sank to the ground to sit beside Gene near the back door with my back against the house and my arms hugging my legs so tight against my chest, I could rest my chin comfortably on my knees. We could hear the sound of angry voices but couldn't make out what was being said until we heard Kinnick stomping through the kitchen to the back porch and calling, "All right! All right!" as he came through the back door looking slightly stunned.

Seeing us sitting near the door, Kinnick paused. "I'll tell you kids one thing!" he said in a tone of grudging admiration. "That mother of yours is a regular buzz saw when she gets her dander up." There was the hint of a smile on his face and he made a kind of chuckling sound as he shook his head and walked on out toward the chicken house.

"Come on," Gene said as he jumped up to go inside the house, but I shook my head, preferring to stay where I was until I knew the coast was clear. The last time I'd heard Mother get so angry was that night in Lynx Hollow when my father hit her and took off down the road. I was scared of walking in on another scene like that.

Gene, always seeming to know what I was thinking, soon stuck his head out the back door. "Hey, quit being a fraidy cat!" he called. "Everything's OK. Maxine got her money."

When I opened the screen door to go inside, I found Mother waiting for me on the back porch. "Here, scrub these potatoes so I can get them cooked for tomorrow's potato salad," she said happily as she handed me the vegetable brush and stood me in front of the sink full of potatoes. "Gene, you bring in more wood. We'll have to build the fire up to boil potatoes and heat the bathwater. We want to be spanking clean for our big day tomorrow." Then spotting Kinnick at the back door, "Oh, John, thank you, dear. Just put the rooster in the bucket and I'll scald him down as soon as the water boils; then Gene can pluck him. You just go on in and listen to your ball game on the radio. The kids and I will soon have things under control here."

This time it was my turn to shake my head. One minute we were on the brink of disaster, and the next minute things were lovey-dovey. I sure couldn't figure out what made these grown-ups tick.

We left the farm for our Labor Day Weekend Festival day in Ronan shortly after sunrise. When we arrived in town, Kinnick parked the car in an empty lot next to the town park, where we would be eating our picnic lunch, and walked over to the barbershop in time to start his workday at 7:00 A.M. The rest of us unloaded the homemade cooler with its big chunk of ice and the food Mother had prepared and put it under one of the picnic tables where it would be in the shade and reserve the table for us. Then, since the stores would not be open for at least another hour, we walked down to look over the carnival grounds.

Gene and I had been to the circus once, but we had never seen a carnival before, and we found it fascinating. We wandered among the booths with their inner workings closed off from view by the canvas drops fastened tightly to the counters or to stakes in the ground, but we could still read the enticing messages painted on the brightly colored facings above the canvas drops. That was enough to whet our appetite for winning prizes as each booth we passed seemed to be offering an even more desirable prize than the one before. There were pictures of stuffed animals, kewpie dolls, jackknives, swords, guns, with lots of TEST YOUR SKILL and EVERYBODY WINS signs. As we ran from booth to booth bragging about how we would toss the ring, throw the ball, or shoot the gun with such speed and accuracy we would probably win more prizes than we could carry, Mother followed along quietly, though Maxine joined in the fun from time to time. It was the carnival rides, however, that pushed our excitement to fever pitch as they stood like eerie giants from another world, temporarily motionless but poised to spring into action when the time was right.

Too soon, it was time for the retail stores to open for business and Mother insisted we head downtown so as to get our shopping done before the stores got crowded. Maxine went off to do her shopping by herself, but Mother kept Gene and me with her so she could fit our shoes and we could help pick out our own school supplies. We each got a pair of shoes large enough to grow into in the hope they would last all year, two pairs of socks, a pencil box, and a tablet, and for Gene two pairs of corduroy pants—my school dresses and Gene's shirts, Mother had already made from material our Aunt Eva had sent from California. When we asked about the underwear we thought we would be buying, Mother told us she had decided to make our underwear out of Kinnick's old long-johns, what with money being so tight right now. That was fine with us— who wanted to waste time shopping when there were so many places to go, so many sights to see?

The rest of the morning passed quickly. We walked back to the car to stow our purchases, then had some cookies and Kool-Aid from our picnic box. We swung on the swings, tried out the teeter-totter, and climbed a tree to watch the opening day parade go by. It seemed like no time at all until Mother was calling us to come and eat. Maxine was at the picnic table with Mother when we got there, and before long Kinnick came hurrying up to join us. Mother chided Kinnick for gobbling his fried chicken and potato salad down so fast, but he said he wanted to get back to the barbershop as soon as possible, for business was brisk and every haircut meant another two bits in his pocket. He even pulled a big handful of quarters out of his pocket to show us how much business he'd done already.

"Come and sit down here at the table a minute," Mother said to us after the picnic dishes were washed and the leftovers put away. "You know," she began quietly, "I didn't want to spoil your fun this morning when we walked through the carnival, but it costs money to play those games and ride those rides. The truth is, we just don't have it. Maybe you can win a prize in the children's games that will be starting right here in the park pretty soon instead."

I felt a black cloud of disappointment wash over me and blinked my eyes to hold back the tears and I could see that Mother was also on the verge of crying—but all was not lost. "Well, lucky for you I've got money left to spend," Maxine said cheerily as she jumped up from the table. "Come on; let's go!" she called as she walked swiftly toward the carnival grounds. In an instant we were up and running to catch up with her; then Mother got up and followed slowly along behind us. When we reached the carnival grounds, Maxine headed straight for the ticket booth, where she bought six tickets and handed two each to me and Gene. She and Gene decided on the two wildest, most adventurous rides there were. Although Maxine assured me the cages would hold all three of us, I hung back to wait with Mother—my heart was set on riding the Ferris wheel and the merry-go-round.

Maxine had another surprise in store for us when she and Gene came back looking flushed and happy after their second ride. "I'll pay for your ticket if you'll go on the Ferris wheel with Runt," she said to Mother. "You've always said that was your favorite ride. That's probably what made her choose it in the first place."

"Oh, I can't let you do that," Mother said. "You had better hold onto your money. It may be a long time before you'll have a chance to earn more what with the way things are."

"Why do you always have to act like such a martyr?" Maxine complained. "You say it's better to give than to receive, but you never let anyone give to you." With that, she marched over to the ticket booth and returned with a ticket she handed to Mother. "Here, use it or throw it away, I don't much care which," Maxine said disgustedly as she walked away.

Mother smiled at me and made a little show of holding back as I tugged and pulled her by the hand toward the Ferris wheel. The attendant took our tickets and held the chair still with his foot as he helped us get seated; then he snapped the bar securely closed in front of us. I thought we were on our way when the Ferris wheel began to move; then it stopped and I looked at Mother in surprise. "Don't worry," Mother whispered. "He has to load up the rest of the chairs. When you hear the music start is when the ride will actually begin."

Start and stop. Start and stop. Up, up we went until at last we were at the very top of the Ferris wheel, and what a beautiful view it was. We could see the entire town laid out below us, and Mother pointed out the high school Maxine would be attending, the granary by the railroad tracks where the farmers came to sell their grain, and the mill next to it where they had some of their wheat ground into flour and oats rolled out for breakfast cereal. To the east, we could see across the river to the foothills with the Rocky Mountains beyond, to the south were vast fields of sugar beets, and to the west was the road we had traveled into town on that morning stretching in the distance all the way to Round Butte, which looked no bigger than a tiny knoll from here.

Maxine had returned and was standing with Gene when we walked over after finishing our ride. "Was it fun?" Maxine asked. As we nodded and agreed it had been fun, a little flicker of triumph flashed across Maxine's face and she said to Mother, "Good. That makes us even then."

"No," Mother replied thoughtfully, "Between parents and children there is no such thing as even. It doesn't work that way. What I do for you you pass on to your children by doing for them, then they in turn do for theirs—and so it goes. My reward will come from seeing you complete your education and make a good life for yourself in this world."

"Lecture. Lecture. Always a lecture," Maxine grumbled. "I'm going back over town and do some window-shopping. I'll meet you at the barbershop at six."

The afternoon went by as quickly as the morning had. We walked around the carnival a while longer, then went back to the park and participated in some of the children's games, though we won no prizes. After that we listened to the entertainers as we rested on the chairs in front of the bandstand, and at six o'clock we walked over to the barbershop to meet Maxine and Kinnick.

Mother had warned us that Kinnick would likely want to head straight home after such a busy day in the shop, but that was not the case. Kinnick was full of energy and smiles as he came out to meet us. "Well, this was a red-letter day in my book," he said triumphantly. "I cut more hair today that I did in the last three Saturdays. This calls for a celebration. What do you say we go for dinner down at the barbecue and stick around long enough for a waltz or two at the street dance later?"

With hoots of delight Gene and I headed for the river, where we'd seen big chunks of beef being turned slowly on spits above huge fire pits. Gene and I had hot dogs, which were a great treat for us, while Kinnick, Mother, and Maxine had barbecued beef sandwiches and coleslaw. It seemed as if Kinnick knew everyone in town, judging by the number of people who stopped by to say hello to him as we sat eating at one of the makeshift tables. It really made me feel important just to be sitting there with him.

After dinner Kinnick surprised us again by suggesting we walk through the carnival while we waited for the street dance to begin. Once we got to the carnival grounds, Kinnick headed straight for the booth with a sign that read: "5 Shots, 10 Cents." He put a dime on the counter and picked up one of the rifles, looked it over carefully, held it up to his shoulder and sighted down the barrel, then handed it to Gene, saying, "Here; aim a little high and to the left." The attendant scowled, but he picked up Kinnick's dime and stood off to the side as Gene aimed and shot, hitting the target four times out of the five tries, which was good enough to win a jackknife.

As we turned to walk away, Kinnick said, "These guys set the sights off on purpose so it's hard to win. You did good, Gene. Now, Glenna Lou, which booth would you like to try to win a prize from?" he asked as he handed me a dime.

"The ring toss," I answered, as I had been wanting one of the Kewpie dolls offered as a prize.

All of the throwing spots were busy when we got to the ring toss booth, so I had time to watch as others threw and missed. It looked like this was going to be harder than I thought. When my turn came I gave my dime to the attendant, took the five rings he gave me, then turned and handed them to Gene, saying, "Here; you do it for me." Gene, never one to back away from a challenge, took the rings, stepped up, and threw all but one with accuracy. Again, four out of five tries was good for a prize. As I tried to decide which Kewpie doll I wanted, I glanced over at Mother just in time to see her move close to Kinnick and slip her hand through his arm and give it a grateful little squeeze—she looked happier, more contented, right then, I think, than I'd ever seen her.

The day after Labor Day was the first day of school, and while Gene and I were excited, Maxine was a nervous wreck. She broke a fingernail; her clothes didn't look right;

90

her hair wouldn't stay in place; carrying a lunch was beneath her dignity. The more Mother tried to reassure her, the more upset she got, and her method of handling anxiety was to attack. When I told her I thought her hair looked pretty she turned on me in a fury. "What do you know about it?" she screamed. "You're happy with that boy's haircut that makes you look like a freak. You look even worse than I do and you don't even care. They'll laugh you right out of school."

"Stop that!" Mother commanded. "Don't try to ruin Glenna Lou's day just because you're in a tizzy. I can see the bus. Here, take your lunch, you'll have to hurry," she said as she handed Maxine her lunch sack and gave her a little pat on the back that Maxine shrugged off as she hurried out the door.

Actually, my haircut had been one of the many family crises that occurred during those first months of adjustment to our new stepfather. Just the day before, on Labor Day, Mother had asked Kinnick, since he was a barber, to cut Gene's and my hair—Maxine had already cut her own to that new windblown style with the little spit curls around the face that was so popular then. Kinnick readily agreed to cut Gene's hair but wasn't too sure he could do a very good job on me, as he was strictly a man's barber, but Mother insisted and in the end he had cut my hair in a style very much like Gene had but slightly longer. Mother and Maxine were horrified, but I liked it—it required little combing, was easy to wash, and was different. That last part, that it was different, was what upset Maxine the most. She felt embarrassed, like it was some sort of reflection on her to have a sister with a boy's haircut, and she was determined to make me feel embarrassed, too, but it wasn't working and that upset her even more.

Because our house was a little less than a mile from the

Round Butte School, we were not allowed to ride the school bus, and on this, the first day of school, Mother planned to walk with us to be sure we knew the way and to make sure our records were delivered and we were properly enrolled. It took no time at all, once Maxine left, to get ready and take off down the road. After climbing the long row of steps to the second floor of the schoolhouse, where the classrooms were, we found a little office just inside the door staffed by a lovely little lady, the school principal's wife, Mrs. Kircoffe, who made us welcome, completed the necessary paperwork, and pointed out our classrooms. Gene said he'd rather go into his classroom by himself, so we walked to the door with him, then across the hall into my room. After the teacher looked at the enrollment papers Mother gave her, she said right away, loud enough for the whole room to hear, that I must be the little girl who had been shot a few weeks ago. I nodded and hung my head a bit, but I could still see the other kids looking at me and felt rather pleased to be awarded, even in this backhanded sort of way, a certain celebrity status.

At first recess, several of the girls from my class gathered around asking me what it felt like to be shot, how it happened, did it hurt, and so forth, but my moment of fame ended quickly when someone yelled, "Fight!" One of the girls asked who it was and when another girl said it was one of the Olson twins and a new redheaded boy I knew it was Gene. Inside I was mortified but I'd already learned it was best to put on a casual front, so I said airily, "Oh, that's just my brother Gene. He has this strange way of making friends." Before anyone had a chance to comment, the bell rang and we could see the boys stop fighting and shake hands and walk back together to fall in line in front of the long flight of schoolhouse steps for the march back into the classroom.

That was the first of four fights, an all-time record, that Gene had that first day. He must have decided the way to head off any misunderstandings about his size—he was one of the smaller boys in his class—was demonstrating right off his skill and lack of fear as a fighter. Apparently he had targeted the four largest boys in the class for this demonstration, and starting with the smallest of the four at first recess, worked his way up with a second fight at lunch hour and a third at afternoon recess. None of the fights were pursued to where anyone got hurt or a winner or loser could be declared, and in all cases the boys shook hands afterward and held no grudges. But Gene was not familiar with the pattern of kids having to board the school buses right after school, and the biggest of the four boys he'd saved for last was one of those who rode the bus. When Gene grabbed one of his books and ran, that boy, who was at least a head taller than Gene and with arms six inches longer, reached out and grabbed him before he could get away, saying in a rather good-natured way, "Don't be a turd. I gotta catch the bus."

Gene, angry at having his plan foiled, dropped the book yelling, "Don't call me a turd, you asshole!" and took a swing that missed as the other boy stepped back.

"I don't have time for this," the big boy mumbled as he dropped his books, stepped in, and with two quick, hard jabs knocked Gene to the ground, then picked up his books and ran for the bus.

As Gene got up and turned around to head for home, I was horrified to see that one of his eyes was already almost swollen shut and his lip was split open, with blood running down from the cut to drip off his chin onto his shirt. I just couldn't get over how he'd gotten hurt so badly in so short a fight, but the only thing I could think of to say was, "Boy, you're sure going to be in trouble when you get home."

*"You shut up!"* he yelled. Then he pulled a bandanna out of his pocket and wiped at the blood on his face. More to himself than to me, he mumbled, "I probably could of whipped him if he hadn't run for the bus." Later, after the bleeding stopped and we were nearly home, neither one of us having said a word, Gene added with a little shake of his head and a touch of admiration in his voice, "I don't know, though. That bugger's got a wicked punch—and the longest arms I ever saw."

When we reached our back door, Gene, putting off the inevitable as long as possible, stood aside to let me go in first. I went straight through to the living room, where Mother and Kinnick were sitting, and Mother glanced up with a look of pleasure that turned to shock as she saw Gene's face, but before she could say a word Gene met the situation head-on. "Well, I finally met my match, like you said I would," he said with a laugh, but he couldn't quite pull off the nonchalance he was striving for due to his badly swollen lip.

Mother leaped to her feet as though preparing to do battle as Kinnick commented mildly, "Now, Gladys, take it easy. The boy's already taken a beating. That's enough for one day."

Mother said only one word, *"Men!,"* then turned on her heel and walked quickly into her bedroom, but she was soon back with a bottle of iodine and some bandages. Without a word she grabbed Gene by the arm and marched him out to the back porch, where she washed his face and applied the iodine with a vengeance, I suspect, for it took a lot to make Gene yell and he yelled quite a bit, though with Gene you could never tell for sure whether he was yelling because it hurt or because he knew it made Mother feel better—he was pretty smart about things like that.

Anyhow, before the evening was over Mother had

wormed out of me the whole story of the four fights and how the boys had shaken hands and seemed not to be angry and how the principal had not called Gene into the office or said anything to him so far as I knew. Maxine, who had come home from school full of stories about the compliments she'd received on her new dress and how the girls had liked her hair and how she'd already made one friend named Sis—can you believe that name—teased me like she always did about not being able to keep a secret, but I didn't care because it was just so nice to have her happy again. Gene went out with Kinnick to do the milking, as usual, and I suppose they talked about the fights, but right after supper Gene went to bed, which wasn't like him at all, so I knew he must be hurting a lot more than he would admit.

When we got to school the next morning, Gene headed straight over to where the boys were playing while I climbed the stairs to go to my classroom. A tall blond girl was waiting for me near the top of the stairs, and as I got near her she stood up and spoke to me. "Hi, I'm Mary Klink, Billy's sister. Our brothers had a fight after school yesterday," she said.

I was hoping she wasn't planning for us to take up the fight where they left off, for she was at least half a head taller than me, though I knew she was in my same grade. "Well, your brother sure won that one," I said quickly. "Just wait till you see Gene's face. He's got a black eye and his lip's all swollen where it got split open—he's a real mess."

"Oh, I don't know," Mary replied earnestly, as though making a valid comparison. "You should've seen how Billy skinned his knuckles!"

While Mary Klink's remark was never adopted as a family saying like some we treasured, it became an all-time favorite of mine and set forever in my memory the name of Mary and Billy Klink.

95

# 7

It turned out there were far more important things happening during those first few days at the Round Butte School than Gene's fights. At first recess that first day, there were boys and girls sitting on the steps or on the grass refusing all invitations to play in the more active games like baseball or hopscotch. When this behavior continued into lunch hour, the teachers appeared to be concerned, and finally the school principal, Mr. Kircoffe, came out to look the situation over and talk to some of the students who were still sitting around. After lunch the teachers announced that going barefoot on the playground would be permitted so long as the weather stayed warm, but shoes must be put back on before entering the building. I was delighted, for I much preferred going barefoot to wearing shoes. It wasn't until I told Mother about the new barefoot rule and she suggested it was probably because some children's feet were hurting from wearing last year's shoes that I remembered there had been a lot of old shoes among those I lined mine up with beside the schoolhouse steps.

Then in the lunchroom where we were required to go and sit at tables to eat the lunch we brought from home, there seemed to be a lot of children with only one sandwich or even half a sandwich, with no cookies and fruit or gelatin like Gene and I brought, and each day several who forgot their lunch entirely or didn't come to school at all. One girl said her mother had suggested we eat picnic-style and put all our food on the table, then share it equally with

96

all the children at our table and maybe some of us could bring a little extra. Right away Mother started packing bigger lunches for Gene and me, even though Kinnick protested that he couldn't be feeding the whole valley. On Friday of that first week, the teachers gave each student a note to deliver to his or her parents asking them to please attend an emergency meeting at the school that night.

At breakfast the next morning, after Kinnick had left for his regular Saturday barbering day in town, Mother told us about the meeting at the school the night before. "Remember when I talked to you about how lucky we are to have a nice house and food to eat and clothes to wear?" she said seriously with an underlying touch of sadness in her voice. "Well, it turns out we are even luckier than I thought, for we were told last night that many families are in danger of losing their homes and don't have money to buy food to eat or clothes for their children to wear to school. Now, the reason I'm telling you this is that you might see youngsters at school in old clothes or shoes and I want you to know that you are not to make remarks about them or poke fun or anything like that. And if anyone else does such a thing you are to tell them they better quit it, for they just might be next, what with the way this depression is going. Do you understand what I'm telling you?"

Gene and I nodded our heads and told her that some of the kids at school had already said mean things, and Maxine said that it was probably even worse in the high school.

"Anyhow," Mother finally stated in a more normal "let's-get-down-to-business" manner, "we decided at the meeting last night that there were at least a couple of things we could do right away to even things out a bit. One is to set up a clothing exchange center at the school, and the other is to establish a school lunch program. So, what I want you to

97

do right now, this morning, is get out all your old clothes and shoes and boots and we'll go through and pick out those that still have wear in them and get them cleaned up to take to the school tomorrow. Then next week I've volunteered to help get a school lunch program going where everyone sends what they can and the mothers take turns preparing a good, healthy hot lunch for all of you. In the beginning it will probably be soup and sandwiches, but by winter we should be well enough organized to provide more variety.

"Now," Mother continued, "you'll be especially happy to hear about our plan to raise money for the lunch program, Maxine. Mr. Kircoffe is going to ask the school board for permission to use the gymnasium for dances once a month—right here at the Round Butte School. Some of the board members were at the meeting, and they all agreed that it was a good idea and thought there would be no problem with it. We'll charge admission and sell donated cakes, pies, and cookies, and there will be coffee and maybe some punch for those who don't drink coffee. Anyhow, we are hoping to get enough of a crowd to pay for a band and still have quite a bit left over to put into the school lunches—and have some fun besides."

Maxine was excited as she leaped up from the table. "I'll have to start practicing up on my Charleston," she said as she started making musical noises and gyrating around the living room.

"Do we get to go?" Gene asked, and when Mother answered, "We'll all get to go," he jumped up and bowed to me with mock politeness, saying, "May I have this dance, Runt, please?" That was my cue to giggle and stand up and curtsy and take his hands and hop around the room with him, though what we were doing could hardly be called dancing.

Mother smiled as she watched our antics for a minute or two before she got up and started picking up the breakfast dishes. "Now that's enough of that. There's a lot to be done if I'm to have anything ready to take to the clothing drive at the school tomorrow," she said as she carried some plates into the kitchen. Knowing she always gave us a few minutes to wind down before the second reminder, but we'd better move quick on that one for there was no third reminder, only action, we continued our dancing until we heard her, "Hey there, let's get to work now." Then we stopped and headed for our bedrooms, hoping she would forget and do our dish-washing chore for us while we dug out our old clothes. She laughed as she watched us go. "OK, I'll do them for you," she called, "but don't think you're putting anything over on me!" I could never understand how she always seemed to know what we were up to.

Toward the end of the following week, harvesting of the wheat and oats began. Kinnick had a neighbor bring in a machine that cut and bundled the grain, and by Saturday the beautiful golden fields were reduced to stubble, with bundles of grain lying every few feet across the field waiting to be stood up in clumps, called shocks, with the spears of grain at the top, up off the ground so they would dry. Kinnick offered to pay Gene and me ten cents a shock to help him with this chore, but I found it much harder than it looked—the bundles were heavy and prickly, and the stubble was hard to walk on. I only lasted long enough to build two shocks, but Gene worked hard for the whole day and by evening he and Kinnick had completed the job. After the grain had dried in the hot sun for a week or so, several neighbors with teams and wagons and a big old thrashing machine came to finish the job of separating the grain from the straw. As the engine was started up and the thrasher, looking for all the world like a giant grasshopper, slowly

99

clicked and clacked to life, we watched with wonder as bundles were thrown from the wagons onto the long conveyor belt and the little kernels of grain came down a chute on the side into sacks and the stems and leaves shot out through another chute at the end to build a great stack of straw. We soon realized why Mother had given us bandanas to mask our nose and eyes from the fine dust, called chaff, that clouded the air around the thrasher. No wonder so many farmers died young from breathing the dust and chaff created by working the soil and harvesting crops year after year.

The following Monday, Kinnick was up early harnessing the horses and getting the wagon loaded with sacks of grain to haul the seven miles into Ronan. He could have hired a truck, but he didn't want to spend the money. He said the horses had to earn their keep and though it would take a trip a day for several days, it was still not costing anything but his time. Anyhow, Kinnick was ready to go right after breakfast, so Gene and I got to climb up on the wagon seat beside him and ride as far as the Round Butte School. It was fun sitting up high behind the horses as they plodded down the road and I was hoping there would be lots of kids on the playground at school to see us, but as it turned out, the buses had not yet arrived, so only a few of the kids who lived near enough to walk were on hand to envy our old-fashioned mode of transportation. Actually, the ones who were there didn't seem too impressed and I doubt the others would have been either, as they had all grown up here and wagons were old hat to them—a bright new shiny truck, now, that would have been a different story.

When school was out that day, I was surprised to see Kinnick standing by the steps talking to the principal, Mr. Kircoffe, and the wagon parked at the side of the road with the horses, looking all shiny wet with sweat from that long haul back from Ronan, still hitched to it. I stood beside the men for a few minutes until Gene came out and Kinnick broke off the conversation with, "Well, now that you're both here, we better get on up the road. Gladys will be wondering why I'm gone so long after I told her I'd be home by early afternoon."

When we got to the wagon and saw it was still almost half-full of sacks of grain, Gene asked what happened.

"It's a long story," Kinnick answered. "Best we wait and go into it when we get home, after your mother asks that same question."

Sure enough, Mother came hurrying out as we pulled in the drive and, seeing the wagon still half-full, asked, "What on earth happened, John? Was the granary full?"

"Like I told the kids, it's a long story. Why don't you fix us some iced tea for talking over while Gene and I get the horses unhitched and taken care of? They're pretty tuckered out from having a load to pull both ways," Kinnick said to Mother, then looking at me, "You jump on down, Glenna Lou, and help your mother. This is men's work."

"Men's work, shmen's work," I mumbled irritably as I climbed down off the wagon as slowly as I could manage. "How come Gene gets to do everything?"

"Hey, Runt, how about playing some baseball with me after supper?" Gene called as the wagon started up again, but I was in no mood to respond to his effort to make me feel better and walked on in the house without answering.

"The first thing I did when I got to town," Kinnick began telling Mother later, after we were settled at the dining table with iced tea and cookies, "was go to the mill to unload the sacks for the flour and rolled oats you ordered. Old Charlie figured the number of sacks, about half what was on the wagon, and helped me unload. After that I pulled into line at the granary and went on in the office, where a bunch of men from up Pablo way were standing around waiting because there was nobody behind the counter. Pretty soon the head of the co-op came in waving a telegram saying, 'Bad news, men—the price on wheat dropped another five cents this morning, and oats went down four.' " Mother gasped but didn't say anything as Kinnick continued. "Now, you know the price has been going down a penny or two a week all summer, but it's held steady since Labor Day, so I thought the worst was over and while it would be tough, we could make it through the winter. But I figured that five cents a bushel came to near a hundred dollars on our crop and that made me mad—real mad, it's just plain stealing—and I wasn't the only one who hauled my load back home."

Mother looked positively stricken as she gasped, "What on earth will we do now?"

"Now don't get yourself all worked up, Gladys." Kinnick said, rather calmly considering he had looked on the verge of one of his political tirades only moments before. "For the past couple months I've been giving this a lot of thought and remembering how my daddy made it through some tough times trading horses. Fact is, he was known at one time as the best horse trader in Bloomfield County back in Iowa. Now, I used to go along with him and he even let me strike the deal a time or two, though I was still too young to turn over any big deals to. Anyhow, he seemed to think I had a natural talent along those lines and said I was lucky to have something to fall back on when all else failed—and it looks like this just might be the time."

"Get to the point, John!" Mother interjected. "Are you saying your going in the horse-trading business?"

"If you'll just back off and let me tell this my way we'll get there a lot quicker," Kinnick said impatiently.

"Sorry. I won't say another word," Mother responded

as she clamped her jaws together in that way she had.

"When I left the co-op, I drove over to the bank and asked to see the head man. I told him about my idea for buying up the good ones of these starving horses being offered at auctions and using my hay and grain to fatten them up, then reselling them. We talked quite a bit about where there might be a market for good horses, even in these bad times, and I told him about some of the talks I've had with the out-of-town men who stop by the shop for a haircut now and then. He liked what I had to say and ended up giving me a line of credit, knowing I was good for it what with owning the farm free and clear and all, to tide us over the winter, 'cause it will take that long to get this thing going. Well, that's it. So now, Gladys, you can have your say. What do you think?"

"I suppose you know what you're doing." Mother said tentatively. "But how do you know you can make it work?"

"Know? Know? We know nothing, except maybe that the politicians are crooked!" Kinnick exploded. "You kids listen to this, now: There are two things you need to make your way in this world. One is the courage to take a chance once you've looked at all sides of a way to go and come to a judgment as to which is the best, and the other is to keep up your credit rating so you can use the bank's money instead of your own to go on."

"They're a little young for that kind of advice, John, but what concerns me is your mention of auctions. It doesn't seem right to take advantage of other people's misery, many of them our neighbors," Mother said.

"Never too young for learning common sense," Kinnick responded. "But about the auctions, well, look at it this way: The more people bidding, the higher the price goes. And if I'm the only bidder, it means a sale when otherwise there wouldn't be one. Anyhow, I can't believe anyone's going to be mad at me for taking their animals off their hands and feeding them and taking care of them even when they know I'm hoping to make a few dollars off it—and don't think they don't know I'm taking a chance on that. Better we try to keep our heads above water so we can help with the lunches and dances and such than join the ranks of the destitute. Now I don't want to hear no more about it."

"Any more about it," Mother murmured by way of having the last word as she got up from the table and gathered up the glasses from our tea. "It's time for me to get dinner started, and you kids need to go on in and get your clothes changed," she said as she moved off toward the kitchen.

The word must have spread fast, for it wasn't more than a week before a boy of fourteen or fifteen came riding up on a horse he wanted to sell. He had a bill of sale from his daddy with him, but it was obviously his own horse and after the bargain was struck he put his arm around the horse's neck and laid his head against it as he said good-bye. Mother felt so bad for him she went out and invited him in for lemonade, but he was having a hard time choking back the tears and said he'd better get on home. Kinnick asked where he lived, then told the boy he had someone to see down that way and would give him a lift if he'd wait a minute while he put the horse in the barn. When I asked Mother where Kinnick was driving off to she sounded both sad and happy as she answered, "Nowhere, actually, he just made up a story so he could drive the boy home without making it seem like he felt sorry for him. He does manage to surprise me every once in a while."

After supper that night, I heard Kinnick telling Mother some of his philosophy on horse trading. "My daddy always held with the notion that horse trading and socializing don't mix," he began. "The seller is always going to think the price is too low, and if you go in and have a cup of coffee with him at his house before you get down to business, he's going to be twice as mad that you accepted his hospitality and still wouldn't pay his price. Then if he comes to your house and you invite him in after, he thinks you're feeling sorry for him about having to sell at a low price, and that's just rubbing salt in the wound. Now, it looks like I might not have to go to auctions at all if there's enough men smart enough to come by to sell their stock, like that boy did today. They can keep the money for themselves if they sell before they get foreclosed on instead of it going to the bank like it does on the auction. What I'm saying is that if they come here, you and the kids better just keep your distance and let me do the dealing in my own way, though I expect most of the time they'll be wanting me to go to their place to look at more than one animal."

"You'll get no argument from me on that," Mother responded. "I want to keep as far away from those kinds of shenanigans as possible. I know we have to do something to keep afloat, but I can't help wishing there was another way."

It wasn't as though we had a stampede of sellers coming to our door that fall, but every once in a while someone would bring a horse by to get a price on—just in case things got worse and he had to sell. Mostly, as he had predicted, Kinnick was invited to go down to a farmer's place to look over several animals, and he started taking Gene with him to ride a horse home in case he was able to strike a deal. If the horses weren't broke for riding, Kinnick would go down in the wagon the next day and tie them to the back of the wagon and lead them home that way, but he was very careful about what horses he bought so the herd didn't outgrow the hay and grain he had. Then, too, as close as Kinnick was with his money, I suspect his offers were pretty low and a lot of the farmers wouldn't sell at his price. He soon earned a reputation as one of the sharpest horse traders in the valley, judging by some of the remarks the kids made to me at school. Mother didn't like it a bit when I carried that message home, but Kinnick was pleased as punch at becoming famous, or infamous, depending on how you looked at it.

One Saturday morning in late October, shortly after my birthday, Junior came riding in on that same little sorrel pony he'd ridden up on before. "Gene, run and tell Mom to come out here right away!" he called out. "I got something to show you all." Gene ran for the house as Junior reined in and pulled a package of Life Savers from his shirt pocket and slid off the pony's back. "Here's a little something for your birthday, Runt," he said as he handed me the candy. "Sorry, I couldn't afford more." I was just tickled he had remembered.

When Mother came out from the house, Junior reached over and opened the pony's mouth saying, "Here, take a look at this." We all gasped with shock to see an ugly misshapen little stump in there where the pony's tongue used to be. "That Old Man Bates is one mean son of a bitch—sorry for the swearing, Mom, but that's what he is. He got so mad at the pony having so much spirit, he used a bridle with a cross-bit and jerked him around so bad his tongue was just hangin' there by a little piece of skin and he would have got out a gun and shot him if I hadn't managed to talk him out of it. Anyhow, I made up my mind right then I wasn't gonna work for nobody that would mistreat an animal that way."

Mother couldn't help correcting him. "Work for anyone," she said softly as she gave a little shiver of revulsion from hearing the story and viewing that awful sight in the horse's mouth. "I was wondering about that when you went to work there. I've heard stories before. Have you got another job lined up? I suppose an apology to John would open the way for you to come back here if you'll go back to school. It's not so late but what you could make up the lessons you've missed so far. You're plenty smart enough, Henry," she added, more to show him she accepted his name change, I suspect, than to pay a compliment. Actually, we had all pretty much converted over to calling him Henry by this time, due to her vigilance about correcting us every time we called him Junior. Mother said it was important to the growing-up process. "He needs a man's name to become a man with," she'd say.

"Naw, that wouldn't work. I made my bed and I'll have to lay in it, like you always say." Henry grinned mischeviously as Mother said, "Lie in it." Then, knowing Mother wouldn't like what he had to say next, he looked down at the ground and started poking the toe of his shoe in the dirt as he continued. "I met a couple guys who've been riding the rails around the country lookin' for work, and they got a ride lined up to Ronan tomorrow and invited me to come along. We can grab a train from there to Missoula, and I can look for work down that way. There's some horse ranches up the valley from there. I'm pretty good with horses, and l figure I got a good chance. Bein' a kid and all, they'll know they won't have to pay me much. I only hung around this long to make sure this baby's mouth healed up OK," he finished up as he gave the pony's neck an affectionate pat.

Mother hesitated a moment, like she was going to say something, then, apparently changing her mind, said, "I'll go in and make up a couple more sandwiches. I was just about to call the kids for lunch. We'll talk more after we've eaten."

We had lunch and visited awhile; then Mother and Henry had a little private talk, but it didn't seem to change anything. When he left he told her not to worry—he'd send her a postcard to let her know where he ended up. She ran to the house in tears after he left, and that set me to crying, too. For a long time after that, whenever I thought about that pony's tongue a shiver would run through me, and sometimes I'd shed a tear or two—it was so sad to think of that beautiful little horse being mutilated like that.

The pony wasn't the only animal I cried over that fall. As the weather turned colder, Kinnick began talking about the butchering to be done before winter set in. One Saturday he came home with news of a deal he'd made. "We'll have two less pigs to slop after tomorrow," he announced proudly. "I cut a deal with the owner of that butcher shop we drive by right there on the edge of town. He's coming tomorrow to butcher one hog for him to sell and one hog for us to eat. I bought that extra hog with the idea of selling it, but with the way things are I'd be lucky to give it away. This way we'll at least get the bacon and hams cured and space in his cooler for the fresh cuts and we'll get the help we need with the butchering for no outlay of cash. That's a pretty fair deal in these times," he ended up triumphantly, looking at Mother as though waiting for praise.

"John, couldn't you just talk this sort of thing over with me ahead of time?" she asked with no hint of congratulations in her tone. "I told the preacher I'd for sure be at church tomorrow for the business meeting after."

"Oh, he'll know something important came up when you don't show up. In these times it's catch as catch can, and I was just lucky Pete had a cancellation. He was all booked up when I asked him before," Kinnick answered brusquely with a hint of disappointment in his voice.

Pete the butcher arrived early Sunday morning, bringing with him the standard gear for outdoor butchering. He and Kinnick unloaded a metal cart, then set a big barrel on top of it, and Kinnick told Gene and me to start filling the barrel with water from the pump on the back porch while he got a fire going out by the butchering site. Pete unloaded some long poles; then he and Kinnick set up a sort of pyramid structure that had a pulley fastened inside at the very top with a rope running through it. When the pyramid was finished, Pete checked the barrel and declared it full enough. Then he and Kinnick pulled it over the fire to start the water heating and headed for the pigpen to claim their first victim.

Although Mother had told me what was going to happen, when I heard that big pig let out a series of high-pitched squeals as they pulled him from the pigpen I burst into tears and ran for my bed and pulled the covers up over my head to blot out the sound. It sounded to me as if he were begging for his life. *Why, oh why,* I asked myself, *does the world have to be so mean?* While it seemed like hours, it was probably no more than a few minutes before the noise stopped and I heard the men come into the house for the breakfast Mother had prepared.

It wasn't long before my curiosity got the better of me and I went back outside to see what had happened. There was the hog's body strung up on the pole structure with blood dripping down from the cut in his throat into the washtub that sat beneath it. Somehow, he didn't look so sad now that he was quietly dead as he had sounded making those piteous sounds when he resisted leaving the pigpen earlier. Still, I vowed to the pig and to myself that I would not eat a single mouthful of it, ever, and rushed immediately into the house to announce my brave decision to everyone who would listen.

After breakfast the business of lowering the hog into

the barrel of water, which by now was scalding hot, and scraping the short, stiff, bristly hairs off his skin began. We all worked at that, though Gene's and my contribution was probably negligible. After that was finished and the skin looked all pink and smooth and shiny, the insides were removed; then the head, the feet, and the tail were cut off and the carcass was sawed in half for easier handling, then hung off the corner of the house in the shade. After that the whole procedure started over again on the second pig. This time, I knew what was coming and went in and covered my head before the pig began to squeal at all, so it wasn't quite as traumatic. By late afternoon, the butchering was over and Pete loaded up his gear and the four halves of pork and headed back to town.

At Kinnick's request, Mother made blood pudding and head cheese and also cooked the heart and liver, none of which I had any trouble resisting. A few days later Kinnick brought home some pork to eat, plus the fat for Mother to render down into lard and the scraps for sausage. Somehow I didn't relate the pork chops we had for dinner that night to the recent butchering, but Gene and Maxine did. Halfway through the meal they burst into gales of laughter, and finally, still laughing some, Maxine said, "Did you know that pork chop came from the hog you vowed not to eat, Runt? Some vow! It didn't even last a week!" And she laughed some more as I jumped up from the table in tears and ran for the back door. "Ah, the poor baby's got her feelings hurt," Maxine singsonged sarcastically. "She's going outside to eat some worms and make us sorry that we picked on her!"

After I cried myself out, I went back into the house, still feeling pouty and sorry for myself. "Why does Maxine always have to be so mean?" I asked Mother.

"The kind of teasing that seems to hurt the most,"

Mother responded kindly, "is the kind that has a grain of truth to it. You did make a point of announcing your intention not to eat the pork. Maybe, instead of trying to gain importance through announcing what you plan to do, you should just keep quiet about it until you find out if you can do it. Best do your bragging after the fact—but then, once you've proven you can do whatever it is, everyone will probably already know about it and there will be no need for bragging."

The butchering of one of the calves took place on a Friday when we were in school, so though I did shed a tear or two in memory of the calf's velvety muzzle in my hand and its big, soft brown eyes, it had already been reduced to two halves of veal hanging in the shed by the time I saw it and the whole thing didn't seem as real as when the pigs were butchered. Even so, again I vowed not to eat the meat and again I broke my vow. While I felt guilty about letting my appetite overcome my good intentions, I was glad I had taken Mother's advice and kept my decision to myself this time.

# 8

The dances at the Round Butte School began the first Saturday night in November. As Mother had promised, we all attended. Gene and I were amazed to see what a good dancer Kinnick was, and I felt proud as I watched him lead Mother around the dance floor with such rhythm and skill that many of the ladies seated on the benches near us commented on what good dancers they were—and such an attractive couple!

Each dance set consisted of three different songs, called numbers, with a short pause between, so we sat for quite a while watching, not only Mother and Kinnick, but the other dancers as well. Some couples were graceful, some not so graceful, and one couple whom Gene found especially fascinating, dipped and whirled and swooped in a most distinctive style.

Finally the first set was over, and as couples started leaving the floor, Mother and Kinnick, looking flushed from the exertion, came back to where we were sitting. "Now, I expect you to ask me for the next dance, Gene. And John's going to dance with you, Glenna Lou. We think it's time you learned the steps so you can join in and have some fun as well," Mother announced happily. I jumped right up and held out my arms in a dancing position until Kinnick reached out and gently lowered my arms down to my sides, saying, "Best wait for the music," as the ladies sitting nearby smiled indulgently.

We were by no means the only children dancing with

their parents when the music did start up again, but I still felt special as Kinnick led me onto the dance floor and started showing me how to move my feet in time to the music. Each of the three numbers in the set was slightly different, but it seemed a matter of following the same basic pattern with minor variations to match each tune. When the set was over, Kinnick told Mother I was doing well and she said she was really surprised at how fast Gene had caught on, then added, "Now, you two go over there and practice in the corner where Maxine's giving her Charleston lessons. You just stay in that one little area, though. I don't want you out on the main floor getting in the grown-ups' way."

We ran for the corner, and as soon as the music started we began, admittedly somewhat awkwardly, to practice the steps we'd learned so far. As each set had a different rhythm, we soon found that moving our feet in that same pattern didn't always fit the music, so we'd stop and watch the grown-ups' feet, then try to imitate what they were doing. Gene was especially good at picking up the foot movement patterns; then he'd show me and off we'd go. Some of the little girls standing around our corner came out to ask Gene if he would like to dance with them, but he just laughed and said he had to learn how first.

We lasted until intermission, but after finishing the punch and cookies Kinnick bought for us we soon fell asleep on the benches along with most of the other children. The next thing we knew, Mother was shaking us, telling us the dance was over and it was time to leave.

It felt like we had barely gone to bed when Kinnick knocked on the bedroom door, then opened it calling cheerily, "Rise and shine! Come on, now; time to get up!" Maxine turned and mumbled for him to go away as she pulled the covers up over her head. Kinnick was so tickled he almost sang the words, "A lesson in life. When you dance you have to pay the fiddler! Breakfast in ten minutes. Don't be late!" and after doing a little flat-footed jig he closed the door.

We were a weary, bleary-eyed group as we stumbled out of our bedrooms that Sunday morning, and we were disappointed when there was no sympathy from Mother, either. "John's right," she said. "There are cows to be milked, horses to feed, pigs to slop, whether you've been up late the night before or not. It's an obligation we accepted, and it isn't fair to the animals to make them wait—they didn't get to go to the dance last night." Gene and I had to laugh at the thought of cows and horses at the dance, but Maxine, more tired from having danced every dance right up to the very end, didn't think it was funny.

"That's another good reason not to live on a farm," she said angrily. "You won't catch me marrying a farmer. I'm going to live in town, where you don't have to get up at the crack of dawn every damn day."

"Stop that, Maxine!" Mother came back with a touch of anger of her own. "There'll be no swearing in this house, as you well know. Don't think you'll get off scot-free, wher-ever you are. The city extracts a payment of its own. It may be different, but mark my words, there'll be a price to pay."

"I'm not hungry," Maxine muttered as she pushed her chair back and got up to march to our bedroom.

"Let it go," Mother said to Kinnick as he turned to order her back to the table. "I'll deal with her later. We'll have to hurry to make Sunday school on time as it is."

Later in the afternoon, after we had eaten Sunday din-ner and taken naps, Gene and I got out the new Christmas catalog that had arrived from Montgomery Ward a few days earlier. We were lying on the living room floor as Kin-nick napped off and on in his favorite chair, and with each page we turned we got more excited and our voices got louder as we declared our choice for this; no that, no, this one would be better. Kinnick, tired of listening to our noisy list of wishes, finally roused up and proceeded to set us straight. "You might as well quit being silly over that book right now," he said. "This big fuss over Christmas is a bunch of foolishness, something the storekeepers thought up to take our money. Best just forget about it this year."

We looked up at him in amazement. He must be kidding! Not celebrate Christmas? Whoever heard of such a thing!

Mother came out of the bedroom, where she'd been napping, in time to hear what Kinnick said. "Don't spoil their fun with that kind of talk, John," she said mildly. "Deep down they know all of those things won't be under the tree on Christmas morning, but it doesn't hurt for them to dream a little, does it?"

"I don't think you got my meaning," Kinnick responded more forcefully. "I'm saying there'll be no tree, no presents, here this year. If you want to celebrate the religious side of it, I'll take you to church. That's all."

If there is a silence so thick it can be cut with a knife, this was it. Gene and I were stunned. Mother just stood speechless for a minute. Then, with a scathing look at Kinnick, in a voice of deadly calm she said, "These children will have Christmas with a tree and presents both. If you want no part of it you can go somewhere else that day or spend it in the barn, but we will celebrate." Then turning to us, "You kids put that wish book away and find something else to do. You do get a little loud and greedy with your dreaming."

As we closed the book and rushed for the bedroom to tell Maxine what was going on, we heard Kinnick ask, "Now just what do you think you'll use for money, Gladys?

Do you plan to squirrel some out of the grocery money and starve us all?"

"Don't you worry about your precious stomach," she retorted. "I'll not touch the grocery money. Where there is a will there's a way, and I have the will; I'll find a way. After this, I wouldn't use a penny of your money for Christmas if my life depended on it."

Maxine was reassuring on this matter. "I have a little money left from summer," she said, "and if I put the word out maybe I can earn a little more. Sis said her family goes up to the foothills to cut their Christmas tree. Maybe they'll let me go with them and get one for us. Don't you worry, when Mom makes up her mind on something, she gets it done. It'll be OK," she finished confidently with a little hug for me, a rare gesture, indeed, for Maxine to make.

When we went back into the living room we found Mother sitting quietly darning socks while Kinnick read the paper. Every once in a while he'd tell her about something he was reading, but instead of joining in with conversation like she usually did, Mother would say, "Mmmm," or, "Oh," and go right back to darning. Gene and I didn't feel much like talking either. Finally, in an effort to get back on Mother's and our good side, I suppose, Kinnick got up and tuned in some dance music on the radio and suggested that Gene and I practice our dance steps.

No one was more fun or could make us laugh more boisterously than Maxine could, when she was in the mood, though, as she was a teenager, that good mood could turn to a bad one in an instant. Now, hearing the dance music playing, Maxine came out of the bedroom and, sensing the tension in the room, was especially lively and full of fun as she took turns dancing with us. She even taught us some Charleston steps to dance to the livelier tunes. She joked around with Kinnick and made a try at getting

Mother to laugh, but the best Maxine could get out of her was a tight-lipped little ghost of a smile.

That night when Mother came in to kiss me good night, I told her I'd prayed for God to bring us a tree with presents.

Mother sat down on the bed and took my hand. "You know, Glenna Lou," she began, "God isn't like Santa Claus with a big bag of toys on his back. He has to look after the whole world, and He can't be bothered with specific requests like that. There is an old saying, 'God helps those who help themselves,' that you will find to be quite true when you grow up. But we can ask Him to help us find a way to get things for ourselves. If you ask for that in your prayers, I'm sure it will help," she went on as she leaned over and pushed the hair up off my forehead and kissed me. "Yes, that will surely help a lot."

November in Montana had turned cold and rainy, sometimes with a bit of snow mixed in, and Gene and I were feeling fidgety from not being able to play outdoors. We took to the dancing partly because we did want to learn but mostly because it was about the only physical activity allowed indoors, so practicing our dance steps became a nightly ritual. Sometimes Maxine or Mother or Kinnick would join in, but mostly it was just Gene and me working off our excess energy as we danced at the far end of the living room, being careful not to knock things off the table or get too close to Kinnick's chair. As we became more skillful it became more fun, and eventually we were dipping and whirling and swooping about with confidence.

"Gladys, come here and take a look at this!" Kinnick called out to Mother one night. "If this isn't a dead ringer for that fellow everyone was watching at the dance last time, I'll put in with you." He was obviously amused.

Mother came in from the kitchen, and Maxine, hearing

what Kinnick had said, came out from the bedroom and they both laughed and clapped their hands when the music stopped. My, we were pleased to have them recognize our imitation of the couple who had so fascinated Gene at the dance on that first night.

On the night of the second monthly dance, the first Saturday in December, Gene and I were so excited when Kinnick parked the car in the parking lot at the Round Butte School we were out the car door and running for the gymnasium before he could turn off the lights. We took off our coats as we passed through the door into the gym, threw them carelessly toward a bench, then headed straight out onto the dance floor, where we dipped and whirled and swooped around with gusto. Though it took most of our concentration to weave our way between the other couples on the floor, we were still aware enough of what was going on to know that people were beginning to watch us. Some would smile and nod, and some of the ladies on the benches were pointing and laughing. We wondered what Mother wanted as we saw her standing at the edge of the crowd looking serious and concerned as she beckoned to us. The next thing we knew she and Kinnick were dancing across the hall like they were trying to catch up with us. Just as the music stopped they did catch up and Mother grabbed each of us roughly by the arm to march us off the dance floor to the benches, where she gave us a push as she told us to sit.

"What on earth were you thinking of?" she demanded, leaning over us, keeping her voice low so the ladies sitting nearby had to strain to hear. "That was a terrible thing to do, making fun of that poor man, right here in front of everyone. Never, never have I been so embarrassed, so mortified, in my whole life. Now you just sit there and think about how you would feel if someone did that to you until

I come back here. And don't you dare move—you hear me?"

We both nodded, although we didn't really understand why she was in such a tizzy, but we knew Mother, and we knew she meant business.

"John, walk outside with me for a minute, will you? I need some air," she said to Kinnick, who was standing nearby.

As they walked away, the music started up again and we heard the man we'd been imitating call out, "That's a couple of great little dancers you've got there!" as he and his partner dipped and whirled and swooped pass us.

"See there?" Gene whispered. "He wasn't even mad."

"But everyone was laughing," I whispered back, beginning to get a glimmer of what Mother was upset about.

When Mother and Kinnick came back, she said, "I'm not taking any more chances on you two tonight. Since that's the only dance you know, you are not to dance any more at all, you hear? I'd take you home right now except that I'm in charge of the refreshments, but we will be leaving right after intermission, providing I can arrange a ride home for Maxine when the dance is over." Then with a straight, hard look, "She shouldn't have to leave early because the two of you don't know how to behave."

There was a scolding when we got home, of course, though it was not as bad as we expected, and after I went to bed I heard Mother and Kinnick talking in the dining area right next to my bedroom door.

"Seems to me you took that awful hard for such a little thing, Gladys," Kinnick commented.

"It was just such a bad way to start off when we're new to the area," Mother said as though resigning herself to being cast out before she'd even made it in. "But, to be perfectly honest, I suppose I was actually madder at myself than at the kids. I never should have encouraged them by laughing here at home—I just can't believe I didn't see it coming. Then, too, I did feel bad for that poor man."

"Don't waste your sympathy on him," Kinnick replied. "I think he took it as a compliment. From what I've seen of him, I doubt he has the sense to know the difference."

Since the time Kinnick had said we wouldn't be celebrating Christmas I'd heard no more about it except during the Thanksgiving holidays, when Maxine asked Mother what was wrong with Kinnick.

"Oh, nothing really. Lots of men don't like Christmas," Mother answered. "I think it's mostly that they don't like having their routine interrupted by all the activity and attention directed away from them. Then, too, it's their responsibility to support the family and they worry about the money going out on what they see as something useless. It's more a woman's holiday with all the baking and buying or making presents and the decorating. Now, I may have found a way to have Christmas with no cost to John, but it's bad luck to count your chickens before they're hatched so we'll just have to wait and see." Then as Maxine and I both started to speak, "Don't ask. When I know for sure, I'll tell you all about it."

With each passing day Gene and I became more anxious, as we were constantly reminded that Christmas was almost here. There were special Christmas programs on the radio. We were practicing our parts for the Christmas program at the school and for another program for the church. And all of the school art projects seemed to include pictures of Santa Claus, reindeer, and Christmas trees. Every day we were a little more discouraged after we asked Mother if she had good news and she answered cheerfully, "Not yet." We were even beginning to lose interest in the catalog—there just didn't seem to be much point in wishing anymore.

Shortly after our December dance fiasco, we came into the house from school one afternoon to find Mother with that happy look we'd been waiting for. "Good news!" she sang out, laughing as she gave us each a little pat on the head. "Now, go change your clothes and I'll tell you all about it when Maxine gets home."

We hurried to do as Mother said, then waited at the window for the school bus to arrive. At last we saw it coming and we ran to meet Maxine, then jumped around excitedly urging her to hurry so we could find out what the good news was.

We sat at the table as Mother got out the Christmas catalog from Montgomery Ward and laid it down in front of Maxine, telling her to read the advertisement she pointed out. The ad said that Montgomery Ward was offering to purchase gold coins, jewelry, etc., to help their loyal customers enjoy a Merry Christmas.

Maxine looked up inquiringly. "You don't have any gold in coins or jewelry that I know about," she said to Mother.

"Aha," Mother laughed triumphantly. "But I remembered I had some gold you didn't know about. When I went to false teeth, the dentist dug out the gold fillings from the teeth he pulled and gave them to me. So, I took a chance and mailed those off with a letter to the address in the catalog and the answer came today—they bought them. Your prayers are answered, Glenna Lou. God is good!"

"Hey, that ad was in the catalog before she ever started praying," Maxine pointed out, then laughed. "Next year she can bypass God and pray direct to Monkey Wards!"

Mother tut-tutted a bit but was too happy to make a real issue of it as she passed the letter of acceptance from the company around so each of us could take a look. Just the feel of that letter in my hands made me feel reverent, as though God was looking out for us, even if one did have to do it for oneself like Mother said.

As I passed the letter over to Gene, my arm froze holding the letter in midair as Kinnick came in through the kitchen to the dining room. "What's that?" he asked.

"Letter from Montgomery Ward," Mother said matter-of-factly. "I saw an ad for gold in the catalog and sent the fillings from the teeth the dentist pulled when I got my plates. They bought them," she added, trying to keep any hint of triumph from her voice.

We held our breath, watching closely to see how Kinnick would react. He scowled. His face turned red. Then, just as we braced for the explosion we saw coming, he relaxed a bit and shook his head. "Well, if Christmas means so much you'd sell the fillings from your teeth for it, I guess I'd best not stand in the way—most likely get run over if I tried," he added, chuckling. Then as he went back to the porch to hang his coat he called, "Just don't expect me to be part of it. I still think it's a bunch of foolishness!"

With little time left between the arrival of the notice from Montgomery Ward and Christmas Day, preparations took on a somewhat frantic air. I think most of the payment for the gold must have been in the form of coupons, redeemable only through the catalog, for Mother often seemed anxious as she waited for packages to arrive by mail. When a package did finally come, she'd hole up in her bedroom, where we could hear the sewing machine going far into the night. During those periods, Maxine took on the responsibility for cooking dinner and seeing that Gene and I did the chores she generously assigned to us. That led, naturally, to arguments with Maxine and complaints about Mother not being available to settle our differences.

"You kids don't know how lucky you are to have a mother who'll work her fingers to the bone for you like that woman is right now," Kinnick said to us one night, then added wistfully, "I never had a mother when I grew up. She died before I was old enough to know her. But with seven older sisters there was always one to tend the house till I left home. My daddy didn't like to stay around at Christmastime. He'd go off on business and take me with him. Sometimes we'd eat Christmas dinner with folks he knew along the way."

"Didn't you ever have a tree and presents?" I asked.

"Oh, I guess my sisters did, but just being with my daddy was enough for me," Kinnick answered as he leaned back in his chair, remembering.

"Seven sisters," Gene finally said as though he'd been considering what bad luck that would be. "No brothers?"

"One," Kinnick replied, "but he was older. Died young, at twenty-one, when I was only five or six. He was the apple of my daddy's eye, good at everything, he'd say. I never measured up," he added softly, but more as a fact to be accepted than something to feel bad about.

Not knowing what else to say, we sat in silence until Kinnick picked up the paper and started reading, so we felt free to go back to wondering what kind of presents Mother was working on right then. We figured it had to be something for us since she wouldn't let us in to see. The mystery only added to our excitement.

Kinnick seemed to have accepted Christmas as something to be endured. Of course, he'd shake his head some and grumble about Mother working so hard and about the money being wasted, but then sometimes he'd help crack nuts for the candy and cookies and he enjoyed sampling the finished product as much as we did. When, two days before Christmas, he agreed to take us into town so Maxine,

Gene, and I could do our shopping, we knew for sure he was coming around.

Hurrah for the joy of giving! Mother gave Gene and me each fifty cents to buy presents for the family. The first thing I found to buy was a book for Maxine. It cost twenty-five cents. Mother counseled me against spending half my allowance on one gift, but I insisted on buying it anyhow. I just knew it would be perfect for Maxine. The marbles for Gene only cost ten cents, and later, when Gene and I traded partners and I went shopping with Maxine, I found a ten-cent pin for Mother and a five-cent cigar for Kinnick. My money was gone, but I had presents for everyone. I was thrilled. I wanted to tell everyone right away what I had gotten for them, but I was determined to resist that inclination and for once keep my secrets.

Right away, Maxine took to teasing me in various ways in an effort to find out what I had gotten her. I held out for quite a while, but eventually I blurted out, "I won't tell you what you got, but you'll sure have fun reading it!" There now, another family saying coined, another lesson learned, no, two lessons, for on Christmas morning I discovered that Maxine had less fun, too, as a result of ruining her own surprise.

It was a perfect Christmas morning. I woke up thinking I'd overslept, it was so light outside from the reflection of the moon on snow that had fallen overnight. As I hurried to wake up Gene, I saw the tree Sis's father had cut for us was piled high with lots more presents than those we'd put under it the night before. Santa Claus came after all!

Maxine got the book from me, of course, a ring from Gene, and clothes from Mother. For Gene there were the marbles, a game of pick-up-sticks from Maxine, and pajamas and a shirt from Mother. I got a bag of jacks from Maxine, pajamas and a dress from Mother, and, best of all, a little grown-up-girl-type doll made of china with arms and legs that moved. At last I knew why Gene was allowed in Mother's bedroom the day before when I was not—Mother was making clothes to dress the doll he had bought. And finally, the grand finale: from Santa Claus, a pair of skates to hook onto our shoes for each of us!

"Hey, look at Kinnick!" Maxine called out after the excitement of the skates subsided. "He hasn't opened a single package, and here we are all through with ours." Then jokingly to Kinnick, she asked, "What are you waiting for, New Year's?"

"Not quite," Kinnick answered as he got up and walked into his bedroom and returned with a paper sack. With a bit of a smile he reached into the sack and said somewhat self-consciously, "Here's something for you kids," as he pulled out a pair of wool socks, unwrapped, for each of us. We were too surprised to say a word.

"Why that's just what they need for skating," Mother filled the silence for us, though she looked as surprised as we were.

Reaching inside the sack again, Kinnick gave a stiff little bow, saying, "And for the ladies," as he handed Maxine and Mother each a pair of real silk stockings.

Maxine laughed with delight as Mother said happily, "How on earth did you manage to sneak those into the house without my seeing you, John?"

"Oh, I got my ways," Kinnick answered with a self-satisfied little smirk as he sat down and started opening up the presents we'd gotten for him. He was obviously tickled at our amazed reaction to his big surprise.

It was all so wonderful: the presents, the tree shimmering in the corner with the sunshine reflecting off the tinfoil icicles we'd spent Christmas Eve hanging on the branches, one by one, just so. And for that extra perfect touch, on the dining table was the square cut-glass bowl Mother and Tom Belts had received as a wedding present, filled with nuts for cracking. Then for breakfast we each got one of the little mandarin oranges Aunt Eva sent from California and, afterward, a piece of peanut brittle from the box of See's candies, also from Aunt Eva.

After breakfast Mother told us to sit still, and she would do the dishes while we each wrote a thank-you note to Aunt Eva and a letter to Henry to let him know we got the card he sent.

Actually, the postcard from him that arrived a day or two before Christmas was the first word we'd had since he left back in October. Henry wrote that he was working on a ranch in the Bitterroot Valley and since he hadn't been there very long he didn't dare ask for time off to come home, but he hoped we'd have a Merry Christmas. Of course, Mother had cried a lot when the card arrived. She said it was from being so happy to know he was all right and feeling sad that he couldn't be home with us to celebrate.

In the early afternoon we all set out for the pond that bordered on the back of our farm. Proudly carrying our new skates, Gene and I ran out ahead breaking trail through the snow as Maxine and Mother, carrying brooms, and Kinnick, carrying a long board he'd nailed braces onto before we left, followed along behind. When we reached the pond, the board was set down with the braces holding it upright and Mother and Kinnick, pushing against it with the brooms, cleared most of the snow off one small area, then used the brooms to sweep off the little snow that was left. In the meantime, the three of us children put on our skates.

Maxine took off skating right away, as she had learned how in eastern Oregon, but Gene and I required some help from the adults to get us started. Although still awkward and wobbly, we were skating back and forth by ourselves by the time Mother said it was time to go. Before we left, Kinnick walked around showing us areas, like where the cattails and other vegetation jutted through the ice, that we were to keep away from when we came out skating by ourselves. The brooms we carried back home, but Kinnick left the board at the pond to be reused when it snowed again.

# 9

It did snow again, and again, and again that winter. It turned out, in fact, to be one of the worst winters the valley had in many years. Shortly after New Year's Day, the temperature dropped so low that Kinnick became worried about his little herd of horses making it through the winter, especially those that had been half-starved when he bought them and were still quite thin and scrawny.

Almost every morning there was new snow to shovel from the path to the barn before the milking could be done. After that was finished and the cows were turned back out into the bitter weather, Kinnick would begin bringing the least healthy of the horses into the barn, where he had rigged up a stove out of an old metal barrel to cut the chill. Every few hours this process was repeated until all of the horses had been brought in out of the snow and cold to be fed and warmed. By then it was time to bring the cows in for the evening milking; then they were left in the barn all night. Kinnick was concerned about having enough hay and grain to last through the winter, as the animals were eating more than usual due to needing more fuel to withstand the cold. Even so, he continued to feed them as much as they could eat. Every evening after settling the animals for the night he'd say, "So far, so good. We'll just have to wait and see what tomorrow brings."

Toward the middle of January, Gene and I got up one morning to a snowstorm with blustery winds blowing the snow into deep drifts around the house. Mother wondered if she should keep us home, as the school bus hadn't come for Maxine at its usual time. Kinnick assured her it would likely be along soon and said she'd better get us on our way or we'd be late for school, as it would take us longer to walk through the snowdrifts.

We were both dressed in our warmest clothes. We wore long underwear with long stockings, and I had on a pair of Gene's old pants pulled up under my dress. At the very last, Mother got out two pairs of Kinnick's long, woolen socks that she pulled over our rubbers; then folding our pants down tight against our legs, she pulled the socks up on the outside of the other clothes. She said that was a trick she learned in eastern Oregon to keep out the snow and protect our feet and legs.

With our wool scarves wrapped around our heads and faces so only our eyes were left uncovered, we headed out into the storm. Gene took my hand when the snowdrifts got so heavy I had trouble getting through them without his help. Finally, as the wind got stronger and the snow fell so fast we couldn't see where we were going, Gene stopped and, putting his mouth against my ear, yelled, "I'm going over to the fence. You hang onto my coat in back and don't let go. It you lose hold, stand still so I can find you!" I nodded and did as he said.

It was rough going across the ditch to the fence, but once he found it, we moved along slowly but steadily through the drifts, some as high as our waists, as he went hand over hand along the barbed wire from fence post to fence post. Suddenly his coat jerked so hard I fell to my knees and lost my hold. As I sat back on my heels I remember thinking how nice it would be to just sit and rest, but I knew Gene would be looking for me, so I struggled to my feet and waited. Sure enough, he came back and found me. "I fell in the gully!" he yelled in my ear again. "We must be at the bridge. We'll have to go back over. Hold on tight, now; we're almost there!"

I don't remember being frightened, for we had no knowledge of blizzards or what can happen to people who get caught out in one, though I do remember that my feet and hands were feeling numb and I was getting very tired. Just when I was ready to ask if we could sit and rest, Gene stopped and turned around. "Here's the gate!" he yelled. "Move around so I can open it."

We made our way across the school yard to the building and fought our way up the long flight of stairs. As we got the front door open to go inside, Mrs. Kircoffe came running up to greet us, calling to Mr. Kircoffe to "come and see who's here." The Kircoffes helped us take off our scarves, mittens, coats, shoes, and socks, then checked our faces, hands, and feet for frostbite. The delight we felt at being there soon turned to pain as we started warming up. They massaged our hands and feet with snow to slow the warming and I cried a little with the hurting, but in the end they concluded there was no real damage and after a while we felt fine again.

There were a few other children who had arrived at the school before the blizzard hit, so the Kircoffes had quite a group to keep busy with crafts and games as the blizzard raged outside. By late afternoon the winds died down, but it was still snowing and the drifts were high. Mr. Kircoffe said we'd better plan to spend the night, as our parents would not be able to come for us before the next morning at the earliest.

"I just wish the phone lines were in up your way so we could call your folks," Mr. Kircoffe said to Gene and me. "But I'm sure they'll know you're in good hands here." His tone was reassuring, but Mrs. Kircoffe looked skeptical as she raised her eyebrows and turned away.

It wasn't too bad with the other children there to keep Gene and me company as we curled up on the floor in the comforters and blankets the Kircoffes managed to rustle up for us, but morning was a different story. One by one, the parents of the children living nearby arrived to take their offspring home until at last we were the only ones left. I was worried. Maybe Mother forgot about us or Kinnick didn't want us anymore. With the weather outside now bright and sunny, I couldn't think of any other reason why they hadn't come.

Just as I felt the tears start welling up behind my eyelids as Gene and I sat dejectedly in a classroom, we heard a tinkling sound of bells in the distance. Running to the window, we saw them at last—Mother and Kinnick sitting high on the wagon, outfitted with runners to make a sleigh of it, gliding over the snow behind the team of horses plunging through the snowdrifts. As Mother looked up and saw us standing waving at the window, she stood up and waved to us, then put her mittened hands up to her face and sank back down on the wagon seat. "Crying again, I suppose," said Gene disgustedly.

As we ran to get ready to head for home, Mrs. Kircoffe told us we had better wait inside. "Your folks will need to come in and warm up," she said. "I'll make some cocoa and toast. I expect they're tired and hungry. Most likely been up all night worrying about you two."

*What on earth did they have to worry about?* I thought. We were safe and sound at school. We were the ones who had something to worry about, what with their taking so long to get here. I guess I really knew, deep down, that Mother wouldn't forget us, but I wasn't so sure about Kinnick. But there he was; he'd come for us just like the real fathers did.

We waited anxiously just inside the door till they came in and Mother gave us each a hug before she burst into tears while Kinnick grumbled, "We'd a been here sooner if your mother hadn't insisted on the sleigh bells. Said she wanted to make a celebration of it. Can you beat that?"

Later, as Mother and Kinnick visited with the Kircoffes over toast and cocoa, "Oh, I was sure they'd be all right." Mother said. "After all we've been through, they wouldn't let a little old blizzard get the best of them," she added with a wink at me. When Mrs. Kircoffe said how smart we were to use the fence to guide us, Mother told the story of how Gene had followed the fence home once before, in Lynx Hollow, after his eyes had swollen shut from a bumblebee sting on his nose. There were other stories and lots of laughter, but while Gene and I were pleased with the compliments and all, we were anxious to be off on that sleigh ride home. I was visualizing Gene and me standing behind the wagon seat with the sleigh bells ringing joyously as we pulled triumphantly into the yard at home. Of course, Maxine would run out to meet us and be happy to hear about our big adventure. And so it was.

The schools were closed down for several days after the blizzard as we waited for the snowplows to clear the roads, and with the snowdrifts higher than our heads and the temperature near zero, none of us went outside during that time unless it was absolutely necessary. It was strange being cooped up in the house all day with Kinnick, for while I had accepted him as Mother's husband, I had never really thought of him as a person who had been married and raised a family long before we met him. He loved to talk and during this week of isolation told us many stories about his childhood in Missouri and how his family had moved to Bloomfield, Iowa, when he was in his teens. He adored his father and always spoke of him with admiration and love. At one point, when I asked him what his middle name was, he said it was Carson, which was his mother's maiden name. Her father, Kinnick said, was a first cousin to Kit Carson, which made him a shirttail relative of that famous man—I was impressed by that. He mentioned his sisters and first wife only briefly but had quite a lot to say about his three sons, all of whom were now grown and married. His oldest son, Barney, lived in the state of Washington, and the other two, Paul and Bill, were in California. I could hardly wait to tell my friends about the Kit Carson connection and was thrilled at having acquired three new stepbrothers. It did not occur to me, at the time, that those young men would find their newly acquired eight-year-old stepsister of no interest whatsoever.

No matter how early I got up in the morning, Kinnick was always up ahead of me. Most mornings he'd be getting dressed by the big wood heater in the living room and we'd all laugh about the order he followed in putting on his clothes. He came out of the bedroom in his long underwear and quickly set about building up the heater fire, which was usually still burning from being carefully banked the night before. As soon as he was satisfied the fire had caught, he'd put on his shirt, the bow tie he wore for working, and then his pants. It was his putting on the shirt and tie before the pants that tickled us, for all the men we'd seen put on their pants first and most didn't even bother with a shirt until they got ready to go outside. None ever wore a tie. But however much we teased him, and we did, his pattern never changed.

One morning late in January, I was surprised to come out of my bedroom and find Mother building up the fire.

"Where's Kinnick?" I asked.

"He's sick," Mother answered. "A little touch of the flu, most likely, so I told him to stay in bed. I'll have to keep Gene home from school to help me with the horses. Do you think you can make it to school by yourself?" she asked. I knew she had already made up her mind I could, so I just nodded.

"How about his precious little Jersey that no one else can milk?" Maxine called from the bedroom.

"Oh, I told him her udder wouldn't cake up in a day or two of Gene's milking her. You know he's got to be pretty sick to agree to let Gene do the honors." Mother laughed.

When Gene came in from milking, Kinnick insisted he bring the pail of milk from the Jersey cow into the bedroom so he could check how much he got. He was surprised, and a little disappointed, I think, to see the pail as full as when he milked her.

It was four days before Kinnick was up and moving about again, and each day there was a little more milk from the Jersey cow. Finally, thinking Gene must be cheating by adding milk from old Bess to the pail, Kinnick started checking both pails and was mystified to find the other pail as full as usual.

"What's your secret?" Kinnick asked.

"I sing to her," Gene answered.

Kinnick laughed, really laughed, which he didn't often do. "That must be one tone-deaf cow, for there isn't one of you can carry a tune," he said as soon as he stopped laughing enough to talk. "If the animals heard you all sing 'Happy Birthday' they'd hang their heads in shame."

I was astounded. I thought our singing sounded fine, but eventually I did come to realize that he was right.

Toward the middle of February, in expectation of spring arriving soon, all of the farmers in the area gathered at the pond behind our property for an ice-cutting party. Families from all directions arrived in their trucks or wagons or whatever vehicle they had for hauling. There were already two big bonfires burning when we got there, and the ladies were busy making coffee while the men staked out the area where they would cut the ice. On the other side of the pond the neighbor children were skating and we lost no time in joining them, so I paid little attention to how the ice was cut, though I did see some of the long crosscut saws like the ones my father had used for cutting down big trees.

At noon we were called to come and eat from the makeshift tables set up with the mountains of food brought by the ladies for a winter picnic. By evening there had been load after load of ice hauled off the pond to be stored in dugouts like ours or icehouses like those the wealthier farmers had. At the last, after the area where the ice had been cut was blocked off by chains strung between big barrels with DANGER signs hung on them and the men's ice-cutting gear and the ladies' dishes from the noontime feast were put away, everyone gathered around the fires to roast wieners and marshmallows.

"Isn't it nice to have so many friends?" I asked sleepily from my warm spot between Mother and Kinnick on the wagon seat, later, as we headed down the road for home.

"There's a difference between friends and neighbors," Kinnick answered. "Neighbors are the people who live nearby like those we were working with today. Some you like and some you don't, but you got to learn to get along and work together 'cause it makes it easier on everyone. Now, there's those determined to 'go it alone' and they might make it work for a while, but there always seems to come a time when they need help and might find it hard to come by. On the other hand, being too friendly with those close by, or the people you work with every day, can create problems, too. Best to maintain friendly relations but keep your distance." Once again, a complex answer to a simple question.

February passed slowly and with March came the spring thaw that gradually melted the snow, creating a sea of mud. Try as we might, Gene and I could not avoid getting our shoes muddy and sometimes our clothes as well, as we picked our way between the deep ruts and puddles of water on the road, though in all honesty, we just might have stepped in a puddle on purpose now and then to test the depth. Each evening as Mother met us at the back door to make sure we took off our shoes and the worst of our muddy clothes before entering the house, she would shake her head and say, "More clothes to wash," as she dropped the muddy clothes in the laundry basket and brought our shoes in to set by the stove to dry.

Washing clothes, at that time, was no easy chore. The water must first be heated on the woodstove in the copper boiler, then carried to the galvanized washtub, where the clothes were rubbed against the washboard, wrung out by hand, rinsed, and wrung out again before being hung outside on the clothesline or about the house to dry. Many of the children at school wore clothes showing spots where the mud had been scraped off, but they had not been laundered, and Kinnick suggested Mother use that same approach, but her pride would not permit it. She would not send her children to school in muddy clothes, and if that meant washing every day, which it did, as we had only two sets of school clothes, then that is what she would do. "You just push yourself too hard, Gladys," Kinnick would say sadly as he shook his head from side to side. "It'll catch up with you one of these days."

Not only did Mother not listen to his advice about the extra laundry; she now launched into a whole new flurry of activity to produce Easter outfits for all of us to wear to the Easter services at our little church. She had her standards to maintain no matter what.

The prospect of Easter brought back the memory of the previous year when my brother Gene and I lived with Aunt

Bert and Uncle Joe on the loganberry farm in Oregon. It was near Easter and we were questioning the existence of the Easter Bunny. All Aunt Bert and Uncle Joe would tell us was to be patient until the day arrived, when we could see for ourselves. We got up early Easter morning and, trembling between doubt and hope, hurried to the kitchen to ask Aunt Bert about the Easter Bunny.

"I haven't seen him," she said, "but then I haven't been outside yet. Uncle Joe's out doing chores; go check with him."

It was one of those mornings so common to western Oregon that time of year when the warmth of the rising sun lifts dew from the grass in the form of mist and moves it slowly toward the sky, in some places thick and heavy, in others as wispy, see-through clouds floating in midair. As Gene and I went outside, our hearts leaped at the sight of a ghostly looking figure standing by the well with the heavy mist rising up around it. As it whirled to face us, we saw that it was Uncle Joe.

"Did you see him? The Easter Rabbit. There, on the other side of the well. Quick! Hurry!" Uncle Joe called excitedly as he pointed into the heavy fog. "He is about my size, gray, with a swallowtail coat and a big top hat. See there! There! Like a shadow. He hopped away when he heard you coming but if you look real hard you might still catch a glimpse!"

"I see him! I see him!" I cried. I did then, and I still do, see a shadowy, gray, man-sized rabbit wearing a black swallowtail coat and a tall top hat with ears sticking up on either side of it as he hops away in the heavy mist.

Aunt Bert must have dyed at least ten dozen eggs to be hidden in the yard, for we filled our baskets twice before going in to eat breakfast and get dressed for church. In the afternoon we found more eggs, and we kept running across the leftovers in clumps of grass, behind rocks, and in the woodpile on into summer.

Of course, there could never be another Easter as magical as that one in Oregon, but this being the first year we were allowed to help dye and decorate some eggs did make it special. There were Easter baskets beside our bed when we woke up in the morning, including one for Maxine, and we had a big Easter egg hunt; then Mother started right out using the hard-boiled eggs to make creamed eggs on toast for breakfast. Following breakfast, we dressed in the clothes Mother had been sewing on late into the night and felt proud of our new finery as we entered the church on Easter morning.

Spring had finally arrived, and as the last of the patches of snow melted off the grass in the pasture we could see that it was turning green. The alfalfa, in the field next to the pasture fence, was greening and growing at an even faster pace. The horses, all of which had made it through the bitter winter, spent many hours a day near the fence eyeing that lush, green carpet of alfalfa in the adjoining field. One morning as Kinnick stepped out the back door on his way to the barn, he let out a howl, then stuck his head in the back door and called for all of us to get our coats on and get out there—he needed help.

It turned out that one of the best of Kinnick's horses had jumped the fence and was grazing in the alfalfa field. Green alfalfa, as it was explained to me later, worked like a poison on some animals, though that same plant after being cut and dried into hay was a safe, nourishing food for them. Anyhow, the horse died and Kinnick grieved for the loss of the animal but even more for the loss of the money he had expected to get when the animal was sold.

"How will you get rid of the carcass, John?" Mother asked as we were all standing by the fence looking at the body of the dead horse lying in the field, then added in a kidding way, "You might try burning it."

With that we all broke into gales of laughter as we remembered the horse that had died in Lynx Hollow and how we had tried to burn the carcass while Kinnick, thinking we were laughing at him, scowled and started to walk away. Mother finally recovered herself and ran after him to explain our odd behavior and beckoned to us to follow them to the house. Once inside, we all participated in telling what we thought was a hilarious story, but Kinnick was not one to poke fun at himself or appreciate others doing so and would not let himself be cheered. A day or two later two scruffy young Indian men came by to pick up the carcass to sell to the fertilizer factory. After they left, Kinnick laughingly suggested there would probably be little left for fertilizer. "Indians eat horse meat, you know," he said—now *that* he thought was funny, but the rest of us didn't.

One of the last horses Kinnick bought was a light gray gelding built close the ground with husky, powerful-looking legs and a broad, flat back, and he had been eagerly looking forward to trying the gelding out on the plow. He hadn't been too happy with the team he'd acquired when he first arrived in Round Butte, and it was his intention to check out all of the horses until he found the best possible team to keep for himself, then sell the rest.

"Today's the day!" Kinnick announced one morning. "I'm going to put the harness on that gray today and plow the garden for you, Gladys. If he pulls as good as he looks, he'll be a keeper."

"Well, how did it go?" Mother asked Kinnick later as he came in the back door to wash up for the noontime meal.

"Good!" he called as he filled the wash pan at the pump. "He's everything I thought he'd be and more. He's willing, smart, and strong as an ox." After he finished washing up, he walked on in the kitchen and, putting his arm around Mother's shoulder, gave her a little peck on the cheek—he was tickled. "How about a cup of coffee while you're getting the food on?"

Mother brought a cup of coffee to the dining room for him. "Isn't it going to be hard to find a match for him? You don't have another gray."

"Color's not important, it's the weight and stride that count," said Kinnick, warming to the subject. "Next to that is temperament. Horses, like people, have a mind of their own. Take that team I got—one's ornery and the other's lazy, and you got to be fighting them every minute to get any work out of them. Now, take Ole Si there—I named him Si after a horse my daddy used to have—he knows what the harness is for and he sets to work, calm as you please, and after the first furrow was dug I didn't have to use the reins at all except to turn him when we got to the end. He's got his pace, slow and steady, and that's fine for plowing and raking, but when you got a team hitched to a wagon you want a little more speed. What I need to match him up with is a horse with more spirit that will set a faster pace for the wagon but let Si set the pace for the plow. I made a deal to send some of the herd to the auction in Missoula in about two weeks, so I'm going to have to move fast."

Gene and I looked at each other in dismay, for this was the first we'd heard about the horses being sold so soon and we had been hoping to talk Kinnick into keeping a horse to ride. "What about a saddle horse for us?" Gene asked.

"We can't afford to keep no horses that don't earn their keep, and I can't see where hauling you kids around is earning anything. You'll just have to ride shank's pony."

We looked inquiringly at Mother as she set the last of the food on the table and moved to sit down. " 'Shank's pony' means walking on your own two feet," she said. "John, maybe you could try to find a partner for Si that the kids could ride when you're not using him."

"I'll keep it in mind. Now, that's enough talk. Let's eat. I still got a lot of work to do today."

Each day Kinnick would harness up one of the horses he estimated to be about Si's weight, and each evening he provided a report on why the horse he'd teamed with Si that day would not make a fitting partner for the gray. After about a week, though, he did find a tall, rangy brown gelding that showed promise and, after trying him out for another day or two, concluded that he would do. Best of all, so far as Gene and I were concerned, he was also broken for riding, so we wouldn't have to use shank's pony all of the time. We named him Jerry after the bay saddle horse we'd had in Lynx Hollow.

Spring on the farm is a strenuous time with plenty of work for all, regardless of age. Gene and I were kept busy helping Mother plant the garden. We tended to the baby pigs and calves and did any other extra chores we could handle that would release Mother and Kinnick for the heavy work. When Kinnick came in from a long day of working the fields, he looked tired and his feet were so sore he would take off his shoes and soak them in hot Epsom-salts water right after supper. He did not complain, however, he was too full of delight with his new team and his satisfaction with the amount of work he'd been able to get done that day.

Mother finally suggested he might go a little slow on bragging about the team, as he was bound to take some ribbing from the neighbors about their looks. She knew a short, heavy gray horse alongside a tall, rangy brown one didn't exactly fit the picture of the matched team most of the farmers had.

"Let 'em talk," Kinnick came back. "They may not look like much, but they'll outpull and outwork any of their matched teams any day of the week, and it won't hardly take a flick of the reins to make them do it. I swear, these horses just seem to know what has to be done and they do it. By the end of spring planting they'll be as good as those big Percheron teams they have back in Iowa."

Mother raised her eyebrows. "That may be, but sure as you're sitting there, talking too much about it is going to bring trouble." And it did.

The trouble started on the Fourth of July when Kinnick suggested we all go across the river to a ranch that was hosting a local rodeo to celebrate the holiday. Actually, what Kinnick was celebrating was the sale of the last of his horses for a profit, as opposed to the loss he would have taken on the crops. Once we got to the ranch, Gene and I were so busy watching the rodeo events and playing with the other kids, we didn't know there'd been any trouble. We wouldn't until Mother started in on the "I told you so" routine on the way home that night.

Apparently, there had been some derisive comments made about Kinnick's new team by one of the grown sons of a neighbor who lived a couple of farms up from us and Kinnick had countered by bragging about how good the team was. The other fellow had been drinking and turned mean, and the upshot was that a bet of ten dollars—a fortune for a farmer in 1932—and a date for a pulling contest were set for the Saturday before the next dance at Round Butte School in early August.

From the Fourth of July until August there was a feeling of tension in our house, though since Mother had vented her anger on the way home from the rodeo we hadn't heard much about the upcoming pulling contest. Kinnick during this time spent every spare minute checking over, repairing, and strengthening the harnesses, for as he told us, "It just wouldn't be fair to these fine animals to have the harness break before they get a chance to show their stuff."

The morning of the contest, Mother announced that none of us were going. She thought it was a bunch of nonsense, and we would not be a party to it. We were all standing at the window watching Kinnick harness and hitch up the team when Mother suddenly broke out laughing.

"Why on earth are you laughing?" Maxine asked.

"Because it's better to laugh than cry, I suppose. I look out there and see a ridiculous-looking team and that old man acting like a kid going off to conquer the world with them—it's just so sad."

Maxine laughed, "A flat-footed old man at that."

"Wearing a bow tie," Gene and I chimed in, and we all stood there like crazy people laughing till the tears rolled down our cheeks.

After Kinnick had the team hitched to the wagon and was ready to move out, Maxine ran for the door. "Let's go wish him luck. Coming, Mom?"

"I can't," Mother said. "John's made a mistake this time. You go on. We'll make some ice cream. He'll be hot and tired when he gets home, and something cold might hit the spot."

Later that afternoon, Mother sent us out to watch for Kinnick's wagon. When we saw it coming up the road we ran to tell her; then we all stood in the shade at the back of the house until the wagon pulled in the driveway.

"He doesn't look too happy," Maxine whispered when the wagon got close enough to see. "He must have lost."

"Gene, come open the gate and help me get the harness off these horses and get them watered and the feed bags on. They're hot and tired. I'll tell you all about it when I get inside!" Kinnick called dejectedly as he stopped the wagon at the gate by the barn.

Mother, Maxine, and I went in the house and got the lemonade poured, the cookies on the table, and the ice-cream freezer set on the floor beside Mother so she could dish it up as soon as the men came in.

Kinnick looked glum as he walked slowly through the kitchen after washing up. He stopped by Mother and reached into his pocket, then slapped a ten-dollar bill on the table in front of her. "Buy yourself a new dress, Gladys, compliments of Si and Jerry," he said as a big smile broke over his face and he danced a little jig. Our reaction of relief and amazement was exactly what he had been looking for, and he walked in his most jaunty manner to his chair at the end of the table and sat there like a king on the throne waiting for his subjects to quiet down before he spoke.

"You shoulda been there! Some of the men came early in a truck with a winch and put a chain on that big log down at the lower edge of the school yard, then pulled it out where the horses could get at it. The rules were five tries and you're out or drag the log ten feet for a winner. If more than one team could make ten feet then there'd be a tie, but no runoff so as to not overtax the horses. There were about ten teams so we drew straws for position and I was in the middle, about fifth or sixth. A couple of teams ahead of me did manage to move the log but they couldn't keep it goin'.

"On our first try Ole Si started out slow and easy, like he always does, but once he felt that weight he knew just what to do; he hunkered down and lunged. Now, that caught Jerry by surprise and he skittered around a little, but I figured, *He's smart and he'll catch on,* so I quieted him

144

down and went for a second try. This time Jerry knew what to do, but he lunged too quick, so I went up and gave him a pat and pulled back on the bit to let him know to slow down and gave Si a pat and got ready to go again. I figured they about had it down by now and this might be the time, and sure enough, when I gave 'em the reins they lunged together and when I saw that log about to move I flicked the reins to keep 'em goin' and they stayed hunkered down and kept right on pullin'. There wasn't so much as a whisper from that crowd, just the sound of the horses snorting and grunting and passing wind, until they passed the ten-foot mark; then a shout went up and I reined 'em in. I tell you, there wasn't nobody snickering about that team after they saw 'em pull that log. A few more teams moved the log, but they'd pause after instead of movin' out, so they couldn't make the haul."

"What about the smart aleck that started the whole thing? Did he have a team there?" Mother asked.

"Yup. He was one of the first—good team, too—but he's no kind of a driver—used a whip on 'em. I was almost ashamed to watch. When my team crossed the finish line he walked over and threw that bill on the ground and jerked his team over to the wagon and headed home. A real sorehead."

"I've a strong feeling this isn't over yet, John. Do try to restrain yourself from crowing at the dance tonight." Mother advised.

A day or two later, as Kinnick and Gene were walking in from the barn, the sorehead neighbor came riding in and jumped off his horse and started yelling about how he'd heard Kinnick was bad-mouthing him at the dance and he wanted an apology. Mother heard the racket and came running out of the house in time to hear Kinnick respond that he couldn't apologize for saying what he meant. I heard

Mother murmur, "Oh, dear, I just knew it wasn't over," as fists went up and Kinnick went down with the first punch.

"If you weren't an old man I'd beat the hell out of you! You just keep that big mouth shut about me from now on or I will, old man or not!" the sorehead yelled as he got back on his horse and rode away.

Mother ran over to help Kinnick to his feet. "John, John, why couldn't you just apologize instead of trying to fight him? He was half your age and twice as big."

"It wouldn't of mattered, Gladys. He had to have his pound of flesh. Best to let him have it and be done."

"Men. I'll never understand this need for fighting," Mother said as Kinnick shrugged off the helping hand she offered and walked unsteadily off toward the house. For the first time I felt sorry for Kinnick. He looked old, really old, and very tired.

A week or two after Kinnick's fight there was an after-supper surprise for us. It was a decorated cake. The words "Happy First Year" were written in red icing on the top with a candle standing up on each side of the "Happy."

"What's this for?" we asked.

"It's an anniversary celebration. You arrived in Montana exactly a year ago today. There's a candle for each of you. Be sure and make a wish before you blow it out," Mother answered happily as she stood up and lit the candles, then walked around the end of the table to give each of us a hug. "I am so happy you're here. It's been a mighty big year for all of us."

# 10

What impact that first year in Montana had on my brothers and my sister I cannot say, but the impact on me was profound. That was the year I adopted Kinnick as my father and I fell in love with my mother.

My memories of my father, Tom Belts, were so unpleasant I refused to be swayed by the stories Mother would tell about their happy early years in eastern Oregon, for this was a man I did not know, could not believe in. The father I had known was an ambitious, driven sort of man, seeking sudden riches; when one scheme failed he moved quickly to find a new angle, try a different approach. He was restless, impatient, quick to laugh, and quick to anger, filled with high hopes or bitter disappointment. Kinnick, on the other hand, set more attainable goals: a modest home, a good wife, and a little money in the bank. He, too, loved to test himself against the world and would take a chance, but only after carefully evaluating the possibilities and laying the groundwork for success. For the most part Kinnick did succeed, which explains the confident, self-satisfied manner he displayed, sometimes to the point of being obnoxious, to be sure, but still based on accomplishments as measured against his modest expectations.

When I arrived in Montana, I had already secretly claimed Kinnick as my father, but my brothers still had a powerful hold over me and I held back. I watched and I waited as Mother had told us to do during that long talk about Kinnick when we first arrived. Where my father had been unpredictable and violent, I found Kinnick to be calm and steady. Where my father and mother had shouting matches with neither of them willing to compromise, Kinnick had a way of accommodating those situations Mother felt very strongly about without seeming to have given in. Where I had felt frightened and anxious around my father, I felt safe and comfortable with Kinnick. And he was there. The day I finally went against my brothers in this matter was the day Kinnick was knocked to the ground by the sorehead neighbor. He looked so sad. I thought he needed a little girl to love him, he needed me, and right then and there I set out to make him love me back like the real fathers loved their daughters, whatever way that was. It would be many years, decades actually, before I would come to realize I had it backward. I needed him, while Kinnick, fifty-five years old with three grown sons, had no need of me at all.

My memories of Mother in Lynx Hollow were of her always working in a somewhat anxious, hurried manner—in the kitchen, at the sewing machine, in the garden, or at the loggers' cook shack. Here in Montana, life moved at a more leisurely pace. It was Kinnick who set the slower pace for he liked to relax in the evening and to have Mother sit with him in the living room after supper, listening to the news and discussing world events, his work in the fields, or some bit of local gossip he had picked up on his barbering days in town. Mother still kept busy, even then, with some sort of handwork, i.e., crochet, embroidery, piecing a quilt, or darning socks, for she was never one to be idle long. Then after Gene and I did the dishes and finished our homework they might play cards with us or we'd all just sit around listening to a radio program. Saturday night was bath night, there was church on Sunday, and once a month came the dance at the Round Butte School. Kinnick always lit up his weekly cigar after Sunday dinner as he and Mother talked while we did the dishes, and later, more often than not, Kinnick would suggest we visit a neighbor or someone would drop in to visit us.

It seemed like almost everything that year was a cause for celebration. Besides the usual birthdays, anniversaries, and holidays, Mother would decorate a cake or fix a special treat when the cow had a calf, when Kinnick sold a horse, when Maxine made the honor roll, or when Gene or I brought home an especially good report card. I suspect she may have been finding excuses to show off the culinary skills she'd acquired working for that wealthy family in Eugene, Oregon, the year before, but no matter; it made life interesting and fun.

For the first time I got acquainted with my mother, and I found her to be wise, generous, cheerful, and loving. She was everything the books tell us a mother should be except for one small flaw—she seemed to cry a lot. Now, if my mother was as perfect as I thought she was, then her crying over the battles with Maxine made Maxine the villain, so I declared war on her, even wet the bed we shared on purpose sometimes to get back at her, and determined I would be so good Mother would never have to cry over me like she did over Henry and Maxine.

How could I not love a mother who delighted my friends by serving Kool-Aid in frosted glasses, with a sugar-covered rim and a wedge of lemon, a cherry, and a sprig of mint on a swizzle stick when we hosted the Girls 4-H Club I'd joined that summer? And how about a mother who launched my sex education by showing me the sexual organ of a rooster? It happened like this:

As the weather warmed in the spring, the chickens

were turned out in the yard and right away the roosters started jumping on the hens and holding them flat to the ground. I was worried they were hurting the hens and started chasing them off until one day Kinnick told me to stop doing that.

"But they're being mean to the hens. They're hurting them," I protested.

"No, they're not. They're fertilizing the eggs so the hens can hatch a batch of baby chicks," said Kinnick as we walked to the house.

"What does *fertilizing* mean?" I asked Mother as soon as we got inside.

"It means spreading fertilizer on the fields to make the crops grow better," she answered. "Why?"

"Because Kinnick said when the roosters jump on the hens they're fertilizing the eggs."

Mother looked surprised and a little cross as she turned inquiringly to Kinnick. "John?"

"She was chasing the roosters because she thought they were being mean to the hens, so I told her to stop it and I told her why." Seeing Mother's unhappy look, he continued, "It's a natural part of life, Gladys. Better she learn about it here with the animals than through those off-color jokes and limericks she's been bringing home from school."

Mother thought about it for a minute or two, then turned to me. "All right. The next time we kill a rooster I'll show you all about it. In the meantime, like John says, quit chasing the chickens."

I just knew this was going to be an important piece of information and could hardly wait through the two weeks before we were to have fried chicken again for Sunday dinner. True to her word, Mother called me in after she started cutting up the rooster and could get at the part she wanted to show me. She also had a piece of paper with a picture on it laid out on the table beside the chicken. She began with that.

"Now, you've seen hens lay eggs and know they come out of a hole in the back, underneath the tail feathers, don't you?" I nodded as she pointed to the bottom of the picture at what looked like a pipe with progressively larger eggs down toward the bottom. "Here's where the egg with a hard shell is waiting to be laid, and above that is the channel with more eggs forming a shell and waiting their turn. Now, up here is where the channel separates into two tubes to make a Y shape, and the eggs in those tubes are smaller. Those circles at the very top above the tubes are the ovaries, where the egg is formed, and you can see a tiny little dot for an egg in there. Only the female chickens, the hens, have ovaries, so they are the only ones who can lay eggs. If you want the eggs for eating, the hens have everything they need to produce them, but if you want to hatch baby chicks from the eggs, a rooster has to be on hand to provide another ingredient," she said as she turned to the body on the cutting board.

"What the rooster uses to fertilize the egg is called sperm. In order to shoot the sperm into the egg channel of the hen, he has this little sac in back under his tail feathers, and he inserts that into the egg channel of the hen and squirts the sperm through it into the channel," Mother explained as she put her hand inside the rooster and poked out a little piece of what looked like very thin skin with grooves on it.

"What are the grooves for?" I asked.

"Well, after he jumps on the hen and grabs her neck with his beak to balance himself, the hen, not knowing what is happening to her, might try to get away, so those grooves act like suction cups to hold the sac inside the channel until he can shoot the sperm," she answered, then turned back to the drawing.

"Now the sperm enters down here and it's like a tiny little fish and it starts swimming up the channel to the tubes and fastens itself to the tiny eggs that are just forming a membrane—that's the little skin we sometimes have trouble getting off the hard-boiled eggs—and that makes the start of a baby chick. You remember how I have to pick out little specks of blood from the egg yolks sometimes? Well, those specks are what grow into baby chicks when the eggs are left under a setting hen for a few weeks. Any questions?"

I was so busy thinking how I'd give my classmates the scoop on Monday that the question caught me by surprise. "How about the animals . . . and people?" I finally asked.

"It works the same. The female has ovaries that produce an egg, though a different kind than birds do, and the male has the sperm, except the sac is on the outside instead of the inside. It's what you kids call a peter. Now, that's enough for one day. I made sure Maxine and Gene were not around when we talked about this, and my advice is that you not rush out to tell them. They'll probably think it's funny and find a way to tease you, and you won't like that. In fact, I wouldn't tell the kids at school either; let's just keep it between you and me. For one thing, if they've been told different by their parents they won't believe you, and for another, they might go home and tell their parents and get me in trouble. Parents can be pretty touchy about this kind of thing. Promise?" I nodded.

Mother had obviously spent considerable time preparing her presentation, what with the drawing, probably copied from one of the medical books she often referred to, and had certainly supplied more than enough information for an eight-year-old to grasp. Then, too, she must have known I couldn't be relied on to keep my promise not to share this knowledge, and sure enough, at first recess Monday morning I set out to educate a special friend. That conversation ended up with my friend shouting, "Everyone knows God makes babies! You and your mother are both liars!" as she stomped away. A few days later Mother let me know that my friend's mother had chided her for sharing the facts of life with one so young; then Mother moved on so quickly to other matters I had no opportunity to explain and it left me feeling guilty about the trouble I'd caused her. This was a tactic of Mother's to let me know she knew what I had done without scolding or punishing me, though I sometimes thought I would prefer the punishment to the guilty conscience.

Early in the summer a bull was brought to our farm to stay with the cows for a few days for breeding purposes, and I felt very smug about my knowledge of what was going on as I watched the breeding process. After that, I lost interest in sexual matters, including the jokes and limericks the kids at school were passing around. There were questions later, of course, but Mother always answered them in a straightforward, honest way appropriate to my age level at the time.

The next four years on the farm in Montana pretty much followed the pattern that had been set in that first year, and our daily life settled down to a comfortable routine.

Mother accepted an offer for part-time employment as the cook in charge of the school lunch program during our second year, as the dances at the school were now profitable enough to get that program on a more professional basis. There would still be a volunteer to assist her each day, but Mother would perform the menu-planning and management duties, much to the relief of the other ladies in the community. It was a relief to the children, too. They had suffered through many unappetizing lunches prepared by mothers who were not good cooks, and looked forward to having my mother cook for them on a regular basis as she had become a great favorite.

Most of what one reads about the Great Depression deals with the individuals who spent those years in a desperate struggle for survival or, on the opposite end of the scale, took advantage of the suffering and desperation to build fortunes for themselves. Perhaps the real heroes and heroines of that period were those somewhere between those two extremes who, through a combination of good luck and resourcefulness, managed somehow to make ends meet and lighten the burden of the less fortunate when they could. My mother and Kinnick were typical of this middle group.

Mother took with her to the new job her genius for preparing delicious, healthful meals on a minimal budget and her enthusiasm for celebration. As she had done at home, she found all kinds of occasions for her decorated cakes and special treats, e.g., when students placed, or won, a debating or glee club competition, some honor was awarded for an essay, or an athletic team did well in a regional tournament. Kinnick, as usual, complained that it was too expensive, too much work for her, and too much folderol for these hard times.

"Oh," Mother would come back, "I stay within my budget. It makes the kids so happy, takes their mind off their worn-out shoes and last year's clothes, for so little effort on my part. I disagree; we need more folderol because it is hard times."

Mother's "extra touches" soon came to the attention of the community, and she was asked to cater a dinner for a local farm organization, then a wedding reception, etc. Although it wasn't on a regular basis, it did give Mother and Maxine, working as her assistant, a chance to earn a little extra money, and as Mother said, "Every little bit helps."

For his part, Kinnick, too, found ways of earning a little extra cash occasionally. After the team pulling contest, the farmers in the area had a new respect for Kinnick's judgment regarding workhorses and he would sometimes be asked to find a good team for them or a match for a horse they already had in cases where one of a team had been injured, had died, or had grown too old to work. At first Kinnick would find a team or a horse to buy and then resell it to them for a small profit, but because the farmer would sometimes be unwilling to pay a fair price, he finally started charging a finder's fee and that worked better. Another venture began when a man from Missoula stopped by the barbershop for a haircut and asked Kinnick how the pheasant hunting was out his way. The result of that conversation was that Kinnick agreed to take the man's bird dog for the summer and try to train it, the man bet it was not trainable, and they would test the dog out on a pheasant hunt in the fall. If the dog worked well, the Missoula man would pay board and training costs for the dog; otherwise he'd pay nothing. Kinnick not only won the bet, but each year after that the Missoula man and friends showed up at our farm for pheasant hunting and hired Kinnick as a guide.

Having had good luck with that first herd of horses, Kinnick continued buying a small herd each fall, feeding them through the winter, and selling them in the spring for much more than other farmers were getting for their crops. Not only were Kinnick and Mother able to stay even, financially, but after 1933, as the economy slowly improved, they were able to start rebuilding their savings, which had been depleted to a dangerously low level during that first year.

In recent years, I have come to the conclusion, although Mother never told me this, that the agreement she and Kinnick reached after the "chasing Henry with the shovel" incident was that Kinnick would, thereafter, bring his complaints about her children to her and she would handle the discipline. In any case, he never again directed his anger at us in a violent way, though he did often complain, rather bitterly, to Mother. This put her in the middle, a burden not always easy to carry but probably the best she could do. She still had three children to raise and little chance of doing it by herself. Then, too, he was a decent man who was willing to support us and she was, from what I observed, fond of him—love, in those days, was not a word often spoken in our house. As for Kinnick, he treated the three of us, and Henry later, as he said neighbors should be treated: he maintained friendly relations but kept his distance.

Maxine soon caught on to the fact that I was seriously competing for Mother's affection, but for the most part, it didn't really seem to bother her much. She was busy keeping up her grades in school, visiting with her best friend, Sis Lavis, and, toward the end of high school, spending time with her "steady" boyfriend. Maxine was at an age when she was trying to break out from under Mother's influence, not compete for it, so she'd just laugh and call me the "goody-goody girl"—except for the bedwetting. It didn't take her long to figure out I was sometimes doing that on purpose, and it made her furious. When Mother would not believe I could do such a thing, Maxine's fury doubled. I was tickled. It was perfect. At last I'd found a way to get at her that only she knew was deliberate, and it helped to make up for all the times she had cut me up with her sharp tongue, for she was much quicker and more adept with words than I was. Obviously, there was more to all this than my protecting Mother from hurt feelings.

In 1934, Maxine graduated from high school with honors and a small scholarship to a nursing school in Portland, Oregon, where she was to be admitted in the fall. Mother agreed to let her stay with friends in town until September to work as a waitress in a café, as she needed to save money to support herself in Portland until she could find a job for her room and board while she attended school. Mother was very proud of Maxine and pleased with her choice of nursing, probably chosen partly because of Mother's own interest in that profession. Mother's sister, Hazel Green, lived in Oregon City, located near Portland, and she promised to keep an eye on Maxine, so the prospect of her being far away was less traumatic than when Henry left.

After Maxine left, the atmosphere at home was calmer, less stressful, than when she was there. I quit wetting the bed almost immediately.

In her first year of nursing school, Maxine maintained her honor roll status, as she had in high school; then disaster struck. She contracted scarlet fever, was hospitalized, went back to school before she fully recovered, and had a relapse. By the time she was well enough to go back to school again, there was no possibility of making up the material she'd missed. The school administrators suggested she wait a few months until the next group of students completed their first year, then reenter school as part of that group. Maxine had no choice but to accept that suggestion, decision really, and found a job as a housekeeper to a wealthy family that provided room and board with a small salary, and she settled down to wait.

A little over two years after he left Round Butte, my brother Henry came home in a rather dramatic fashion. It was Christmas morning. I got up at dawn and looked out the bedroom window to see if it was still snowing; it wasn't, but I did notice the figure of a man moving slowly, unsteadily, up the road. Every few yards he'd stop and lean over and put his hand over his mouth for a moment, then sort of gather himself together and come plodding on. Suddenly I realized it was Henry and went tearing through the house yelling, "Henry's coming up the road! Henry's here!" as I hurried to put my galoshes on over my bare feet and throw a coat on top of my pajamas to run out to meet him. He saw me coming and tried to speed up to meet me, but he couldn't. When I finally reached him, he put his arm around my shoulder and gave me a little squeeze. "Merry Christmas, Runt. I think I'll just hang onto you and let you help me on up this here road," he said in a low, scratchy voice that didn't sound at all like Henry. He didn't look much like I remembered either, as his face was gaunt and old-looking. Still, I was thrilled to see him and felt proud to be the one to help him, but scared by the fits of coughing he had before we reached the house.

Mother met us at the back door, and Henry said "Merry Christmas," as she grabbed him in her arms and hugged him hard.

"It is a Merry Christmas with you here, Son. You're skinny as a rail," she added shakily with tears in her eyes as she stepped back to look him over. Seeing his face was flushed, she put her hand on his forehead and went from tears to her best nursing manner in an instant. "You're burning up with fever. Here; sit by the fire and let me get your coat and shoes off. Then it's off to bed with you."

Between coughing fits, Henry told us he'd been walking all night to get home; what with the snow and it being Christmas Eve, there were few cars to thumb a ride with.

As Mother pulled off his shoes, she held them up to

the light and saw there was just a little jagged edge of the sole left around the outside edge. She sounded shocked. "Good heavens, you've walked the soles right off your shoes, though I doubt there was much there to start with. These look like the same shoes you left home with."

Henry reluctantly admitted that they were. He said they did have some small holes in the sole before and he'd padded those with cardboard, but the cardboard didn't hold up long in the snow.

It was his strong will and determination that carried Henry through those last few miles, for he was very ill with pleurisy. Mother nursed him day and night for days before his fever broke, and it was a tribute to her nursing skills that he survived at all. It took him a month to get well and another month to regain his strength. Sometime during that period he made his peace with Kinnick, and though he was never fond of him, as Gene and I were, Henry did accept him as Mother's husband and paid him the respect due that position. Henry also, during that recovery period, told us many stories about the places he'd been, the things he'd done, but the one I remember best was the story of where he'd been just prior to coming home.

It seems Henry had boarded a freight train going east out of Missoula and met some fellows on their way to Butte, Montana. They planned to get a job in the mines there; the miners were on strike for higher wages and better working conditions, and the mine owners were hiring anyone they could to replace them. "I didn't really give it much thought," Henry told us. "I was half-starved and they had money for food, so I went along. Sure enough, there were men at the train yard waiting to sign us up, and we signed on to go to work that night. The boys bought me a meal and paid for a bed in the flophouse where we went to get a few hours' sleep before goin' to work. Let me tell you, that was the toughest twelve-hour shift I ever put in or ever want to. I hadn't been down there ten minutes before I saw why the men were striking for better conditions, and by the time those twelve hours were over I figured they should get double the pay. Anyhow, we finally got out of there and were headed to the flophouse to get washed up and go to breakfast when some union guys jumped us in the alley. Before I knew what hit me, there was this big guy sitting on top of me using my ears as handles for pounding my head on the pavement while he yelled at me about bein' a sleazy little son-of-a-bitch scab who didn't know his ass from a hole in the ground and he'd probably be doin' me a favor to put me out of my misery. Well, I was about to agree with him on that, 'cause I was already seeing double and my head felt like it was split in two. Anyhow, he went on about how they weren't just striking for themselves and their families but for workingmen everywhere, including me, though I wasn't worth the powder to blow me up, let alone striking for. It ended up with him tellin' me to get out of town, pronto, as he bounced my head a couple of more times and I passed out. The other guys were gone when I woke up, so I went on down to the paymaster to get my wages and there was the biggest bunch of beat-up guys ahead of me you ever saw." Henry smiled ruefully. "The paymaster just laughed as he paid us off, said they'd have another crew of dummies when the train pulled in. I wasn't in shape to hop a freight, so I bought a bus ticket to Missoula and had enough left for coffee and a sandwich; that was the last I had to eat till I got home."

We were all outraged that those union guys would treat our Henry like that.

"Ah, I doubt I'd of done it in the first place, if I wasn't so hungry, but I don't blame them. I'd probably do the same thing if I had a wife and kids to support and saw a bunch of young punks comin' in to take my job."

I don't recall exactly when Henry took off again, probably because the circumstances were different. He was sixteen now and had already been off on his own for two years, and Mother had more confidence in his ability to survive so was less upset about his leaving.

Gene changed from a boy to a teenager during these years. That first summer he joined the Boys 4-H Club and began the club project of raising a calf with enthusiasm, but it wasn't long before he was complaining that he already knew more about raising calves that the adult adviser to the club did. Then, too, Gene thought the other boys in the club were a bunch of babies "playing farmer," he'd say in disgust. By the middle of summer he had quit the club, though he continued caring for his calf, and started working for the farmers in the area at any sort of odd job he could get. He liked earning money for himself—there was no such thing as a child's allowance at our house. He also, early on, quit going to church with Mother and me.

Gene did well in school, enjoyed the athletics, especially the track-and-field events, was well liked by both the girls and the boys in spite of his quick temper leading to many fights, and for the most part treated me in a kindly, if somewhat superior, manner. It was that superior manner that never failed to get to me. Henry used his knuckles on my head—the Dutch rub he called it—for putting me in my place as "the little sister," but Gene developed a far more effective technique. Gene had always, for his age, had exceptional strength in his arms and hands, which he utilized by grabbing my wrists and crossing them, holding them tight together between the thumb and forefinger of one hand; then, holding me at arm's length, he'd reach out with the other hand and twiddle my nose. It was so demeaning, a cheap show of superior strength; it infuriated me. I was helpless. If I tried to break his hold, he'd tightened his grip until it hurt my wrists, and at arm's length, with Gene's arms being so much longer, I couldn't reach him with a kick, though I surely tried. The only way I could retaliate was to wait my chance until his back was turned and then run up behind him and hit him as hard as I could. He never gave me the satisfaction of letting me know I hurt him, if I did, for he would just laugh or prance around on his toes saying something like, "Oh dear, oh my, did I just feel a fly land on my back?" Still, it did make me feel better.

Gene was smoking by the time he was twelve and not much older when he started leaving the dance at Round Butte School to go outside with the older boys to have a drink of whiskey. At that time, at least in Montana, any boy who could see over the bar in a saloon could slap his money down, order a drink of whiskey, and be served. Prohibition had been repealed by then, and drinking whiskey was an even greater symbol of a real man than smoking cigarettes—and Gene was in a hurry to be a real man. Mother would hear reports of his activities and be upset, but Gene had developed some good-humored ways of deflecting her anger. He'd put his arm around her and tell her how pretty she looked by way of changing the subject or right away tell her he had been foolish to do whatever it was he did and it wouldn't happen again, but it always did.

For the most part, my life was probably very much like that of any other little girl living with her family in a rural area. I saw my friends every day at school and once or twice a month at the 4-H Club meetings in the summer. In the early years, Gene and I had our chores to do but still had plenty of time left over to play, dream, skate on the pond, and swim in the irrigation ditches. It was a happy, comfortable life.

As we got older, however, Gene was more in demand to work for neighbors, and once Maxine left I was assigned more boring household chores to do. We were getting restless.

# 11

In the spring of 1935, Kinnick announced that we were going on a trip that summer, in June, as soon as the first cutting of alfalfa was stacked for hay. He wanted to visit his sons in California and Washington, and Mother, Gene, and I would be visiting our relatives along the way as well. It couldn't have come at a better time for Gene and me.

Our first stop on the trip was American Falls, Idaho, where we visited our Grandmother Belts, who still lived with her son-in-law, Mr. Barlow, and her three grandsons, left motherless so many years before.

Grandma Belts, crippled with arthritis, her gray hair pulled into a bun on top of her head with wisps fallen loose to float against her long, heavily lined face, seemed very, very old to me, but I found her to be still energetic and full of fun. There are two things I remember about that visit. One is that she opened a jar of real mincemeat and let us eat it all, right out of the jar, and the other is the story she told about her middle grandson, Clyde, nicknamed Moony.

All three of my Barlow cousins were now handsome young men, with the oldest, Charles, graduated from high school and holding down a job, Moony a senior in high school, and the youngest, Jim, a high school junior. It seems the senior class had planned a "skip day" to have a picnic in honor of graduation. Permission for the outing had been denied by the school principal, but the class was determined to have their picnic anyhow.

After laying the groundwork for her story, Grandma

said, "Now, that Moony is a straitlaced, goody-goody, kind of boy, and he said he planned to go to school no matter what the rest of the class did."

"What did you say?" Mother asked, smiling as though anticipating an unconventional answer.

"Well, I told him he had two choices. He could either go to the picnic and get in trouble with the principal along with the rest of the class, or he could go to school and get in trouble with me."

"What did he do?" Gene and I asked anxiously.

"He went to the picnic, of course; he knew his life around here wouldn't be worth a nickel if he didn't," Grandma finished up triumphantly.

We all had a good laugh over that. Mother laughed because she was happy to find Grandma Belts still young at heart; Gene and I laughed because we were tickled to have a grandma with such modern, up-to-date ideas of how these things should work.

After we left American Falls, Mother told Kinnick the story about Grandma Belts and Moony, but Kinnick, without so much as the ghost of a smile, said flatly, "Hmmph, I figured your kids had to get their feistiness from somewhere."

We stopped at Salt Lake City and what was then called Boulder Dam, now Roosevelt Dam, as we drove south, but all the other sights Mother wanted to see Kinnick adamantly refused to consider, as he was in a hurry to get to Los Angeles and see his boys. The plan for our arrival was to go first to Huntington Park, a suburb of Los Angeles, where my father's sister, Eva Belts Field, and her husband, Thorp, lived, as Gene and I were to stay there for a few days while Mother and Kinnick visited with Paul and Bill Kinnick and their wives.

We arrived at Aunt Eva and Uncle Thorp's house late

in the afternoon, so Mother and Kinnick spent the night. After they left the next morning, Aunt Eva took Gene and me out for lunch, a great treat for us; then we boarded a streetcar to visit Uncle Thorp's butcher shop, located in a business district a few miles away. The assistant butcher employed by Uncle Thorp was a Japanese man with a son about our age who had agreed to entertain us for the next few days.

Now, I had seen pictures of Japanese people in my books at school, but this was the first time I'd seen an actual person of that race, and I was fascinated. I thought him by far the most beautiful boy I had ever seen. He was smaller than me, perfectly proportioned, with a small, round face and delicate, almost feminine features. Where we had freckles and rosy cheeks, his face was all of one color, a smooth light tan, with high cheekbones and dark, sparkling, almond-shaped eyes, topped by a head of jet-black hair cut very short. We must have looked confounded when his father, in broken English, introduced him by his Japanese name, for he broke into a smile that lit up his whole face as he told us to call him Tosh like the kids at school did, then asked us, with none of the shyness Gene and I were feeling, if we'd like to go outside and walk around the neighborhood with him.

Tosh was an animated little fellow, friendly, cheerful, and a wonderful tour guide. He seemed to know all of the shopkeepers in the area, and we wandered in and out of several Japanese stores where he showed us the difference between items that were strictly for American consumption and those the Japanese would buy for their own use. The proprietors all seemed to know and like Tosh, and they would smile and bow and greet us, mostly in Japanese; then Tosh would interpret what they said for us and we'd try to smile as we ducked our heads, for we felt shy and a little foolish about looking through their stores with no intention of buying anything. After the tour, we went back and played in the alley behind the store until closing time, when we would be riding home with Uncle Thorp.

We spent two more afternoons with Tosh. The first was at his home, where his mother served us a Japanese-style lunch. We didn't like it too well, but we ate as much as we could to be polite, and Tosh showed us around the house explaining the symbolism of the Japanese pictures and artifacts. The house, on the outside, was a typical small California bungalow, but inside it was furnished and arranged in a Japanese style that made it seem far more spacious and elegant than Aunt Eva's house of about the same size. I thought it the loveliest home I'd ever seen. Later we went outside to play, but Gene and I spent most of the afternoon answering Tosh's questions about the farm and our life in Montana. Tosh got very excited when he found out we lived on the Flathead Indian reservation and asked all kinds of questions about the Indians and their way of life, most of which we could not answer because we knew very little of their culture, as there were no Indians actually living in our area or attending our school. Although we thought we were too old to play cowboys and Indians, Tosh was so anxious for us to play, so delighted when we did, we spent the rest of the afternoon at it. The next day, Uncle Thorp brought Tosh home with him at lunchtime to spend the afternoon with us at Aunt Eva's house. This time he was visiting us, so we chose the games. After Aunt Eva served us lemonade and cookies in the midafternoon, we sat around talking about our families, our schools, etc. We were amazed when Tosh told us he went directly from public school to a Japanese school for two hours each afternoon; then after dinner he did homework until his bedtime at ten o'clock. Even in the summer, he spent four hours each morning in the

Japanese school, then went to the store, where he helped his father and played with the children of the other merchants. He was required to do no chores at home at all.

Early on, Gene and I conceded that Tosh's academic knowledge far exceeded ours, but we felt quite superior about the practical knowledge we'd acquired from our mode of life. Little did we know that our knowledge of how to care for a runty pig or an orphaned lamb would not be exactly what one needed, later on, when it came time to enter a profession.

Overall, it had been a remarkable experience for two farm children from Montana. It had given us the opportunity to evaluate life in the big city (it was fun to visit but we didn't want to live there) and provided a chance to learn about some elements of a very different culture that caused me, at least, to want to learn more about the Flathead Indians whose reservation we shared.

From Los Angeles we traveled north to Stockton, California, to spend the night at Mother's Uncle Bernice Wyman's house (he was a brother to our Grandfather Wyman), then on to a motel in Eugene, Oregon, where we paid short visits to several relatives and friends of both Mother and Kinnick. After that it was on to Oregon City, where our Aunt Hazel and Uncle Ralph and our favorite cousin, Alan Green, the one we knew best, lived.

Mother barely took time to exchange hugs and say hello to Aunt Hazel and her family before she was on the telephone to call Maxine, for she was the one we were most anxious to see. Maxine told her she was living at the summer home of the family she worked for, located at Lake Oswego, not far from Oregon City. Her employers were out of town but had given her permission to invite us over to visit and had even suggested she might want to ask Gene and me to spend the night.

We had no trouble finding Lake Oswego, but when we turned onto the street Maxine had given as her address we thought there must be some mistake. The houses were very large and permanent-looking, not at all like the summer homes we'd seen on the banks of Flathead Lake back home. Mother insisted we keep driving until we found the proper house number. A little farther on we did find the number and Kinnick turned into the long, circular driveway, but instead of proceeding to the house, he stopped. It was so big—at least twice as big as Aunt Hazel and Uncle Ralph's house in Oregon City, the nicest, biggest home of any of our relatives. This house was very long and low to the ground, with only one step up to the front porch, but two stories high, with the upstairs rooms tucked into a series of gables across the front beneath a dark green roof. It was painted white, not the clean, crisp white of smooth wood siding, but a weather-beaten white on rough shingles set in an uneven pattern to give it an informal, casual look, despite its size. There must have been an acre of grounds, with long, sloping lawns and shrubs and trees, but no formal gardens like we'd seen in some of the yards we'd driven by, and we could see a tennis court set off to the side beyond the driveway that curved in front of the house.

"Gladys, check that address again, I think we're lost," Kinnick said worriedly. "I just can't see folks living in a neighborhood like this for only the summer."

"The neighborhood I worked in at Eugene was just as nice as this, and there were families who lived there only a few months of the year," Mother came back impatiently. "I'm sure this is the right address. Oh, it is the right house. There's Maxine now; she's waving for us to drive on up."

"Quite a little shack, isn't it?" Maxine said as she laughed delightedly at our awestruck faces when we got out of the car. There were hugs and greetings all around;

then Maxine said, "Let's go on in. I'll give you the two-dollar tour before lunch—that's cheese soufflé, by the way," she added mischievously, watching Kinnick's face for the look of distaste she expected from the meat-and-potatoes man. Then, slipping her arm through his as she led us through the front door into the spacious entry hall, she added, "Oh, you know I wouldn't do that to you, Kinnick. Actually I fixed up a scrumptious ham casserole, especially for you."

"Well, this don't look too rich to me," Kinnick said as we turned from the hall into the big living room furnished with rather ordinary couches and chairs, slipcovered in various patterns of chintz fabric, slightly faded, and with tables and lamps that looked very much like those we had at home.

"Oh, it's chic in the rich-bitch circles to furnish your summer house with a run-down look," Maxine responded. "You should see the house they live in through the winter; now that's a mansion. It's not much bigger than this, but with a view out over Portland and Mount Hood. It's furnished with antiques and paintings they pick up on their trips to Europe now and then—ta-da!" she ended, flinging her arm up with her little finger extended in a tea-drinking pose as though making fun of them.

We went on to tour the library, the music room, and the formal dining room, then up the stairs to look at the bathrooms and huge bedrooms, some bigger than all three of ours at home put together. At the far end we finally reached Maxine's room, and even that was larger than the room we shared at home. Next to Maxine's bedroom was a set of narrower, steeper stairs—the back stairs, she called them—so we went down those to the kitchen at the back of the house. Sure enough, the table in an alcove off the kitchen was set for lunch.

"You can sit there at the head of the table, Kinnick, and you don't have to say a word, but we're going to have some conversation with our food!" Maxine called as she leaned over to open the oven door and extract the casserole. "How's Aunt Eva, Mom, and Grandma Belts? Did you stop in American Falls like you planned? Sit anywhere," she indicated as she set the casserole on the table and pulled out a chair for herself. "I can't wait to hear all about it."

Gene and I did stay and spend the night. After Mother and Kinnick left, Maxine took us to the lake to swim, and after we got back she gave us a tennis lesson on their private court. Later that night we asked about the family she worked for, and, among other things, she said they had only one child, a son, William the Third. He was sixteen years old and a bit of a practical joker, so he often got in trouble with his parents.

"Bill's latest escapade," she said, "was a few weeks ago when he installed a musical toilet paper holder in the powder room—that's what they call that bathroom under the stairs in the front hall—just before people arrived for a big party." Maxine laughed remembering the scene. "After they all had a cocktail or two, the ladies started using the powder room and you could hear that tune playing clear as day. The men caught on to what was happening and they laughed and clapped and the ladies were embarrassed till Bill's mother finally got so mad she yelled at his dad, right there in front of everyone. 'Go find that damned thing, whatever it is, and kill it!' " By now Maxine was laughing so hard we could barely understand what she was saying.

"Where was Bill when this was going on?" Gene asked.

"He was peeking down from the top of the stairs to see what was happening."

"Did his folks catch him?" I asked.

"Oh, of course, he knew they would. He thought he might get by with it 'cause his dad is a 'boys will be boys' kind of guy, but his mother was so mad she made him stay in the house for the next two weeks. But he's a good kid; he didn't tell them I was in on it before the party. If he had, we wouldn't be sitting here talking about it, for I'd of been fired for sure."

I was surprised that a rich kid would do such a thing. I'm not sure what I thought rich kids were like, but I'd never thought of them as having an offbeat sense of humor or an inclination to get into trouble like my brothers did. Then, too, a lady who could afford to have a summer home like this using a word like *damned?* And people with not one but two houses of this size for just three people? This whole experience would take some heavy thinking on my part.

Aunt Hazel's house looked less luxurious to me when we drove in the following day—both the house and yard seemed smaller than I remembered—but it was good to get back on familiar ground and we looked forward to spending time with our cousin Alan, although his older sister, Eleanor, we were not at all anxious to see. Eleanor was a senior in high school, very petite—barely five feet tall, about ninety-five pounds—with the most beautiful head of naturally wavy dark red hair I have ever seen, and that, combined with her fair complexion and brown eyes, made a very attractive image, and she knew it. We called her uppity. She called us hicks from the sticks. Alan was a good-looking boy, a year younger than Gene but a head taller, a slower-moving, kindly, take-charge type of fellow who had a calm, friendly way about him that made us feel comfortable and happy to hang around with him.

The greatest points of interest in Oregon City, for Gene and me, were the public swimming pool and the elevator at the bottom of the hill that you could ride up and down in, for free—both new experiences for us. Oregon City was a rather unique town in that the business district was situated on a long, quite narrow strip of land between a high, solid rock cliff and the Willamette River. The residential section extended from the top of the cliff up a long hill behind, and there at the top, on the edge of town, was the cemetery we'd visited on Memorial Day during that year we lived with Aunt Bert and Uncle Joe. Aunt Hazel and Uncle Ralph lived about halfway up the hill on one of the few streets that ran all the way from the top of the hill to the face of the cliff below. Here the street turned sharply to the right, down along the edge of the cliff as it dwindled away to level ground, then made a sharp left turn to intersect with streets leading back to the business section in front of the cliff. From the beginning there had been a set of stairs up the face of the cliff so pedestrians could avoid the long detour, but once the elevator was installed the steps were rarely used.

The days we stayed with Aunt Hazel and Uncle Ralph were the most pleasurable of the whole trip for us. Alan went with us as we visited Mother's sister Bertha, her brother Paul, her father, Granddad Wyman, and various of her aunts and cousins, as they were his relatives as well. In between visiting, Gene and I rode the Oregon City elevator, swam in the pool, played baseball on the school grounds, helped Alan rake the leaves and mow the lawn, visited relatives on his father's side that lived nearby, and did any other activity, within limits, that struck our fancy. We even spent one day in Portland exploring the city with Maxine, on her day off, while Mother and Kinnick visited Kinnick's sister, Minnie, and her husband, Lee Emerson, a railroad engineer who had chosen to retire there.

Our next stop was Chehalis, Washington, a small town

about one hundred miles north of Portland, where Kinnick's oldest son, Barney Kinnick, and his wife, Hazel, lived. It was a boring two nights and a day for Gene and me, for they had no children and lived in a house on a busy highway, so we were confined to the yard while Kinnick and his son went out to look things over.

From Chehalis we traveled another hundred miles north to Seattle, Washington, to visit Mother's youngest brother, our Uncle Henry Wyman, and his wife, Aunt May. We thought it a little strange that first night when Uncle Henry cooked dinner for us, but Aunt May just laughed and said he was a better cook than she was, so she did the dishes afterward instead. As Uncle Henry cooked, Aunt May sat with us at the kitchen table telling us how happy she was to finally meet us, how much she loved Wyman, how kind, generous, wonderful he was, etc. Mother, from a family who would rarely hug, let alone talk of love, looked askance at May's effusiveness at first but was soon won over by her cheerful disposition and sincerity.

After breakfast the next morning, Uncle Henry took us for a drive through downtown Seattle, where he showed us the various points of interest, including the Smith Tower, an awesomely tall building for that time, drove by historic mansions on Capitol Hill, and stopped at a scenic point overlooking, to the east, the University of Washington, Lake Washington, and the Cascade Range in the distance. We drove around Lake Union, where we saw a great variety of boats tied up to the docks, across Queen Anne Hill to see the westward view over Puget Sound with its many islands and the Olympic Mountains beyond, then down a very steep hill—Uncle Henry called it the counterbalance—and on to a waterfront café for a seafood lunch. Uncle Henry told us we were going, after lunch, to the home of his first wife to visit his twelve-year-old daughter, Violet, the only one of our cousins we had never met.

When we arrived at Violet's house, Uncle Henry told us to wait in the car while he went in to get her. Violet did come out of the house to stand for a few minutes on the sidewalk near the car—long enough for Mother to snap a picture of her—then Uncle Henry walked her back to the house, and that was the end of the visit with our cousin Violet Wyman.

The only one of Mother's immediate family she had not visited was her baby sister, Vera, but Aunt Vera and Uncle Ernie Andrus, with our cousins Dorothy and Charles, lived in Port Angeles, located a short day's drive northwest of Seattle, but the road to Montana was to the east. It would be a two-day detour and Kinnick would not hear of it—so we headed east for home.

Several times after we left Los Angeles I'd asked Mother about her experiences with the Indians on the Umatilla reservation in eastern Oregon, but she had put me off—said we'd talk about it when we got home. I suspect it was because she didn't want to discuss it in front of Kinnick, for he was prejudiced against all but the white race and even there seemed to dislike some nationalities.

My interest in learning more about the American Indian culture had been aroused by Tosh in California and had not gone away, so as soon as we settled in at home I pursued the matter with Mother again. She told me of her experiences with the Umatillas and about their belief in being one with nature, of not harming the land, and of killing no more animals than they needed for meat to eat or skins for clothes and tepees, and she showed me the beaded bags, the shawl, and the blankets given to her by the Indians. When Mother saw in the paper there was to be an Indian celebration in Saint Ignatius, thirty miles away, in late August, we conspired to talk Kinnick into taking us. We asked, I begged, Mother insisted, and we finally badgered him until he reckoned he could use a day of playing cards in Saint Ignatius with someone other than the Ronan crowd. He agreed to take us.

What a glorious celebration it was! This could not possibly be the same apathetic people I'd seen sitting outside their shacks on the fringes of Ronan—these people glowed with health and happiness as, wearing native costumes, they visited back and forth or danced or chanted to the beat of native drums. The women wore beaded headbands that matched their brightly beaded buckskin dresses and moccasins. There were older men dressed in buckskin outfits wearing the long feathered headdress of a chief or a shorter version as befitted the elders of a tribe, and there were medicine men in scary masks, but what fascinated me most were the young warriors, many of whom wore nothing more than paint on their faces and bodies, with small loincloths set low on the hips and feathered bracelets on their wrists and ankles.

For most of the morning Mother and I watched the general dancing, where everyone, men and women, most aged to tiny toddlers, would dance awhile then return to their seats to watch the special dances performed by the medicine men or warriors. My eyes popped a time or two as the warriors leaped so energetically their loincloths swayed and flapped around and I glanced at Mother to check out her reaction, but finding no indication of embarrassment or outrage, I took my cue from her and concentrated on the dance itself. What fascinated me most was the way the warriors danced on the balls of their feet so that each time they landed the foot and ankle worked together like a spring to propel them back up into the air with what looked to be no effort on their part at all—it seemed they could go on like that forever.

Toward noon, we left the dance compound to find a café to have some lunch, then spent considerable time going through an area where the various Indian tribes who shared the Flathead reservation had set up displays of native artifacts and craft items, then back to watch the dancing until it was time to meet Kinnick at the car for the trip home.

I changed my favorite dream, from beautiful princess in a faraway castle to Indian princess, roaming the land and sleeping in a tepee; I spent weeks perfecting my version of the warriors' dancing method, and I started tanning the hide of a calf that had been butchered recently, determined to make myself a buckskin dress. The more I worked on the hide, the more brittle it became, and since I didn't take to the idea of chewing it like the Indians did to make it soft, I abandoned the project.

This was the first year since I started first grade that Gene and I were in different schools. Gene took the bus to town, where he was a freshman in Ronan High School, while I walked to my eighth-grade classes at Round Butte. Anyhow, I called it walking; Mother called it dawdling. Admittedly, I was easily distracted—I'd see a frog, a snake, or a bird to be watched or a horse or cow by the fence to be petted and talked to. Then, too, I had much to ponder and to dream about, for my eighth-grade teacher, Mr. Kircoffe, the school principal, had a passion for poetry and literature, with a unique ability to communicate that passion to his students. He would have us each read aloud a verse of an epic poem, e.g., "Rime of the Ancient Mariner," "Horatius at the Bridge," or a sonnet like "How Do I Love Thee" or the "Rubaiyat," or take a part in Shakespeare's *Hamlet* or *Romeo and Juliet*, then help us relate these works to our own life. I chose *Ben Hur* to read for my first book report and was absorbed for weeks by the stories of the Roman army, the plight of the Christians, the chariot races, and the crucifixion of Christ.

Maxine gave up her plan to become a nurse and moved back to Montana that winter, not to live with us, but to share an apartment with a friend in Ronan, near where she worked. I have always thought Maxine came home to marry her high school sweetheart, Leonard, whose proposal of marriage she'd turned down to go away to school. When she arrived, however, she found he had become engaged to someone else. If Maxine was disappointed by that news, she covered it well, for she, like the rest of us, bought into the spirit of the poem Mother often recited:

> Laugh, and the world laughs with you,
> Weep, and you weep alone,
> For the brave old earth must borrow its mirth—
> But has trouble enough of its own.

Maxine laughed, offered her congratulations to Leonard and his bride-to-be, and went on with her life.

# 12

Almost a year to the day after Kinnick announced we were taking a trip to California, he began talking about selling the farm and leaving Montana.

"You know, Gladys," he said one night after dinner when we were seated in the living room, "it looks like I'm going to come out pretty good on the horses this year. I've been thinking about selling the crops in the fall and putting the farm up for sale."

Mother was obviously taken by surprise. "Whatever for? We're doing so well here."

"Well now, you know I'm not much of a farmer. I don't have that feel for the land that a good farmer has. It was just a stopgap to weather the depression, give us a place to grow our own food, to stay afloat, and we've done that and more these past two years. Seems like it might be a good time to make a move."

"How come you didn't mention this before? Where will we go? What will you do?" Mother asked anxiously.

"Now, don't get excited, Gladys, nothing's been decided yet. We're just talking about it." But Kinnick was warming to the subject. "That trip last summer wasn't just to visit. I wanted to look things over for myself to see how much of the recovery those lying thieves in Washington brag about was true. I was surprised to find it looking pretty good in California."

"You can't be thinking of moving to California!"

179

Mother interrupted sharply. "That's not a fit place for man nor beast."

"You're jumping to conclusions; have some patience." Kinnick paused, waiting for Mother to settle down. "There was quite a bit of building going on down there. Of course, with all the white trash moving in from around the country these last few years I guess they got to make someplace for them to live. Most of the building's being done by big outfits, though; a small builder wouldn't stand much chance, so the answer is, no, I'm not thinking of moving to California."

"Thank goodness for that, so . . ." Mother relaxed a bit.

"What I'm figuring is this: If they're building in California now, then they'll be building all the way up the coast before long, and that's good for the lumber business, put loggers and mill hands back to work and improve things all around. I kept an eye out through the timber country on our way up, and about the best place I saw is that little town in Washington where Barney lives. There's several mills cutting finished lumber, so I could save some money buying direct. I talked to a couple bankers that day I was there, and they seemed to think they'd be ready to back a house on speculation in a couple of years, so moving there next year is about right. I can always get some barbering to do at first till I get the building going. What do you think? It'd be halfway between your folks in Oregon City and Seattle and it's a nice, neat little town, plenty of churches to choose from."

"What's the name of that place? Chehalis? I have to look up how to spell it every time I send a note to Barney and Hazel." Kinnick nodded as Mother went on. "I don't know what I think yet. We've built a good life here, but after our trip last summer I have been thinking it would be nice to live a little closer to my family. Dad's not getting any

180

younger and the girls are there."

Gene and I looked at each other in dismay—leave Montana? We had never even considered such a thing, our life here seemed so permanent. Still, when we talked about it later, we found a part of us would be sorry to leave, but another part of us was looking forward to a change of pace.

There was much talk about this matter later, but, to all intents and purposes, it was settled, right there in that first conversation. But moving was a year away and I had more immediate problems to contend with.

When she wasn't working, Maxine often visited us on weekends, and with my graduation from eighth grade coming up, she decided it was time for me to quit being a such a tomboy and start acting like a girl. She wasn't at all impressed by my athletic prowess on the basketball court or my winning ribbons for the sixty-yard dash and the baseball throw at the county track meet—she wanted to groom me for a life of boyfriends and parties. The first step, she thought, was a store-bought dress for graduation, although I was perfectly happy wearing the dresses Mother made for me.

In spite of my objections, Mother and I met Maxine in Ronan for a shopping spree, and they bought me a tan rayon crepe dress, new shoes with a little heel, and silk stockings to wear with them. The day of graduation, Maxine came out early and had me try on my new dress. "You look terrible," Maxine directed as she made a face. "Stand up straight, pull in your gut, tuck in your butt. Here; put this book on your head and walk back and forth like this." Maxine said as she walked in front of me. Later she polished my fingernails, made up my face, and claimed I was a great success, as the girls gasped and the boys raised their eyebrows and smirked at me as I walked in for the graduation ceremony. I felt like an idiot and was happy when she

181

lost interest in the project and I could go back to my normal tomboy self.

That fall, Gene and I took the bus together to Ronan High School, where I was a freshman and he was a sophomore. A few weeks after school started, Gene was waiting for me one afternoon beside the school bus and led me aside to talk to me.

"You know, Runt, I've been skipping school quite a bit lately and I got called into the principal's office today, so I just walked in and told him I was quitting school." Gene laughed and shook his head. "Know what he said? 'I'm sorry to hear that, Belts, I was really looking forward to kicking you out.' Anyhow, if I was to go home now, you know Mom would bawl and Kinnick would say I told you so, and I don't feel up to that. I figure it's time for me to move on, anyhow."

"Where will you go?" I asked.

"Ah, I don't know; maybe I'll head down Texas way and be a cowboy. You tell Mom I'll write often and let her know how I'm getting along. Take care of yourself," he added with a playful punch at my arm as he turned and walked away.

The lump in my throat was so big I couldn't even say good-bye as I stood watching Gene striding confidently down the street toward the railroad tracks, and I could barely keep from crying as I walked over to board the bus, dreading the moment when I would have to tell Mother that Gene was gone. Of course, she cried and Kinnick did say, "I told you so," but things got better after a few days when a letter arrived from Gene. For a long time after that he wrote every week, long, cheerful letters about where he was and what he was doing. With times being better now, it was easier for Gene to find odd jobs to pay his way than it had been for Henry when he left. Eventually, Gene did send a picture of himself, looking healthy and handsome in his cowboy gear as he held the reins of the horse beside him, though I don't know if he was in Texas at the time or not.

The Saturday after Gene left, Kinnick came driving into the yard in a brand-new 1936 Ford coupe. Mother and I came out of the house to meet him as he got out of the car wearing the biggest, most delighted smile I'd ever seen.

"How do you like it? I've been waiting quite a while to see if it would sell before the new models came in, and when it didn't I made an offer and I got it. Isn't she a beaut?"

Mother's tone was icy. "It only seats three people."

"Well, that's enough. There's only three of us."

"What you're really saying is that you're glad my kids are gone. We'll never be able to offer anyone a ride. How could you, John?" Mother cried, lifting her apron to her eyes to catch the tears as she hurried toward the house.

"Hey, there's a big trunk back there and the lid lifts up high enough the kids can ride in that if we have extras. It may not be luxury, but it'll get us there!" Kinnick called.

I'm sure it hadn't occurred to Kinnick that Mother would take his decision personally, for he was not a sensitive, perceptive kind of man. All he saw was a brand-new car at a very special price that he could drive to Chehalis when we made our move—it probably had nothing to do with us at all. Throughout the many years Kinnick drove that car, I don't think Mother ever got into it without feeling some part of the hurt she felt that day, and I don't think Kinnick ever understood why she felt that way. It was one of the few things she was never able to laugh about.

Kinnick stuck with his plan of completing the harvest, selling the crops, putting the farm on the market, and waiting through the winter for it to sell. He was not prepared when the farm sold quickly and the buyers wanted to take possession by December. Mother and I wanted to stay in Montana through the school year and Kinnick wanted to stay until the roads were clear enough to make the trip across the mountains to Washington, so we rented a little house in Ronan. Living in Ronan, Kinnick could work full-time at the barbershop through the winter and go on ahead to Chehalis in the spring to look for property to build on and find housing for us, and we could stay until school was out, as Mother would be able to manage there, in town, without a car. I was glad we would be in a different house for Christmas, because without Gene I knew it would be a dreary holiday on the farm.

I was twelve years old when I started high school in Ronan, thirteen when we moved to town after my birthday in October. I liked living in town. With no animals to care for, no outdoor work to do, I had fewer chores, could participate in after-school activities, and could attend the school dances. I was barely entering my adolescence and still thought that mushy girlfriend/boyfriend stuff was silly, but I was beginning to think I'd like to have a special friend, a boy, to go with to the dances so I would have someone to stand with between dance sets. Finally, it happened! The boy who sat next to me in study hall asked me to go with him to the next school dance. I was thrilled. I had a date—not just any date, but a date with a high school junior, a football star well liked by all who, so far as I knew, had never asked a girl out before, though I knew lots of girls who hoped he would.

"Guess what!" I called excitedly to Mother as I came through the back door of our little rental house. "I have a date for the dance on Friday night. That boy I told you about in study hall asked me to go with him, and he'll come by to pick me up. How about that!"

"You mean the Indian boy?" Mother asked with that tight-lipped, disapproving look she had.

Before she could say another word, Kinnick came storming into the kitchen. "What do you mean, an Indian's coming here to pick you up?" he asked in a loud voice. "Gladys, I told you to set that girl straight when she first started talking about that Indian friend of hers. I'll not have one of those dirty little lowlifes near my house or any of my family. That kind of thing gets around, my reputation's ruined and my life in this town won't be worth a plugged nickel. Tell her no! Any Indian comes sniffing around here gets run off with a shotgun, so put an end to it right now."

I was shocked, furious, hurt, as I stood there speechless, unable to move; then I burst into tears and ran for my room. After I had finally cried myself out, Mother came in and sat beside me on the bed.

"I know, honey, you're thinking that it isn't fair, and in a way, it isn't. But life just isn't always fair and you have to learn to deal with that. Aside from the Indian matter, you're too young to be dating. You're only thirteen and the other girls in your class are two years older, but to my way of thinking even that's too young. If we'd stayed on the farm, this wouldn't have happened, but I can see where in town, with less to do, more hours to kill, it's a bigger problem. You will have to tell him you can't go. You do see that, don't you?"

I nodded numbly—even I could see the situation was impossible—but I was too distraught to think beyond that point right then. Mother reached over and gently brushed my tear-sodden hair back off my face.

"Dinner's in half an hour. I'll help you with the dishes and we'll talk more then."

"You think a daughter of yours is too good for an

Indian boy, don't you?" I asked sullenly as I stood beside Mother at the kitchen sink with a dish towel in my hand, waiting to dry the dishes as she washed them. My fury was directed at Kinnick, but the hurt I felt came from the disapproving look on Mother's face when I told her about my date. I thought she like the Indians, and I thought her two-faced for not wanting me to go out with one.

"It isn't a matter of good or bad," Mother said carefully. "It's a matter of race." She paused as I slammed down a plate with my dish towel on the counter and turned to walk away. "Now, that's enough of that, young lady. You just come on back here and listen to what I've got to say before you make up your mind about whether I'm right or not." I reluctantly walked back and picked up my dish towel and put the plate away. Mother continued.

"It isn't just a matter of a person's skin being white, or yellow, or red, or brown; it's a matter of heritage, of different beliefs, different values. To be friends with a person of another race, to be interested in their culture, is one thing; going on a date that most folks see as a prelude to marriage is something else entirely."

"But I'm not going to marry Tommy; I just wanted to go to the dance with him!" I cried. "Besides, he already told me he's going on to college and when he's a lawyer he's coming back to marry a full-blooded Indian girl because he'll be the chief of his tribe, one day, like his grandfather is now."

"You see? The responsible Indians don't want their sons and daughters to marry outside their race either, for they understand as well as we do the kinds of problems it can bring."

But I didn't understand. "Why can't we just all be people and not worry about that stuff? Tommy is the nicest boy I know, and it just isn't fair."

But Mother still said no. I knew I would have to break the date and that presented a dilemma. Tommy thought I was the same age as the other girls in my class, so I couldn't tell him my mother wouldn't let me go because I was too young, and to tell him I couldn't go because he was an Indian was unthinkable. The only solution I could come up with was to give no reason, make no excuse.

After study hall the following day, I motioned for him to wait until the other students left the room. "I can't go with you," I whispered, feeling miserable. Tommy stood stock-still, like a statue, for a minute, and seeing the hurt look in his eyes, I felt the tears well up in mine. I hadn't given him a reason, but I could see he knew.

He reached out and took my hand. "Don't cry. We can meet at the dance, this one time, and pretend that everything's all right."

On the night of the dance, when I came out of my bedroom to join my friends who had come by to walk with me, I was wearing my graduation outfit and Mother looked surprised but didn't say anything except to enjoy the dance. Mother must have known I was planning to meet Tommy, as I'd only worn that outfit the one time before, but she had this way of letting a situation play itself out without her interfering, providing there seemed to be no real harm in it.

Tommy and I danced and danced, not just with each other but with other partners as well. At intermission we went hand in hand outside, as many couples did, and walked around the schoolhouse to a dark corner and Tommy kissed me. It was a soft, tender little kiss, and afterward he put his finger on my lips and said, "Hold this to your heart and remember me."

Tommy never attended the school dances after that, nor did he ask me out again in the months before we moved to Washington, but we stayed friends and sometimes had long talks during lunch hour at school. I asked many questions about the Indians, and he always answered me like a wise old man talking to a child.

He told me stories his grandfather told him about the ancient times, about the war with the white man and moving to the reservation, but mostly he talked about the problems the young people faced, being raised as Indians in a white man's world.

"If we were emigrants of a different race from a faraway country who came here to make a better life, we could adopt the new ways and still retain our culture, for we would always have our own country to go back to," Tommy told me. "But it was here, in this country, where our forefathers lived in harmony with all living creatures and did not claim ownership or leave their mark upon the land. Our ancestors were a proud people, and to accept the white man's ways, so opposite of theirs, would be to spit upon their image, to be nothing, neither Indian nor white. We know their style of life is gone forever, that we must move on in the world as it is, but how do we do this? My grandfather hopes my becoming a lawyer will help us find a way to resolve this problem. I think it will be very difficult, but I will try." Tommy ended with a sigh.

On the last day of school, after study hall, I said good-bye to Tommy and told him I would write to him.

"No," he said. "It would end badly, for we'll be on different paths. Let's say good-bye now and remember each other with happy hearts."

Later, I said good-bye to my best friend, Ada Atkinson, and we promised to write and visit each other. There wasn't really a party, but I ate lunch with a whole group of friends, both boys and girls, that day, and we made jokes and we laughed a lot and they wished me luck. The following day, Mother, Kinnick, and I were on our way to Chehalis, Washington.

Kinnick had driven up to help Mother with the packing, make arrangements for a moving truck, and drive us to Washington in his new Ford coupe. Kinnick told us he'd bought a house on Fourth Street in Chehalis. It was an older home, he said, but he'd had it cleaned and painted and it was in a good neighborhood, two blocks from the athletic field and grade school, three blocks from the junior high, and six or seven blocks from Chehalis Senior High, where I'd be starting school as a sophomore in the fall.

I sometimes wonder if Kinnick had some paint left over from the farm, because the house we moved to was painted the same light gray with white trim that the farm buildings in Montana were. The house, built in the early 1900s, was tall and narrow, with a front hall, bathroom, and kitchen along one side, an open stairway and dining/living room on the other side. There were three bedrooms upstairs with sloping ceilings against the steep pitched roof. The house sat on one side of the lot, with a large lawn on the other side all the way down to the garage in back. In the front was a cement sidewalk next to a parking strip of lawn out to the curb, and the street was paved. The other houses in the neighborhood were also clean and neat, with well-kept yards. Mother and I were delighted with our new home.

The first few days were spent getting settled; then we attended services at the First Baptist Church on that first Sunday. Mother had been raised a Baptist in Oregon City and was pleased to be able to rejoin that denomination. After church, the minister welcomed us and invited me to join the Baptist Young People's Union (BYPU) meeting that evening while Mother attended evening service. I accepted the invitation and met two girls, sisters, about my age but behind my grade in school, who lived just up the street from me. Through those two girls I met other young people in the neighborhood, and I had a wonderful summer, being lazy, eating everything in sight, reading two or three books a week, playing kick-the-can, and hanging around with the other teens in the neighborhood.

By the end of summer, when school clothes become an issue, I had grown three inches taller and gained thirty pounds. I was in shock—from a petite five feet, one inch and 100 pounds to a giant five-foot-four and 130 in just one summer? I felt ridiculous, big, fat, another person altogether. I needed a whole new wardrobe, for none of the clothes from the previous year would fit, so there was considerable shopping and sewing to be done.

"How do you feel about starting a new school?" Mother asked as she sat on the floor pinning a hem up on my new dress. "Big and ugly," I answered dejectedly.

"I've been thinking; it might be a good idea to take it slow at first. Sometimes those most friendly right away are not the people you may want to associate with later, and that can lead to hard feelings and resentment down the road. Why don't you try being friendly with everyone but not too close with any particular person until you've had a chance to look things over?" she suggested.

I snorted. "I won't have to worry about that—I'm so fat nobody will even want to look at me."

"Well, then, fat and happy is the way to go," Mother said laughing at me for feeling sorry for myself, and the next thing I knew, she had me laughing, too.

So, that's the way I started school in Chehalis— feeling ugly, pretending to be happy, and keeping my distance. To my surprise it seemed to work, and why wouldn't it? I was pleasant, posed no threat to established friendships, and required no more from my classmates than a friendly smile or a wave. Keeping my distance gave me a chance to identify those students who belonged to a "crowd" and those who didn't. The "elite crowd," mostly sons and daughters of the professionals and businessmen in town, ran the serious activities—the school paper, student government, debate club, etc.—as their parents ran the town. They were preparing for college and success in later life. The "fast crowd" consisted of students with that elusive quality called popularity. The boys either were athletes or good-looking or had a great personality and the girls were slender, cute, and made of honey that attracted boys like flies. It was this group that concentrated on the social life, in school and out. The rest of us were only students.

I turned out for after-school athletics and met a girl, Dorothy, who was also cheerful but kept her distance, an excellent athlete, better than I was at most sports, and over time we became friends. Knowing Dorothy was to also know another girl her age, her niece, Marjorie, who had come to live with them after Dorothy's much older sister, Marjorie's mother, died. It was through Marjorie, a very popular girl, that I had an introduction to the fast-crowd social life.

Now, I only had to look in the mirror to know I didn't fit the image of the popular students, but that didn't keep me from admiring the boys and wishing I were the kind of girl who did belong. When Marjorie asked me to attend a party as the date of a boy I admired, I didn't even stop to wonder why he hadn't asked me himself, for I'm sure I didn't want to see the obvious. I agreed to go. I got to the party late and sat on the couch waiting nervously for my date to appear. Finally, he came out from the kitchen with a bottle of beer in his hand, stumbling about, looking tipsy, then spied me on the sofa. "Oh, here's my date," he said as he flopped down beside me and with a rather blurry version of a wicked grin said, "Let's make out," and began to paw me. It was as though he'd suddenly grown ten more hands. When I moved one hand away, another would be tugging at my blouse or trying to pull up my skirt, until I finally broke loose and grabbed my coat and ran for home.

I didn't tell my mother why I'd come home early—I was too embarrassed and confused to talk about it—but she must have guessed because a few days later she asked if I'd heard anything about a certain girl being "in trouble," a term used then for unmarried pregnancy. I told her that I had.

"It's just so sad," Mother said. "If only they knew more about the growing-up process, they'd understand that boys of this age have a strong sexual drive and are mainly out to satisfy that need and the girls, desperate to be liked, anxious to please, give in to that desire without realizing it's more like the rooster jumping on a hen than the kind of adult love they'll experience, and enjoy, later."

Mother went on to say all the usual things like "it's the girl who pays, her life is blemished, she gets a bad reputation," etc., but the message she really pushed was a more subtle one about respect, the coming together of two people with respect and feeling for each as opposed to satisfying a purely physical need, and that was the one that made most sense to me. Throughout this conversation, and others later, Mother always talked as though I was an older, more knowledgeable, responsible person who would, of course, agree with her.

I wish I could say that I had learned my lesson and gave up my desire to be a part of the crowd, but that was not the case. I was occasionally invited and could not resist, but it always ended up, whether at a party or in the back-seat of a car, that the boy wanted to go "all the way," though none were as crude as that first fellow, and when things started getting passionate I would think of the rooster and the hen and laugh.

Now, most teenage boys have learned to take a joke or a razzing from the fellows, but let a girl laugh when they are trying to make out and they take it as a slur on their technique—it stopped them cold. Needless to say, those boys never ask me out again. Before the year was out I accepted the fact that I was not meant for the fast lane and found the courage to say no.

Maxine got married that winter to a fellow in Ronan, Charlie, and sent a wedding picture of the bride and groom, but I was so involved with my own adolescent problems that I don't remember taking much notice of that event.

We hadn't heard a word from Henry in a very long time, two years or so, when he showed up one spring day on our doorstep. He said he was working at a chicken ranch up toward Randle, a village located east of Chehalis near Mount Rainier. When we were still living on the farm in Montana, I remembered overhearing something about Henry marrying an older woman and about Mother having the marriage annulled because he was only eighteen years old at the time. I assumed he had not communicated with us because he was angry at Mother. Anyhow, we were all glad to see him. He had become a man, without that boyish look he had when he came for Christmas some years before, and told Mother he had found a lady he was interested in, a schoolteacher in Randle, and would like to bring her in sometime to meet us. Mother told him to let her know and most any Sunday would be fine.

After school was out that year, I went strawberry picking to earn money for school clothes and was glad I had when I received a telegram from Gene later in the summer.

193

RUNT, CLOTHES & MONEY STOLEN. IN JAIL VAGRANCY, PHOENIX ARIZ. SEND $50 BAIL AND BUS TO EVA'S, GENE.

The Western Union delivery boy must have known what was in the wire, because he made a point of getting me outside before he gave it to me. As soon as I could think of an excuse to get away, for I knew I wasn't to tell Mother, I went to the police station to find a policeman I knew Kinnick liked. I showed him the wire and explained I only had about thirty dollars. He called the bus depot to check bus fare from Phoenix to Huntington Park, California, where Aunt Eva lived, then adding some on for food decided twenty-five dollars would do it. Sending money to get out of town would satisfy the vagrancy charge and, since he knew Kinnick, he'd vouch for Gene so they'd cancel the bail. I gave him the money plus the cost of wiring it to Phoenix and went home hoping we heard from Gene before Mother found out I had no money left for school clothes.

A week or so later, Mother got a letter from Aunt Eva with the news that Gene was there and ready to come home and go back to school, if Mother and Kinnick would have him. Aunt Eva offered to buy Gene some clothes and pay his way to Chehalis on the bus and, fortunately for me, enclosed the twenty-five dollars to repay the money I'd sent to Phoenix. And so it was that Gene came back to live with us and finish high school.

# 13

Gene's entry as a sophomore to Chehalis Senior High went smoothly. He was a nice-looking boy, not handsome as Henry was, but with curly reddish brown hair, brown eyes, a nose slightly damaged from being broken a time or two, and a cute lopsided grin. Though of a shorter, stockier build than Henry, Gene was attractive in a rather rugged way, and he had that magic characteristic: a winning personality. He was quick to acknowledge he'd made a mistake in dropping out of school. He said he'd learned the hard way, bumming around the country, that you didn't get far in life without a high school diploma. It was a line that made him popular with both teachers and students.

Not long after school started, as Gene and I were walking home one day, I told him one of the fast-track girls had asked me if he was coming to her party that weekend.

"Nah," he said. "I don't think I'll get involved with a crowd. You know, I hadn't been home ten minutes till Kinnick took me aside for a little chat, said if I was going to do any helling around to do it out of town; he didn't want any local girl's reputation besmirched by me." He laughed, "*Besmirched*, that's the word he used, but it's not bad advice. The local Romeos won't take kindly to me movin' in on their territory, anyhow, and they're the ones I have to get along with."

It was good to have Gene home to talk to about all the things I'd been confused and troubled about this past year. I told him about the parties I'd gone to, that I hadn't fit in.

"Good. You just keep your nose clean, Runt. Foolin' around with those guys'll bring you nothin but trouble. They're out for all they can get, then they laugh and brag about their conquests, mostly lies—of course. You don't want to mess around with that."

"How do you know so much?" I asked. "You just got here."

"Hey, I'm one of them, that's how I know, except I've learned to keep my mouth shut better'n them. They've already given me the scoop on the easy marks. I know more about the girls here in two weeks than you've learned in a year."

"You're all a bunch of pigs," I said disgustedly.

Gene laughed and leaned his shoulder over to give mine a nudge. "That's true, but we're so cute and cuddly you little gals can't live without us, can you?"

Gene's message, cruder but much the same as Mother's, brought back those feelings I used to have with the nose twiddling: Boys thought they were so smart, so superior; they were so smug. Not only did they take advantage of girls, but they kept them in a dither—and sat back and laughed about it. I had been to the girls' pajama parties, and all they could talk about was boys and how to attract them: what perfume to wear, the color nail polish or lipstick, the hairdo this one liked, but the other one didn't, and on and on. These were not things I'd ever been much concerned with. Besides, it seemed to me that a boy should like you for the kind of person you are, not for your perfume or hairdo. Well, I'd just go my own way, not waste my time on the dating game. I'd become a serious student.

The serious-student decision was prompted, actually, by a visit from the Baptist minister to our house one evening. He'd come by, he said, to tell us about scholarships available from Linfield College, a Baptist school in

McMinnville, Oregon. Mother was very enthusiastic, and I, feeling like a maiden aunt in the midst of a girls-versus-boys world, was also interested. The minister talked about the importance of good grades, participation in school activities, and being active in the church. It would help if I were to be baptized and become a full-fledged member of the church, he added as though it were an afterthought, but either way I could still apply for the scholarship. Being baptized was something Mother had brought up before, but I didn't think it would be right because I liked to dance and the church did not approve. The minister gave us some Linfield College materials to read, told us application forms would be available in the spring and must be submitted by the end of this, my junior year, then bade us good night.

The next two years for Gene and me were fairly typical of most high school students of that time. Gene attended classes regularly, turned out for sports, found a variety of odd jobs to do after school and weekends for spending money, and after a few months acquired a more permanent part-time position with the telephone company. I concentrated my efforts on winning a scholarship to Linfield College, as the minister had suggested, and worked at a variety of housework/baby-sitting jobs until I was offered steady employment caring for a first-grader while her mother worked the last four hours of a split shift, evenings, as a telephone operator. Weekends Gene and I went to school functions, dances, plays, and athletic events, I with my friend Dorothy or sometimes other girls and Gene with the buddies he'd made at school by then. Most of the girls with older brothers envied me because Gene would always ask me to dance, once or twice, at the school dances and stop by and chat a minute at the football or basketball games, while their brothers acted as if they didn't have a sister. Afterward, we girls would go straight home, as was expected of nice girls, while the boys would head out to, as Gene put it, "raise a little hell."

It was fairly easy for Gene to keep his hell-raising activities out of town, as Kinnick had told him to do, for Chehalis was only four miles from a larger town: Centralia, Washington. Chehalis had a movie theater, but aside from that, the sidewalks were effectively rolled up when the stores closed at 6:00 P.M., while Centralia offered many nightlife opportunities like dance halls, all-night restaurants, and professional fights on Saturday nights.

Occasionally Gene would take me with him to one of the dance halls in Centralia if one of his older friends was driving so he could be sure I was taken straight home afterward, though Gene always left with someone else. These dances were much like those Gene and I had grown up with in Montana, where the men went out to their cars to have a drink from time to time. Sometimes we'd see Henry there, and more often than not, after several trips outside and several drinks, Henry and Gene would get into an argument and decide to straighten each other out by fighting. The first time this happened, I tried to stop them, but they pushed me aside and after that I stayed inside and pretended I didn't know them. I just couldn't stand to see them fight. The off-duty policeman acting as a bouncer at the dances finally suggested to Gene that he try boxing in the professional arena in Centralia, where he'd at least get paid for fighting. During his last two years of high school, Gene did just that.

In the spring of my junior year, Henry and the schoolteacher from Randle, named Doris, were married. They had been going together off and on for more than a year, but Doris said she would not marry a drinking man and it had taken Henry some time to believe she meant it and be willing to quit. Doris's parents gave them an acreage near

Randle, where Henry would build them a house, clear the land, and farm it while Doris continued her teaching job. Doris was a lovely person, we all liked her a lot, and Mother was happy to have Henry finally settled down.

In the spring of my senior year, Maxine arrived from Montana, without warning, with her two-year-old daughter, Connie. She had left her husband, Charlie, who worked a large farm with his immigrant parents and brothers.

"Work, work, work, that's all they do, all they want to do, all they'll ever do," Maxine told us. "Charlie's folks are from the old country, where they had to work hard to survive, and now that they've got a nice farm and a good income, all they can think of is getting more—more land, more tractors, more money in the bank. They keep control of every penny and only pay the boys barely enough to live on. No way am I going to kill myself to help them get any more, and Charlie won't hear of leaving them—so here I am."

"I know it's been hard—I could tell that from your letters—but maybe you just need a vacation," Mother said soothingly. "I am glad to see you. I've felt just terrible to be so far away, not able to see my first grandchild grow up. My goodness, it doesn't seem possible she's two already—"

"Mom, you can forget that vacation crap right now," Maxine broke in angrily. "I told Charlie he had a month to get over here or I'm filing for divorce. I am not going back to living like that, and that is that!"

"Well, what do you plan to do?" Mother asked calmly, ignoring Maxine's anger.

"I called Aunt Eva before I decided to come, and she said she'd pay my way to business school. I thought if Connie and I could stay here awhile, it shouldn't take too long to brush up on my steno skills; then I can get an office job and take an apartment in town somewhere. Even if Charlie does decide to come here, which he won't, it'll take a while for him to get a job, so I'll need to work regardless."

Gene suggested Maxine and Connie take his room—he'd sleep on the couch since he wasn't home that much anyhow, and I had plenty of closet space for him to share. So, Maxine and baby Connie moved in with us. Actually, it was fun to have Maxine there. The years of marriage and having a baby had mellowed her, to say nothing of the fact I'd that grown up a lot as well, and once she started classes at the business school in Centralia we were all in school and had more in common. We all doted on baby Connie, except maybe Kinnick, who didn't seem to notice her.

Late in May, Charlie arrived from Montana but not to live—he'd come to take Maxine and Connie home to Ronan with him. Maxine would have none of it. After a few days of arguing with her, Charlie gave up and said he'd be going back the next day, a Sunday. Kinnick picked Mother and me up from church that day, and as he parked the car at home Maxine came running from the house to meet us. She was crying and screaming so loud we hurried her into the house, away from the neighbors' curious eyes, trying to calm her down so we could understand what she was saying. Gene was inside and told us Charlie had stopped in to say good-bye and asked if he could take Connie for an ice-cream cone so she'd have good memories of her father. He assured Maxine he'd have Connie home in half an hour. That was two hours ago and they figured he'd just headed straight out for Montana. Maxine, beside herself with fright and worry, finally settled down enough to tell us if Charlie ever got to Ronan, with all his brothers there, there would be no chance of getting her baby back except through the courts, and even then they would find a way to keep her. She had to find a car and catch him before he got that far.

It was a miracle—Kinnick offered Maxine the use of

his car, which both she and Gene had driven before, and the three of us, Maxine, Gene, and I, drove off in hot pursuit of a man with a two-hour start on a five-hundred-mile trip with no idea of what his plans were, what route he would take, etc., but it was better than doing nothing. We took the closest route from Chehalis, up through Randle to White Pass, and down the southeast side of Mount Rainier to Yakima. Gene did the driving through the pass, giving Maxine time to settle down, and I studied the map of Washington to find the best route from Yakima to Spokane. We hadn't been on the road very long before Gene made some remark about our needle-in-the-haystack search, and that set us all to laughing and joking, wondering how Kinnick would react to his car going seventy miles per hour and all in all having a great time. Of course, we were keeping a close watch for Charlie's car, though none of us thought we had much chance of catching him in the first three hundred miles or so.

At Yakima we stopped for gas and food to eat along the way, as it was already midafternoon and we'd had no lunch. Maxine took over on the driving across the flatlands toward Spokane, and we reminisced about Montana and later Gene and I started filling Maxine in on the Chehalis years and our various school activities.

Maxine listened quietly for a while as she concentrated on her driving; then, "Hey, I haven't heard a word about the prom. Did you guys go?" she asked.

"Not only did we go," Gene answered. "We double-dated."

"Well, Runt, how about your date? Was he cute?" Maxine pressed when I did not respond.

"Oh, he was cute all right, tall, handsome, junior class president, no less, and me a senior. A buddy of Gene's who couldn't dance worth sour apples. Then, to top it off, they

201

took us girls out for Cokes afterward, so generous, then hurried to drop us off, anxious to move on to whatever all-night party they had planned. I'll bet we were the only two girls in town who went straight home."

Gene laughed, "Hey, we had a couple hot little numbers waiting for us in Centralia. It wasn't the kind of party you two girls should attend."

"Why did you go with him?" Maxine asked, ignoring Gene's remark.

"Because he was the only one who asked me." I answered reluctantly, embarrassed to have to make such a confession.

"Well," Gene started off slowly, "now that school's out I guess I can tell you that a couple of other guys asked if you had a date for the prom yet, so it isn't as though there weren't others wanting to ask you."

"Then why didn't they?" I asked, thinking he was making up a story to make me feel better.

"Now don't go gettin' mad and throwin' a fit, but the first thing I did when I started senior high was put out the word that anyone who wanted to date my sister went through me. When they asked me about the prom, I told them you already had a date; they were too high-powered for you." Gene grinned as he put his arms up to protect his head from the attack he expected me to launch.

"Hey, no fighting while I'm trying to drive!" Maxine yelled before I had a chance to hit him. "We can't take a chance on wrecking Kinnick's car, and we got serious business to attend to here."

Maxine spoke just in time, for I was surely ready to beat Gene about the head and ears. Instead I looked moodily out the window for the next few miles trying to sort out my feelings. On the one hand, I was used to Gene looking after me; on the other, how dare he! I had a right to make

202

decisions for myself, though, in all honesty, I hadn't fared too well in that department. Ah, well, he meant well, what was done was done, and right now we had a baby girl to find.

I was the only one of the three of us who felt sure we would find Charlie and Connie. I'd been pondering the problem from the standpoint of driving and caring for a two-year-old. Charlie was not used to caring for a child, it would slow him down, he'd be exhausted with the effort by the end of the day, but he'd be smart enough to get out of reach of the Washington State Patrol, just in case we had reported him, so he'd try to get into Idaho before he stopped. That was a point of contention—both Maxine and Gene were sure Charlie would try to drive straight through; I was equally convinced he'd stop in Idaho to spend the night.

In Spokane we paused for gas and another hamburger; then we drove on through Coeur D'Alene, Idaho. It was getting dark when we arrived at Kellogg, Idaho, and I insisted we drive by the motels—there were only two—and see if Charlie's car was parked by one. After all, it would only take a few minutes. Gene and Maxine were not enthused but, to shut me up, turned off the highway down a side street toward the first motel and *bingo*, the second miracle of the day—Charlie's car was there. Being on the outside nearest the door, I ran in to get the room number from the office; then Gene went to the door of the unit and knocked. Charlie opened the door looking tired and sleepy, then seeing Gene at the door and Maxine and me standing by the car stepped out and said, "Sorry, Gene, but you're going to have to fight me for her."

"Oh, God," I whispered, "men and their never-ending need to fight." But I was scared, too, for Charlie was a much bigger man, older, more mature than Gene, though Gene had been boxing in the ring at Centralia for over a year by then.

Gene backed off the porch onto the lawn with Charlie following him; then Charlie threw a punch. Gene ducked and came in with a right to the jaw that lifted Charlie clear off the ground, and he went down. The minute Charlie moved away from the door, Maxine had run into the motel unit to get Connie, so, leaving Charlie sitting on the ground rubbing his chin, we all got into the car and headed home. We were delighted to have our little girl back, but once that first flush of triumph subsided, I remembered the disconsolate look on Charlie's face.

"I felt kind of sorry for Charlie, sitting there. She's his child, too, and he must feel bad to have her gone," I said.

"Don't waste your sympathy on him," Maxine retorted sharply. "He's more worried about what his folks will say than losing a daughter. She's nothing more than another possession to them, and what belongs to them they hang onto. He'll catch hell when he gets home, but he won't come back." And he never did.

I graduated from Chehalis Senior High in June 1940 and at the graduation ceremony was awarded a scholarship to Linfield College. It was not a full scholarship, for I was not an honor student, but it paid the tuition, no small item, and there was promise of a job with the college to cover room and board. I was very pleased, and Mother was ecstatic.

Right after school was out, Maxine went to work for a local insurance agency and I went out to the strawberry fields, where, by working hard, I could earn more money than was being paid for housework or child care, the only other kind of work available to a girl my age. After that, another girl and I went to the raspberry fields in Kent, Washington, and stayed in the bunkhouses with other migrant workers, and again, by working hard we did quite well and it was an interesting experience, almost a vacation in a way, being away from home. By the end of July the berry season was over, but college was still two months away, so I took a housekeeping job in the home of a doctor and his wife.

Now, in those last two years of high school I had become not only a serious student but a serious person as well. The candle of youthful idealism had been lit and burned inside me with a pure, bright flame. I could not reconcile my love of dancing with the Baptist philosophy, and when the minister suggested I should go ahead and be baptized anyhow I was outraged. Even worse, he suggested I could not continue as the president of the BYPU, since I was not a member of the church, so I resigned that office—I would not be blackmailed. When I went downtown to attend an outdoor Christmas celebration where gifts and baskets of food were passed out publicly to needy families, I felt sick to see the look of humiliation on the faces of the needy and the smug, self-satisfied look of the donors—there had to be a better way. I followed the progress of the war in Europe and was incensed at the treatment of the Jews, though we had no idea then of the real horror of the Holocaust. I thought all people should be treated with dignity and respect regardless of race, religion, or financial status.

It was the doctor's wife who gave me a personal glimpse into the prejudice of those with better-than-average financial status against those with less, those willing to work at menial jobs. I'd been raised by a mother who believed in the old saying: "If it's worth doing at all, it's worth doing well" and had spent my childhood redoing what had not been done well. As a young child, I'd resented this constant emphasis on perfection, but by now, after finding employers appreciated my abilities, I felt confident that I could handle the job I'd been employed to do in the doctor's home. I expected a period of training, a period of adjustment, an establishment of schedule, but this did not happen. I was treated like a robot responding to oral commands. It was, "Do this, do that, no, not that, do this right now, that can wait till later," leaving me no opportunity to get my bearings or anticipate demands. But it was more than that: it was a way of gazing off to the side instead of looking at me directly, a tone of voice, a curl of lip, inferring lack of intelligence or capability on my part, an inferior-person status. Before the end of the first week, I was ready to tell the woman off and quit the job.

Mother sympathized. "I've had similar experiences so I do know how you feel, but to tell her off, as you put it, will not make her change; she probably doesn't even know she's offending you and wouldn't believe it even if you told her. She'll just see you as a difficult girl, a whiny baby, and she'll spread the word and you'll be the one put in the wrong. Then, too, you did take the job and you have a responsibility to fulfill. You stick with it two more weeks, then give a week's notice due to a change of plans, which will be true because you will have a change in plans for getting the school clothes you want without that last month's pay you were counting on."

Kinnick also had his piece to say: "Don't ever quit a job for reasons of anger or dislike. That's false pride, bad business. It'll come back to haunt you. Do as your mother says."

I held my tongue and quit at the end of the month.

I was sixteen, almost seventeen, in the fall of 1940 when I went away to college. The week before school started, Kinnick drove Mother and me to McMinnville, Oregon, to get me registered and settled in the dormitory.

Because I was a working student, I had to be there the week ahead to help with general cleaning of the dormitories and be evaluated for a more permanent assignment. It was an interesting week, meeting other students who were working as I was, some in their junior or senior year. They were very helpful with information about classes, teachers, sororities, and other aspects of college life at Linfield. My permanent job for the year turned out to be preparing breakfast, weekdays, for the fifty or sixty girls housed in my dormitory, so I worked three hours each morning before classes, for fifteen of the twenty hours I'd signed up for, and the other five hours on Saturday doing miscellaneous jobs. It was an ideal schedule.

That first year in college was a pleasant, reasonably successful experience being on my own. I maintained the grade average required by the scholarship, pledged a sorority, dated various young men, students, but only one was special, and that went awry though I never did know exactly why, and I enjoyed the serious discussions of religion, history, psychology, and life that went on in one or more of the girls' dorm rooms late into the night. There was only one problem: Talking late into the night then getting up at 5:00 A.M. to fix breakfast wore me down to where, when school was out and I moved home, I was so exhausted I could do nothing but sleep for the first two weeks.

It had also been a year of changes for my family. Maxine had done well on her job and was studying to move up in the insurance business. She had saved her money and bought a car, a brand-new 1940 Studebaker coupe, and moved to an apartment of her own. Gene, well liked by the men he worked with at the telephone company, had been offered an apprenticeship in the electrical wiring business and had been attending night classes required for that vocation through his last year of high school. Now that he had graduated, he had moved to a job with a company in Longview, Washington, and was already gone from home when I got back. By far the biggest development, however, was that my parents had sold our house on Fourth Street and moved to a nice, new home on the outskirts of Centralia. Kinnick had finally built the house he'd promised Mother when we left Montana.

Mother was concerned about my health, due to my being so tired and sleeping so much, and so was I. I could not seem to get interested in the idea of finding a job to earn the money I needed to go back to school. It had been fun, in a way, I had learned a lot, but to what purpose? I simply had no idea what I wanted to do, where I wanted to go with it.

An ad in our local paper for a temporary summer job as housekeeper in a waterfront summer home on Three Tree Point, near Seattle, caught my eye. My friends Dorothy and Marjorie had an apartment in Seattle, where they attended business college, so I'd have someone to visit on my days off, living on the beach sounded romantic, and a new environment might help me make up my mind about my future. At the employment agency in Centralia I got the job, plus the train ticket to Seattle that went with it.

After getting off the train in Seattle, I went into the depot to the information booth, where I'd been told someone would meet me, and a lady got up from a bench nearby and approached with outstretched hand.

"You must be Glenna Belts from Chehalis," she said as she shook my hand. "I'm Mrs. Russell. Welcome to Seattle; I'm so glad you decided to come and work for us this summer." Then turning slightly, she called in a pleasant voice, "Porter! Would you get these bags to the car for us, please?"

"Oh, I can carry them," I said quickly.

Just as quickly, she leaned close and whispered, "No, no, they need the work," and leaving the porter gathering up my bags, she touched my arm to indicate I should follow her as she walked out toward the parking lot.

I was amazed and pleased with Mrs. Russell's welcome. In five minutes this little lady, no more than five feet tall, with that buxomy dowager look very similar to that of the queen of England, had effectively established our working relationship for the summer. She was in charge, a thoughtful employer, and I was a valued employee.

As we drove south from Seattle toward Three Tree Point, Mrs. Russell explained she was a widow and her husband, bless his heart, had owned a steel supply business that left her well provided for when it was sold. She chatted amiably as she defined my work schedule, asked if I had plans for my days off, said I could catch a bus into Seattle to visit my friends or ride with her those days, if she happened to be driving in, and told me I'd have lots of free time to enjoy the beach, as she and her son, William, would be gone a lot.

"That Bill," Mrs. Russell said ruefully. "He's hardly been home five minutes since he got back from UCLA for the summer. He's taking an advanced degree in cinematography that leaves little time for a social life, so he thinks he deserves to have some fun. Actually, a little too much fun when he lost $500 at the races the other day. I'm a little miffed at him for that. Oh, here we are." She paused as she made a hard right turn onto another street. "This is Maplewild Drive; it runs along the sound down to our house near the point. Keep a close watch on the right for a cream-colored house with a red-tiled roof set in the middle of acres of lawn and native shrubs and flowers. It belongs to Mrs. Peet, of the Peet, Palmolive, Colgate Company. She could live anywhere in the world she wants and chose this as the most beautiful place to live out her later years; she must be in her eighties now. Anyhow, I think that's quite a compliment for the area."

Mrs. Russell's summer home was an older home, neither large nor fancy, but it did have a commanding view of Puget Sound and the shipping lane from Seattle to Tacoma, so there were often large ships to watch as they made their way back and forth between those cities. There were also steps down to the beach, where one could swim or sit on a rock and dream, and I had plenty of time to do both, for Mrs. Russell and her son were gone most of the time, as she had said they would be.

The first memorable happening of that summer was when Mrs. Peet came to lunch. Mrs. Russell didn't tell me she was coming until the day of the luncheon. It was a casual affair, she said, nothing special to get ready; she'd fix the main dish, and I could do the salad and serve.

After lunch Mrs. Peet picked up the last of the dishes off the table and followed me into the kitchen, where she picked up a dish towel and proceeded to dry the dishes as I washed them. She asked me about my family, what did they do, had I always lived in Chehalis, what I was taking in college, what my opinion was regarding the United States entering the war in Europe, what I thought of President Roosevelt's handling of the economy, and various other matters. Once the dishes were done, she suggested I pour us each a glass of lemonade and continue our visit at the kitchen table. Finally, an hour or so later, she got up to leave.

"Thank you, my dear; it's been a real privilege to have this opportunity to talk with you," Mrs. Peet said in a most charming manner. "When Mrs. Russell said she had a college student from Chehalis here for the summer, I couldn't resist the luncheon invitation. I have so little chance to talk to young people these days. You've quite restored my hopes for the younger generation. I can't say I agree with you on everything, but you did give thoughtful answers and that's the most one can expect; times are bound to change. The change I need right now is to get home for a nap. Good-bye. The best of luck to you."

The second memorable happening, late in the summer, involved Mrs. Russell's son. After Mrs. Russell told me on that first day about the money Bill had lost at the racetrack and his partying style of life, I'd been avoiding him during those few times he was home. Now, apparently partied out, he spent more time at home, and as we got better acquainted I found him to be much nicer and more serious-minded than I had expected. We had the college experience in common and often sat on the rocks or walked along the beach together, talking about a variety of things, much like the talk sessions in the girls' dorm at Linfield. Mrs. Russell was gone one evening and I was relaxing on the beach when Bill arrived with a few friends and I got up to leave.

"Hey, don't go!" Bill called as I started up the steps. "We're just here for a wiener roast. Why don't you join us?"

"Oh, yes, do stay; it will be fun." the other young men and women said, and I, knowing I should not stay, stayed anyhow. Before darkness fell, they all left for another party.

The next morning Mrs. Russell told me, as kindly as she could, that there had been talk in the neighborhood and she'd appreciate it if I'd make a point of not going to the beach when Bill was at home.

"All right, I'll stay off the beach. Excuse me," I croaked, so full of resentment I could barely speak as I brushed by her on my way upstairs to my room. *Oh, no,* I thought, *it's not the neighbors that are offended, it's the mother of one of the girls at the wiener roast—one like the doctor's wife.* But after running the gamut of emotions over that, I eventually faced up to the fact that I was at fault for joining the group—I was an employee, and they were guests of my employer's son.

The following morning I apologized to Mrs. Russell and, seeing she was still distressed, offered to leave right away. The job was nearly over anyhow.

"Perhaps that would be best," Mrs. Russell agreed. "But the end of the month is only three days away. Let's wait till then so I'll be able to drive you to the depot." She reached over and laid her hand on my arm. "Thank you, Glenna. You're a remarkable young lady. You will do well in life."

It had been an interesting summer, an opportunity to see the inner workings of a very different way of life than the one my family lived. I'd met two women, one a socialite, one the widow of a millionaire, both truly ladies as my mother was, and like her they accepted who they were and lived their life the best they could. My mother was right when she said, "It isn't the amount of money people have, it's what's inside that counts."

# 14

Exactly why I didn't go back to college in the fall of 1941 I do not know, but I suspect it was partly because I was anxious to enter the working world as my brothers and sister had. I would be eighteen in October and eligible for a regular forty-hour-a-week type job, no more being tied to housework, and I was very proud to be accepted for employment as a clerk in Doane's Drugstore in Chehalis.

Since Mother and Kinnick now lived in Centralia and I had no transportation to the store, I stayed a month or so with Maxine in her apartment in Chehalis, then rented a furnished apartment for myself. What fun! What freedom! Working eight hours a day was like being on vacation compared to the live-in housework I had been doing, and I was delighted to have an apartment of my very own. The work at the drugstore was all new to me. I learned about the merchandise in the store by stocking shelves, reading directions to familiarize myself with items new to me, and, like any young girl would be, was especially fond of dealing with cosmetic lines—Coty and Max Factor were very big back then as I recall. My working hours were noon to closing time at nine o'clock, with an hour for dinner between five and six.

One evening as I left the store on my dinner break, I saw a man, the father of one of my classmates from high school I knew quite well, walking toward me carrying a bag of groceries in one arm. As he got closer, a look of recognition crossed his face and he started to smile, then suddenly stopped, stood still as the smile turned to a stunned, uncomprehending look and the bag of groceries dropped from his arm to the cement, spilling out two oranges that rolled toward me as he sort of crumpled, ever so slowly, to the sidewalk. I stopped, shocked, not knowing what to do as people ran out of from nearby stores to help him, then, feeling grateful to those older, wiser individuals for taking charge, I walked quickly around the group on up the street. Later that evening, I learned the man had died of a heart attack.

This was one of the most significant events of my young life. The death was so sudden, so unexpected; one moment the man was there, smiling and getting ready to say hello, and the next moment he was gone. It could happen to anyone, at any time. What had I said to a member of my family or a friend that I would regret if it was one of them, or me, who died? There were no second chances, no time for apologies or making up for one's spiteful words or careless actions. And what of me, my own life, so fragile, so temporary? Should I be cautious and protect it or should I live it fully, feeling every moment dear and precious?

When the announcement came of Japan's attack on Pearl Harbor, December 7, 1941, it turned our gradual-recovery-from-depression mentality into a mobilization frame of mind. There was a sense of urgency—every citizen was needed; we all had a part to play, we must join together to keep our nation and the world free. There was a feeling of excitement, an intensity of purpose, that made us feel more self-righteous, stronger, and more capable that we had ever been before. It made me even more aware of how good it was to be alive.

By Easter of 1942, our hopes for an early victory had been dashed when the battles for Bataan and Corregidor were lost. Japan had taken the Philippines, and news of the

Bataan Death March was trickling in. For Gene and me, it was difficult to reconcile what we were hearing with our memories of Tosh and the other friendly Japanese people we'd met in California. When Aunt Eva wrote that Tosh and his family, along with thousands of other Japanese Americans, had been sent to a relocation camp, we were even more confused.

We were all at home that Easter Sunday, knowing it might be the last time we'd be together, ever, for the war had pretty much taken over our lives by then. Gene had signed up for the navy and was due to be called up soon. Maxine had applied for a secretarial position with the Oregon Shipyard near Portland. Being a married man, Henry had decided to let the draft board make the decision for him; he'd go when he was called. All of them encouraged me to go back to Linfield in the fall. If I couldn't make it on my own financially, they said they would help. I agreed to give it a try, though I still had no specific goal in mind. Since all raw materials for building houses had been requisitioned for military use, Kinnick could not continue building houses—there would be no market for them anyhow—so he'd decided they should sell their house and move to a country place. There would be a need for full-time barbers, he thought, with all the young men gone to war, and raising most of their own food would at least contribute something to the war effort—the national campaign promoting victory gardens was already in full swing.

Early that summer, having gotten the job she applied for at the shipyard, Maxine moved to Portland, Oregon, and as soon as possible I went to visit her with a plan for college in mind that she could help me with.

"Hey, Glenna!" Maxine called from the kitchen of her little apartment, being careful not to call me Runt, as I'd asked the family to use my real name instead. "How do you like my little home, sweet home?"

"It's keen, and such a nice location, it'll be good for Connie when you bring her down from Mom's. You were really lucky to get a place with a yard like this. How's your job? What exactly do you do?"

"I'm the receptionist in the personnel department right now, but my boss's secretary is leaving for Texas next month and I'm first in line to get her job. So, if you decide you want to go to work instead of school, I'll be in a good position to help you get a job," Maxine answered as she handed me a cup of coffee.

This seemed an ideal time to make my pitch. "Speaking of school, I was hoping you'd be willing to drive me out to see the college, since you've never been there. I've been wanting to look the drugstore in McMinnville over; maybe I can get a job there instead of working for the school. I think my biggest problem that first year was living in the dorm; there's just so much going on all the time it's hard to concentrate on studying." I laughed as Maxine raised an eyebrow. "OK, let's face it, you know me, I can't say no, so the only way to make it in math and science is to stay away from the temptation."

"Math and science?" she inquired. "How did all this come about?"

"It's been in all the papers and on the radio about the shortage of engineers and scientists. And that soldier from Fort Lewis I've been dating—you know, the one who took me to the Ice Capades in Seattle—said they talk a lot about that in his classes on the base. Anyhow, that's what I get my best grades in, so I thought it might be worth a try."

"Well then, finish your coffee and 'let's git to gitten,' " as Gene says. The store probably closes at six on Saturday. We can talk more on the way."

When we got to McMinnville, the proprietor of the drugstore was in. He had a vacancy for a clerk coming up on August 1. If I'd have the owner of the drugstore I worked at now, Mr. Doane, call or write him with a reference, the job was mine. How lucky could I get? Luckier still, it seemed, for when I visited my sorority adviser it turned out she had a room for rent and would be delighted if I'd consider living there.

By the end of July I had moved into the room I'd rented in McMinnville and was ready to start work at the drugstore on the first of August. Two weeks later I met a young man from the McMinnville area, Edgar Rich, six feet tall, what today would be called a "handsome hunk," and we came together with that sense of respect and caring for each other Mother had talked to me about some years before. We were married in October 1942. While we waited for Ed's call to serve in the Army Air Corps—he had already been accepted for pilot training—he worked at moving logs from the millpond onto the conveyor belt at a lumber mill, and I, anxious to spend every minute possible with him, dropped out of college—there was so little time, so much to learn about each other.

I don't recall that we discussed the possibility of his not returning from the war, but the memory of that heart attack victim in Chehalis was always with me. With that in mind, though not spoken of, Ed and I agreed to spend as much time together as possible before he went overseas. Ed got his orders to report to the Air Corps base right after Christmas, and I took Maxine up on her offer to find a job for me in order to save money to join him, wherever he might be, as soon as it was feasible.

Seeing Maxine in her professional capacity at the shipyard gave me a new appreciation for my sister. I was still seeing her as the pudgy girl she'd been in high school, but when I looked at her like this, in a new environment, I realized she'd turned into quite a beauty. Not beautiful in the classical sense—she was too short for that, only five foot two, looking very slender in a navy blue suit with a gored skirt that flared above shapely legs and high-heeled shoes, a fitted jacket flaring slightly over slender hips, topped off with a bright red blouse that complemented her round, pretty face, brown eyes, and naturally wavy dark brown hair. As I sat waiting to be interviewed, I watched as Maxine moved around the office in a quick, efficient, friendly manner (she'd been promoted to office manager by then), and it was obvious from the responses of the other women that she was respected and well liked in that capacity. *Wow,* I thought, as I sat there in my severely tailored olive green suit and white blouse, *how does she do it? She's managed to retain her special flair, her femininity, that aura of dynamic energy, and still look sharp and businesslike.*

I stood up when Maxine came over to where I was sitting with a gentleman in tow. "Glenna, meet my boss," she said in an irreverent, saucy way, but I could see he liked her manner. "You're in luck. He only interviews the really important people." She laughed as she made more formal introductions.

The boss was businesslike and to the point. "Maxine tells me you aren't interested in typing or general office work, so I made an appointment for you with a man downstairs who is looking for operators on some machines they use for running payroll. I told him if you're half the worker your sister is he'll be lucky to get you. I don't think there'll be a problem; we already have you signed up at IBM school for the training you'll need. Maxine will show you where his office is. I'm happy to have met you. Good luck," he said as he shook my hand.

The department I went to for my interview was called

the Electrical Data Processing (EDP) Department, and the machines being used for the processing were called unit record machines. I was taken on a tour of the facility beginning with the Keypunch Room, where payroll data from hand-written source documents was keyed in through a keyboard similar to a typewriter. The output was a card with little oblong holes punched into it, representing up to eighty numeric or alphabetic characters (numbers or letters). Once the data had been transcribed to cards, each containing a unit of information, the manager said, they were loaded by the handful into the big machines in the Unit Record Room to be processed all the way through printing payroll checks. In the Unit Record Room we looked first at the sorter, approximately five feet long by three feet high with a hopper at one end to load the cards and thirteen pockets, one after the other, to receive the sorted cards. There was a multiplier machine for doing calculations, a collator for merging files together in a specific order, a reproducer to punch new cards for specific purposes, and a tabulator for printing reports for the accountants and checks for shipyard workers. All but the sorter had a removable board with electrical contact prongs on one side and holes on the other side with removable wires plugged into them. He said I would be going to school at the International Business Machines (IBM) Company offices in downtown Portland for classes on how to wire the boards. The operation of the machines I'd learn through on-the-job training.

It was fascinating work. I used to describe it as a combination of waitress work, being on your feet all day feeding machines, and accounting, as some knowledge of mathematics and accounting principles was required.

During the first few months of working at the shipyard, I shared Maxine's apartment with her and Connie. It was convenient for both of us, as we could share expenses and Maxine could pursue the party life she so enjoyed while I, being married, stayed home with Connie. Since Maxine and I worked different hours, I joined a car pool to ride back and forth to work.

A lady in the car pool with me—I think her name was Caroline—had lived for many years in the Philippines, where her husband held an important position with the government. She told us about her life in the islands, the American compound where she had lived, and how they had known for many months before the invasion that Japan planned to attack. She said letters had been written, warnings given, and still our government did nothing.

"I was fortunate to get away," Caroline informed me. "Right after the invasion, there were literally hundreds of us waiting with our children to board what we knew would be the last ship for the United States. The steamship company refused to book us passage, for they weren't sure the ship from Hong Kong would even come in to dock. The Japs were getting close by then. At any rate, there would be nowhere near enough space for all of us, but just in case the ship did dock, my husband arranged a lottery so boarding would be quick and orderly, for time was definitely of the essence. We were to line up in the order established by the lottery, have our money for passage ready, and be prepared to move quickly with our children and luggage when the time did come.

"A little band was playing patriotic music on the dock while we waited, and when we finally saw the ship was coming in to get us a mighty roar went up from the crowd and the band played 'America the Beautiful' as loud as it could. The steward met us at the gangplank to collect our money and assign space—if you couldn't pay, you couldn't go—and after a while he announced they were full up.

Only about half had boarded, and I was one of those left on the dock." Caroline paused to wipe away the tears that had gathered in her eyes.

"Suddenly, to our amazement, all the men who had boarded the ship in Hong Kong came marching single file down the gangplank, each carrying a coat and hat, no luggage, giving up their berths to women with children, including me and mine. It was the most dramatic, most awesome, moment of my life. They were so gallant, so brave, so heroic, for they knew as well as we did they'd likely end up dead or taken prisoner—we all knew the Philippines would fall. I say a prayer for those men every day."

A few weeks later Caroline told us she'd like to read us part of a letter she had received from a lady who was a friend of hers in the Philippines. "The letter begins with some family stuff, so I'm skipping that," Caroline said, then began to read something similar to the following: " 'After the ship pulled away, without us on it, Jack and I talked with some of the others who had been left behind. We agreed the lottery had been fair—at least we were still together as a family—and we talked about how we might be able to stay together. Being civilians, we were free to make a choice. The result was that we and five other couples decided to pack the absolute minimum we would need for camping out and head for the hills. We were a little band of twenty, twelve adults and eight children. It was like a camping trip at first, but after Bataan the Japs sent out scouting parties to round up any Americans or Filipinos known to be American sympathizers, and we had to stay on the move. We had agreed that anyone who could not keep up would be left to fend for themselves, and finally one couple said they could not keep up. That night we heard shots and screaming, so two of the men worked their way back to the top of the cliff overlooking the valley where the family was. When they got back they told us the Japs had shot the little girl and hung the couple on a tree limb by their feet and built a fire under them. We didn't dare go back and bury them for fear the Japs were waiting for us.

" 'We changed our pact to suicide, after that; then one man injured his leg and he and his family fell behind. He shot his wife, two children, and himself, but this time we were able to bury the bodies before moving on. Two days later, one of the women who had been pregnant when we started out gave birth, under the most primitive conditions, to a healthy baby boy, bringing our number up to fourteen. After a while there were fewer search patrols and life eased up a bit. Of course, I can't give any details of where we were or how it happened because it would put others in danger, but eventually we made contact with the navy and they picked us up.' "

Caroline quit reading from the letter and went on to tell us all fourteen people had made it through this harrowing experience. They had been taken to Australia, where they were all doing well.

Stories of this kind made our own problems in those troubled times seem very small indeed.

Near the middle of March 1943, Gene wrote a letter to Maxine and me from San Francisco. His last shore leave before going overseas was coming up, and he thought if we were in the mood to travel, he'd be more than happy to show us the town before he left.

Ed had also made a move, to San Antonio, Texas, for the first phase of his pilot training. After the first four weeks, he'd written, trainees were allowed to live off the base, and his four weeks would be up the end of March. He really hoped I would be able to come to San Antonio then.

I gave my notice at the shipyard and bought a train

ticket to San Antonio, with a stopover in San Francisco to meet up with Gene and another in Los Angeles to visit Aunt Eva. Near the end of March, I was on my way.

Gene met me at the train in San Francisco, as he'd promised. He put my luggage in a locker at the depot, as he had not been able to get a hotel reservation, and we happily took off to see the sights, feeling sure we would be able to find a hotel room for the night along the way. We rode the cable car, visited Fisherman's Wharf, and walked through Chinatown, and when evening came we still had not been able to get a room. Not that we hadn't tried, but in those few hotels that had a vacancy they asked for a proof of marriage. When Gene would say I was his sister, they'd laugh, "Yeah, sure." They'd say, "I thought I'd heard 'em all, but that's the worst. No dice." At midnight we gave up and went to an all-night movie theater, where I managed two hours' sleep on a couch in the ladies' room before I was asked to leave and the rest of the night slept off and on in a theater seat. But we had fun, an adventure of sorts, and the chance to say good-bye.

For Ed and me, from April to December of 1943 it was two months here and three months there, mostly in Texas, where we were introduced to the southern drawl and a multitude of insects. Our first night in our rented room in San Antonio, we woke up in the night to a rustling sound and the feel of something skittering across the sheet we were sleeping under. I turned on the light and was horrified to see a horde of big beetlelike bugs scurrying off in all directions. Ed laughed as he told me they were cockroaches, found everywhere, he said, including the barracks on the base. I spent the rest of the night in a chair with the light on and first thing in the morning went looking for a compound to rid us of that infestation. I was also introduced to chiggers and spent days in an agony of itching, for they are known to settle in where clothes are tight and I was wearing a full-length girdle.

Our life during this period was much like that of thousands of other military couples clinging together for as long as possible. We moved from San Antonio to Chickasha, Oklahoma, then I went back to Portland and the shipyard for a time, then back to San Antonio again for the final phase of pilot training. In December, Ed received his pilot's wings, his commission as a second lieutenant in the Air Corps, and we went on furlough back to the Northwest.

We were with Mother and Kinnick at their little farm in Centralia that year for Christmas. Ed and I were listening to a radio program from overseas while we decorated the Christmas tree in the living room when I heard a special announcement.

"Now, from England, representing the United States Air Corps, here is Captain Alan Green of Oregon City, Oregon," the announcer said.

"Mother, come quick!" I called as I ran to the kitchen. "That's Alan on the radio."

"Are you sure it's *our* Alan Green?" Mother asked as she walked in to listen.

"Of course it is. I'd know that voice anywhere." I put my finger to my lips to indicate we should listen quietly.

We were all very excited, more excited to know Alan was still alive and well than about the honor of his of being chosen to represent the Air Force on a program being broadcast to millions of Americans.

My cousin Alan, always big for his age, had now become a man, six feet, four inches tall, still handsome, still slightly pigeon-toed, which only added to his charm, and still with that friendly, take-charge manner that had endeared him to me when we were children. I was not surprised that he was chosen for such an honor; he was the "All

American Boy" who didn't drink nor smoke, a clean-cut, likable fellow who had joined the Air Corps shortly after Pearl Harbor and had been flying bombing missions in Europe for some time. Alan told us later we had it wrong.

"The fact is," he said, "I was chosen for that broadcast quite by chance. We'd just gotten back from a bombing mission and I was tired, so I went to bed while the rest of the gang went out to party. The next thing I knew someone was shaking me by the shoulder, telling me to get up and dress—I was going to be on the radio. It seems the program people had forgotten they needed an actual member of the Air Corps to read the script and sent that fellow to the barracks to dig one up. I just happened to be the only one there. Anyhow, I went in and they handed me a script and showed me how to use the microphone. When they gave the signal, I read the script, and then I went back to bed."

I spent a part of that Christmas holiday reading Gene's letters to Mother from overseas, he was a prolific letter writer. After I'd visited him in San Francisco, Gene had been shipped out to work with the Seabees on Guadalcanal shortly after the marines had taken the island back from the Japanese. The goal was to build a huge airfield where planes could be launched for bombing runs on other Pacific islands as our military worked its way up toward Japan. There were still many Japanese soldiers on Guadalcanal who had not surrendered, vowing to continue the fight until their death. It was dangerous duty, but Gene's letters, often looking like paper doilies due to the holes where military information had been cut out, were still cheerful, with that special way of putting things that was uniquely Gene's.

"If anyone should happen to ask you," Gene wrote in one letter, "you tell them these little buggers are using real bullets over here and I can prove it. The other day a sniper's bullet whizzed past my head into a tree and I dug it out to keep for a souvenir. It was real all right. Once they learn to aim a little better, they could be downright dangerous."

When his furlough was up, Ed left for Liberal, Kansas, to be trained for combat. He wrote that I should come there right away, as the Air Corps had assigned a barracks on base where officer's wives could live. This was my first experience with the military firsthand, and it was here I developed an aversion to that mode of life. It was a dual system. The visible system was the colonel issuing orders to the major, who gave orders to the next in line. The invisible system was the colonel's wife issuing orders in the form of invitations to the wives of lesser officers. I could understand the need for a chain of command for military action, but having our social life controlled by command performances infuriated me. Still I went along with it for Ed's sake, knowing it was temporary.

Our next stop was a month in Salt Lake City, Utah, while Ed waited for his assignment, then on to Tucson, Arizona, for training on the Liberator Bombers (B-24s) he'd be flying overseas. In July 1944, Ed left for duty in the European Theater and I left for Portland to go back to work on the unit record machines at Oregon Shipyard.

About this same time, we heard from Aunt Hazel Green in Oregon City that Alan had been severely wounded. He had taken off on a bombing mission and his plane exploded in midair, due to sabotage. He was hospitalized for many months but recovered fully, except the use of one badly damaged leg was still impaired.

My cousin Charles Andrus, the son of Aunt Vera, who lived in Port Angeles, Washington, had joined the navy a year or more before the war. Luckily he was not at Pearl Harbor when the Japanese attacked, but he had seen action on a navy cruiser in both the Atlantic and Pacific. His ship had been damaged in a naval battle with the Japanese and was being repaired in Portland during that time when Ed was overseas. Charles and I saw a lot of each other while he was there and had great fun bowling and going to movies, and he had fun kidding me about trying to kill him all those years ago when he was visiting us at Aunt Bert's house. It happened like this:

We were about six or seven years old at the time, playing King of the Mountain on an old wagon in the barnyard. When my turn came to be the king, I grabbed the iron bar used as the wagon brake, to make up for my smaller size, and brandished it unsteadily above my head. Now, my brother Gene knew me well enough to keep his distance, but Charles was used to his gentle sister, Dorothy, and he came charging straight up onto the wagon bed. I've never been quite sure whether I lost my balance, as I claimed I did, or I was retaliating for his having pulled the chair out from under me at the breakfast table that morning, but that bar came down smack on the middle of Charles's head. I was frightened as I saw the blood gush down his face, but there was a wee sense of satisfaction, too, as we helped him up the path toward Aunt Bert, who was rushing down to care for him.

Charles told me he was trying for a transfer to the submarine corps. He was tired of being on a cruiser like a sitting duck, he'd rather take his chances underwater. I teased him that the bar I lowered on his head must have addled his brain, as he was as tall as Alan, six-foot-four, and would have to be a contortionist to move through that cramped space. He did, however, get his wish and finished out the war in a submarine.

My brother Henry must have been inducted into the armed forces about this time, though I'm not exactly sure which branch of the armed forces. Actually, we had little contact with Henry during those years, as he had a wife and responsibilities while the rest of us were single.

My three cousins on my father's side, the Barlow boys from American Falls, Idaho, also served in the armed forces. The youngest, Jim, was in the Tank Corps and served under General Patton in his march through Germany. I'm not sure what branch of the service Charles and Moony were in.

Being the historian in the family, Mother kept a scrapbook with news of our young men in the service, friends of Gene and mine from high school, plus any wartime happenings related to them or those she judged to be of great importance. She wrote literally hundreds of letters, sent packages, knit scarves, folded bandages, and did anything else she could do to make life more tolerable for those who served, as did most of the mothers in America.

Ed finished his mission quota in the spring and was scheduled to come home the end of May 1945, which, as it turned out, was shortly after Germany surrendered, bringing the conflict in Europe to a close.

We had a marvelous two weeks of rest and relaxation at a fancy hotel on the beach at Santa Monica, California, at government expense, then reported for Ed's stateside duty at Walla Walla, Washington. A few months later Ed was discharged, and shortly after that the atom bombs were dropped and Japan surrendered. World War II was finally over.

# 15

The period of letdown, disillusionment, and discontent that often follows a lengthy, all-out effort such as World War II did not affect my family—we had our lives to live, and we were anxious to get on with them. Maxine stayed on at the shipyard to keep things going until the government decided what to do with those industries no longer needed. Henry had his wife, Doris, and a life in Randle to go back to. Gene returned to electrical wiring work, and Mother and Kinnick stayed on the farm. As for Ed and me, we headed for Seattle to attend the University of Washington.

The first order of business, on our arrival in Seattle, was finding a place to live. Our resources were limited, for we had lived those war years together as much as possible, as opposed to my staying put and saving money. Not that either of us regretted that decision—it had been a grand adventure—but it did leave us a bit short on the financial side. I spotted an advertisement in the *Seattle Times* for a small houseboat on Lake Union to rent. It was a price we could afford, the idea of living on the water appealed to us, and the address was close to the university, so we drove right out to see it. The owners of the moorage, Bud McCarty and his wife, Ruth, were pleasant, younger than we expected the owners of such a property to be, and the houseboat, no larger than a house trailer, was neat and clean. We rented it and moved right in.

As soon as we had a telephone installed, I called my

Uncle Henry, Mother's younger brother, as Mother had asked me to do, to tell him we were in town and to say "hello" from Mother. He was delighted to hear from us and invited us out for dinner on the coming weekend. The next call was to the university for information regarding registration. I was told there would be no problem, providing we passed the entrance exam, with starting school the beginning of fall quarter. We both passed the exam and registered for fall quarter, though I'm not sure what our major subjects were.

It turned out Bud McCarty also ran a marine repair and tugboat business. Through him, Ed got a job on weekends salvaging logs off the beaches of Puget Sound with Bud's friend, also a tugboat owner. In the summer and early fall, salvaging logs was a weekend operation for extra cash, but through late fall and winter, the stormy season, it was a full-time job as the high winds caused big waves to sometimes break apart the log booms being towed to mills, so new logs were washed up on the beaches every day. With hundreds of miles of beach on Puget Sound, it took a lot of savvy, knowledge of tides and winds, to know where to look. Ed, still longing for the Air Corps and not really interested in his studies, enjoyed the salvaging operation and dropped out of school to work at it full-time.

The following Easter, Ed and I went down to visit Mother in Centralia. After I'd told her my big news, that I wasn't going back to school next quarter, she had her cry, then asked me about Uncle Henry. Yes, we'd seen them several times, I told her, and both of us liked Uncle Henry and May a lot.

"Mother, did you know Uncle Henry's first wife at all?" I asked.

"Not really well," she answered. "She was quite a bit younger than I was. She was a friend of Vera's and about her age. Now, why do I get the feeling there's more to this than idle curiosity?"

"You're right, as usual," I responded. "There's this girl, Laurie, living at the end of the dock. I've gotten quite well acquainted with her, and the more I get to know about her, the more I think she might be Uncle Henry's daughter, Violet. Her last name isn't Wyman, but then it wouldn't be because she's married. We just saw her that once, on our way back from California, but I don't remember what she looked like. Anyhow, there are just too many coincidences. Everything Uncle Henry tells me about Violet matches what Laurie tells me about herself."

"Well, for heaven's sake," Mother laughed nervously. "This is getting strange. How old is this girl?"

"A year and a month older than me. Her birthday is in September. I know because we were looking at an astrology book one day and it turned out she was a Virgo and I was a Libra. Do you have any pictures of Violet's mother?"

"No, I'm sure I don't, but Violet was older than you, so we should be able to find out when her birthday is by looking at the Wyman family tree. I'll get it." Mother hurried off to look in her box of treasures. In a few minutes she was back, waving her copy of the family tree. "Sure enough, Violet was born September 1, 1922, and listen to this: her full name is Violet Lorraine, so the Laurie also fits. I can't imagine a young girl these days wanting to keep a name like Violet, though Henry always loved that name. Why don't you just ask her who her father is when you get back?"

"Because she thinks family is a drag. She is always saying how glad she is she doesn't have one. Her mother is dead and she never mentions her father. I'm afraid if I told her I was a relative that would be the end of that."

Gene was also home for Easter. He had quit his job in electrical wiring for the big money in electrical construc-

231

tion and was now stringing wire on the huge poles and towers heading off in all directions from the newly constructed Coulee Dam in eastern Washington. While Mother and I were talking about Laurie, Gene was telling Ed to buy a surplus army truck—they were selling cheap—and come to work at Coulee Dam hauling the big spools of wire and other supplies needed by construction crews. The lure of big money had gotten Ed's attention.

On the drive back to Seattle, Ed and I talked about the pros and cons of doing as Gene suggested. It might give us a chance to save some money. Maybe we could start a family—we both wanted children—and it might be fun to live in Eastern Washington for a while. On the other hand, there was not much of a future in such work and it would require a lot of traveling, a few months here, a few months there, and there would be no chance to buy a home or put down roots in one location like a family needs. In the end we decided to shop around for trucks—if they were as cheap as Gene said they were, we'd give it a try.

A few weeks later, the surplus army truck we had acquired was packed, ready to leave for Coulee Dam, and now was the time to find out if Laurie really was my long-lost cousin, Violet Lorraine Wyman. I had spent a lot of time imagining a variety of conversations with her, mostly anticipating rejection, but since I was leaving anyhow, what did it matter? It turned out that all the worry had been for nothing because Laurie wasn't home, but her friend Jimmy was home and confirmed that her father's name was Henry Wyman. I told Jimmy the rather complicated story of how I had become aware of the connection, then left a note for Laurie with a General Delivery address at Grand Coulee, Washington.

My memory of what happened next is that Ed and I climbed in our truck and drove off toward eastern Washington and that a letter from Laurie, expressing delight at finding a blood relative she liked, arrived in Grand Coulee almost as soon as we did. Laurie's memory is that she got back to her houseboat before we left Seattle and I announced, in person, that I was her cousin and that we had a chance to talk about it right then. What is surprising to me is that we were both attracted to the houseboat way of life at the same time, in the same place. It does make one wonder if such inclinations are at least partially due to heredity.

Things went well in Grand Coulee, but Ed was restless, talking more and more about flying airplanes and the advantages of military life. This was not new, actually, Ed had not really wanted a discharge from the Air Corps; it was I who forced the issue.

I thought a lot about what my Indian friend, Tommy, in Montana had said about the letter writing, that it would end badly for we'd be on different paths, that it would be better to let it go and remember each other with happy hearts. Over the months, I talked to Ed about divorce, not because I was angry at him but because he had found his niche in life, a source of satisfaction and happiness in the Air Corps, while I detested that mode of life, so perhaps it would be better to go our separate ways. Ed was adamantly against divorce, saying we loved each other, so we would work it out.

When a friend offered me a ride to Seattle in January 1947, I accepted the invitation and left a note for Ed— admittedly a cowardly thing to do, but the only solution I could think of at the time. After I found an apartment and a job, I had no trouble finding work, as experienced unit record operators were in short supply. I wrote a letter telling Ed I was filing for divorce and tried to convince him again, in writing, that it would be best for both of us.

Sometime later that year, each of us Belts kids received a letter from Mother saying that she was going into the hospital for an operation. The doctors had not been able to determine the exact cause of her pain but had narrowed it down to gallbladder or cancer. Maxine's job at the shipyard had ended and she was planning a move to California, Henry and Doris were in the process of divorcing, as Ed and I were, and Henry was building towers for electrical lines out of Coulee Dam with Gene, but we all made it home to be with Mother before her surgery, all very scared by that word *cancer,* especially me, accused by the others of being overly dramatic, as usual.

The night before the operation, Kinnick sat with Mother through the dinner hour, then came home early to take care of Connie while the four of us went up to visit Mother, perhaps for the last time, I thought. The other three were full of jokes and laughter while I stood numbly by with little to say but trying to laugh along with the rest of them. When a nurse came by, she said it sounded more like a celebration than the usual visit to a prospective-surgery patient.

"In a way it is; we should have a toast," Gene said as he grabbed some paper cups to fill with water for each of us. "To Mother," he said as we held high our cups. "She saw us through!"

"Or saw through us!" Maxine, Henry, and I chorused, three minds with but a single thought as we broke out laughing.

Mother laughed with us, but her lip was trembling and there were tears in her eyes, though she looked happy to have all her children there. The nurse said she was sorry to break this up, but it was time for us to go.

Maxine, Henry, and Gene went straight into the kitchen to get a beer when we got home. They offered one to me, but I said no. I'd never acquired a taste for beer, though I did have a cocktail now and then in a social situation, but it didn't seem appropriate right now. They all laughed at me and went in to sit in the living room while I got myself a cup of coffee. Actually, I'd been getting concerned about their heavy drinking—*alcoholism* was not a word one often heard back then. Henry had gone back to drinking in the army, and he and Gene both had that hard working, hard-drinking image of a real man. Maxine, the party girl, seemed determined to keep up with them.

"Why don't you guys get smart—go to college on the GI Bill and get out of that rough construction life? That's no way to live," I said to Gene and Henry as I entered the living room.

"Watch out, boys," Maxine warned. "Your baby sister's trying to make gentlemen out of you."

"Hey, I'm proud to be a workingman. Yea, my children, though you walk through the valley of darkness now, the power lines shall bring you light." Gene made a motion meant to look like the Messiah blessing his flock. "Seriously, though, those gentlemen aren't going to get anywhere with the recovery if somebody doesn't get these power lines built to get electricity to their plants. We're sort of heroes when you look at it like that."

Henry chimed in, "Gene and I both working on this project, hell, we're liable to own the company soon. That'll make us gentlemen in a hurry."

"It won't matter anyhow," Maxine said. "We'll probably all die young like the rest of the Belts crowd. Let's just live it up and 'let the devil take the hindmost,' as Mom says."

We talked far into the night after that exchange, reminiscing about our childhood, exchanging stories about the war years, catching up on current events, and sharing our aspirations and dreams for the future. There was a togetherness, a closeness, heightened by our concern for Mother, that we never had again, quite like that, as single people, though it was always there in the background. We all went our separate ways after that, we married, or married again, had children, and we got together now and then, could always count on one another if we needed help, but the focus in later years was different, as it should be.

Gene and Henry went back to their construction job and, at one point, were each offered supervisory positions. Gene said he liked being a workingman; he'd stay with his union buddies on the line.

Gene married, had two daughters, divorced, married again, and had a son. When the boy was eight months old, Gene, at age forty, died of a heart attack. He'd just climbed down from a pole where he'd been repairing a power line to bring the lights back on in the homes of nearby residents. He was on the job, doing what he liked best.

As soon as I was notified, I caught a bus for Pasco, Washington, to be with his wife and baby and help with funeral arrangements. I went by myself to the funeral parlor to view the body, as I needed a moment alone with Gene to say good-bye. It was easier than I expected, for there he was, lying in the casket with that little lopsided grin on his face as though he were saying, "Well, what do you know? This time, the joke's on me," and I couldn't help but smile—dear Gene, my lifelong friend, my buddy.

Henry accepted the supervisory position offered him and, while he didn't own the company, did go on to become the top executive of a large electrical construction firm, spending much of his time on airplanes flying between his offices in Ohio and California and his home in Oregon.

Henry married again and had one daughter. He died at the age of sixty-one, in Greece, where he'd gone in search of a cure for his recurring cancer. It wasn't the cancer that caused his death but a bleeding ulcer he'd had trouble with before.

A few days after I got the news of Henry's death, I received a postcard in the mail from Greece. It had the picture of a very sad-looking donkey on the front with a little note above where Henry had written: "This looks like I felt when I first arrived." How like him. As with Gene, I had to smile, remembering how Henry had carried me home, piggyback, from my first-grade classes at Lynx Hollow School—it was as though he was still looking after his little sister and had written to ease the burden of my grief.

It was Maxine, actually, whom I was closest to through later years. She had been a big success in the group insurance business in California, married again, and had another daughter. It was a disastrous union, too complicated to go into here, but in the early fifties she sent her older daughter, Connie, to Seattle to live with me, then, a short time later, moved with her young daughter to Seattle and filed for divorce.

We didn't really get along too well. Maxine with her sharp tongue and me with my goody-goody attitude often clashed, but our shared heredity and childhood formed a powerful bond, for better or for worse, and we always managed to put our differences behind us and continue on.

Maxine had changed in those years in California; there was a hint of hardness, a brittle edge, to her that she hadn't had before. I attributed it to her drinking. It had been worrisome before she left and was now excessive, though she refused to talk about it or admit it was a problem. Henry, who had turned to Alcoholics Anonymous, tried to talk to her, as Mother and I did, but Maxine insisted it was her life and she'd live it as she damn well pleased. What could we do? She was still sharp and capable, did well in real estate, the mortgage business, and various other pursuits—financially better than I did—and it was, as she said, her life.

Whether it was her vitality, her willingness to take a chance, or the family philosophy of "do something, even if it's wrong," that we all subscribed to, Maxine seemed to attract unusual happenings in her life, some so bizarre they're hardly believable. Still, she always helped me if she could, I did the same for her, and we had many good, some hilarious, times together.

Maxine contracted cancer at age sixty-eight. She had sold her house in Seattle and moved to Tacoma, Washington, by then, to be near her daughter Connie. I went down and stayed with Maxine through the operation and chemotherapy, then some time later through a second operation and therapy session. A year or so after that, she called me to tell me the cancer was back.

"It's like wildfire," she said. "They put it out one place and it flares up in another. It's time to put a stop to it. I'm not going for further treatment."

The last time I saw Maxine was in the hospital in Tacoma. As usual, she was direct and to the point as she told me the doctor had been in that morning to tell her she had little time left and if I had anything to say to her or questions to ask, I should do it now. I shook my head, no, nothing.

"I said the same thing to Connie earlier this morning, and you know what she asked?" Maxine smiled expectantly.

"I can't imagine."

"She asked how I keep the tomatoes I raise from seed from falling over and rotting on the ground." She laughed, obviously tickled by this exchange. "I told her I put a little circle of toothpicks around to hold them up."

Her younger daughter, Charlene, who'd moved up

from San Diego to be near her mother during this period, was there to take Maxine home with her, as Maxine requested, and we talked and laughed some, about nothing in particular, until it was time for me to go. Maxine was sitting in a chair beside the bed. I walked over to say good-bye and put my hand on her shoulder as I said, "I love you, Sis." She picked my hand up from her shoulder and held it to her cheek. I could feel the tears and knew she loved me, too, but she couldn't say the words. She died a few days later at her daughter's home.

I married again, had three children, a boy and two girls, divorced, and married a man who had five children of his own, and that marriage lasted, off and on, until he died some thirty-five years later. One day, after I retired at age sixty-three, I was reviewing my life, my marriages, in an effort to come up with a new direction for the retirement years, and as my thoughts drifted on back to my childhood and memories of Kinnick and Montana, a light in my head came on. Good grief, I'd been trying to make my husbands love me like I wanted Kinnick to when I was eight years old, I thought. Those poor men, but on the other hand, they also brought baggage with them from their childhood years, so who's to say?

I continued working with IBM unit record equipment until, in 1959, I moved into computer processing in the Engineering Department at the Boeing Aircraft Company. I started as an operator on a first-generation UNIVAC-1103A computer. I moved, over time, from operations into programming, analysis, management, and teaching/administering a computer technology program at a community college. With the steady stream of new developments in the field, there was rarely time to be bored or discontented with the work. If I did get tired of it, I changed companies, opened an antique store, or studied drama at the university for a year. I retired from the computer field, a second time, in 1996 at the age of seventy-two.

The process of writing this story has been a worthwhile journey of discovery, seeing how those early years developed the qualities that made the four of us successful at our various careers, though not rich or famous, but also sent us into the world with a taste for adventure, no tolerance for boredom, and that "do something even if it's wrong" approach that led us into the many interesting experiences we had along the way. We never stopped finding some element of humor in our successes, our failures, our tragedies, and our disasters. We laughed and we loved, many times. We accepted responsibility for our actions, though we didn't always act responsibly, and we wasted little energy on regrets or blaming others for our problems. I have come to think of us as a very ordinary family with an extraordinary zest for life, and I feel privileged to have been a part of it.

# 16

Kinnick built a little gray-and-white house in Chehalis where he and mother lived in later years, and it was here, at eighty-three, he died of a heart attack.

I had taken the children down to visit one weekend and on Saturday had driven Kinnick to see a house being built by a young man under his direction. It was a satisfying day. Kinnick was pleased the house was coming along so well and happy to have his skill as a builder still taken seriously. The next morning as we sat talking—Mother had taken the children to Sunday school—Kinnick leaned over, gasped, straightened up, laid his head back on the chair, took a few deep, ragged breaths spaced far apart, and was gone before I realized what was happening. He was, as he'd always said he hoped he would be, fully dressed, still capable, sitting in the living room of a house he'd built.

Mother made two moves of interest after Kinnick died. She painted the house bright yellow, and she went back to practical nursing, caring for a baby born with a terminal birth defect, seeing the elderly through their last days, or staying with family members who needed help. Her energetic, cheerful, no-nonsense manner in taking charge of a difficult, sometimes sad, situation endeared her to all who knew her.

In her late seventies, Mother started acting in uncharacteristic ways. After a thorough mental/physical exam, she was diagnosed with arteriosclerosis of the brain, hardening of the arteries, that would gradually shut down her various bodily functions and eventually some vital organ. At eighty, she made the decision to enter a nursing home because of her inability to control her occasionally bizarre behavior. "This is not something for amateurs like you kids to try to deal with," she said. "Best turn me over to professionals."

Mother and I went together to look at nursing homes, and finding one she liked, she moved in immediately, leaving me to go through her things and dispose of furniture and other belongings as I saw fit. It is amazing what one can learn about a person through this process. I'd lived with Mother, known her all my life, and still discovered much about her that was new to me. I knew she had a deep respect for education, but about her quest for knowledge on her own I knew nothing. There were notes in the back of books, in margins, and on scraps of paper in boxes and magazines like: "*Phlox*, Greek word for fame"; "Phrygia was country King Midas ruled. Troy was in Phrygia"; and "Sebastion Melmoth, pen name of Oscar Wilde." There were also journals, kept for a week or two from time to time, with records of money sent to Aunt Hazel and Aunt Bert to defray the expense of keeping Henry, Gene, and me in the 1930s, and some entries reflecting worries and anxieties, often followed by reaffirmation of her faith in God. There were lots of cards and letters, saved over the years, from her mother, the four of us, and others.

There were many things about my mother that mystified me. Over the years she sometimes told me about a dream she'd had and within a week we'd get word that what she dreamed had, in fact, happened. Her intuition also seemed more finely tuned than the average person's. She seemed to know our thoughts, plans, and actions long after we were grown and under circumstances that could hardly be explained as commonsense conclusions.

Mother was in the nursing home for fifteen years. Her condition gradually worsened, as predicted, and by the seventh year she could no longer put words together in an understandable way. It was then the most mysterious event of all occurred. One day she was listening, smiling, trying to talk, and the next day there was nothing there but her piercing dark brown eyes. In the eight long years before she died she never spoke again to an adult, to my knowledge, but we knew she still could speak, for my daughters brought their babies to visit and Mother cooed and talked as she always had to babies. It was as though Mother willed the essence of herself away, leaving her body there to do what must be done. The nursing staff was as amazed as I was. The medical staff had no explanation.

Before Mother died, in 1991, I had no desire to visit Lynx Hollow, although I'd made the effort to find our place on Butter Creek and been back to our farm at Round Butte, Montana. After Mother's funeral, I mentioned this to my cousin Alan Green, who with his wife, Louise, now lived at Port Ludlow, on the Olympic Peninsula, a short ferry ride from Seattle. Alan expressed a desire to take another look at the big white house in Lynx Hollow where he had spent part of one summer with us, and we continued to talk about it, every now and then, over the next few years. Finally, in October 1996, Alan, still the take-charge type, called me with my marching orders.

"Louise and I are all set to make that trip to Lynx Hollow this next Thursday and Friday," he said without so much as a hello. "You come over on the ferry Wednesday afternoon and spend the night so we can get an early start. We'll put your car in the garage like we did when we went to Oregon City and drive down in ours."

We arrived in Cottage Grove early in the afternoon on Thursday, got directions to Lynx Hollow, and drove out in search of any buildings I might recognize. It was a lovely little valley, mostly farmland now, instead of woods, surrounded by hills that seemed smaller than I remembered. We found a big white house I thought was the one we used to live in, and I asked permission from the lady of the house to take pictures. She told me I was welcome to do so and if I had any pictures or materials about Lynx Hollow from when I lived there her husband would appreciate my sending copies, as he was interested in the history of the area.

In addition to the pictures of the white house and barn, I got pictures of the house my father built, the loggers' bunkhouse, the cook shack, and the Lynx Hollow School building. We also located where my father's lumber mill had been; it had been torn down some years before, but we took pictures of the site. It was a successful trip.

When we left Port Ludlow on this trip to Oregon, Alan, Louise, and I had been in a carefree mood, like college students on spring break, but the closer we came to our destination the more anxious and unsure I felt. Was there still such a place as Lynx Hollow? Would the name be changed? I was only six years old when we moved from there; would it be as I remembered it? As we left the valley, my camera filled with pictures of my past, I felt incredibly happy, joyous, light, free of those feelings of anxiety and the fear and resentment of my father I'd carried with me all my life.

The following week, I sent the lady we'd met a picture of myself at three years old on the porch of the big white house, noting square posts in my picture versus round posts on the house as it is now, and enclosed the story of my family's early years, which included the section about Lynx Hollow.

My telephone rang about eight-thirty Halloween night. It was the lady in the white house in Lynx Hollow, calling to thank me for sending the materials. She told me it was the right house; the original posts were square, but the porch had been rebuilt. She had read my story and thought it wonderful: her husband also enjoyed it. They'd heard rumors of bootlegging in the valley during prohibition and were pleased to have them verified, and so forth and so on.

Finally, changing the subject, she said, "I don't suppose your mother is still alive, is she?"

"No, but she lived a long life, to ninety-five," I answered, thinking that a rather strange question for someone I didn't really know to ask.

"When did she die?"

"Five years ago, in 1991." This question was stranger still. "Why?"

There was a long pause; then the lady said hesitantly, "We've been wondering if she might be our ghost."

I was in shock. Had I heard her right? "You have a ghost?" I asked.

She went on to tell me it was a very friendly ghost, first seen by a logger staying in the house while the owners were away and later by members of the family. She described the ghost as female, five feet tall, wearing a housedress, with her hair pulled back into a bun. I was too stunned to do anything but listen as she told of noises like footsteps on the stairs and doors opening and closing, all somehow connected with a yellow room.

I sat for a while, trying to calm down and collect my thoughts. I wasn't at all sure I believed in ghosts. On one hand, I'd never seen or heard one, myself. But on the other hand, I'd always been intrigued by ghost stories and couldn't say for sure I totally disbelieved. Coming on Halloween, could this be a hoax? I didn't think so, but there might be some sense of fun in the timing of the call. But Mother as a ghost? I'd better call my kids.

My youngest daughter, Kylin, asked when the ghost first appeared.

"I was too shocked; I didn't think to ask," I answered. "But it sounded like more than the five years since Mother died."

"Yes, but remember, Grandma actually went away all those years before." Kylin was very excited.

My middle child, my daughter Erin, did not interrupt my story, but she did gasp or giggle now and then.

"How bizarre," she said. "Did you tell her about Grandma's yellow house?"

I admitted that I hadn't.

I put off calling the oldest of my three, my son, Brian, until last, him being the most conservative one. He listened quietly and was so slow responding I had to prompt him.

"Well, actually, it makes me feel kind of sad," he finally answered. "The theory of a ghost as a person's spirit, troubled, trapped between two worlds with something left to finish up, is not something I like to associate with Grandma. She was always helping, taking care of others, and deserves to rest in peace."

I gave that some thought. My dislike of my father had always worried Mother. Those years in Lynx Hollow had been traumatic for her, perhaps in ways I had no knowledge of, but there was little to be gained by speculation.

"Ah well, we'll never know for sure," I said to my cousin Alan when I phoned him later, but I'll always cherish the memory of our trip to Lynx Hollow and meeting the family in the big white house. If the ghostly presence in their home is Mother, they are very lucky indeed.